Pride Publishing books by Megan Slayer

I0663111

Single Books
Constant
Permanent
Vaulting
Drive my Car
We Belong Together
Finding Michael

Must Love Dogs
The One I Want
You and Me Again
The Real Me

Cedarwood Pride
Home to Cedarwood
Ripples in Cedarwood
Scoring in Cedarwood
Rainbows over Cedarwood
Rocking Cedarwood
Cedarwood Manny

Anthologies
Out of Bounds: Crossing the Line
Out of Bounds: Making the Play
Aim High: Lifetime Hitch
Brothers in Arms: One Night with You

Collections
What's his Passion?: Wild Card

FINDING MICHAEL

MEGAN SLAYER

Finding Michael
ISBN # 978-1-83943-852-3
©Copyright Megan Slayer 2018
Cover Art by Erin Dameron-Hill ©Copyright February 2018
Interior text design by Claire Siemaszkiewicz
Pride Publishing

Published in 2020 by Pride Publishing, United Kingdom.

Pride Publishing is an imprint of Totally Entwined Group Limited.

FINDING MICHAEL

Dedication

For everyone looking for that special someone…
keep searching. Your Michael is out there.

To SM, for accepting and editing this.
Love you. I really do.

For MS, because you kept after
me to finish this story. You rock.

For JPZ, because without you,
I'd get nothing done. Love you, too.

Chapter One

"I'm so stuck it's not even funny." Tristan stared at his computer screen and groaned. He hadn't written a word in more than a week. Writer's block wasn't his enemy and the occasional day without writing wasn't the end of the world. But he hadn't been able to work out an idea or even sketch a thin plot for anything.

He glanced over at the doorway. He hadn't seen his butler in a while and didn't like talking to himself. "Dennis?" He drummed his fingers on the desk top. "Are you there?"

The dry spells in his writing were getting closer together. He hadn't produced a bestselling novel in the last two years. His last three books were well reviewed and had sold a good number of copies, but none were the fourth breakout book he needed. If he didn't come up with a novel that sold well, he'd lose his contract with his publisher.

Part of him wanted to be angry. How dare they dump him? He'd sold over a million copies of his first three books and made the expected lists with all four. His publisher should have been grateful to have him on the roster.

Then there was the other part of him that never could quite come to terms with his ability to write. Throughout his life, all he'd wanted to do was make stories seem real. He could spin a yarn with the best storytellers, but he tended to downplay his talents. All the people who'd told him writing a book was easy would come to mind and he'd give in to his fears that he'd never produce another great work.

God, he needed a drink, a vacation and a good fuck. Unfortunately, he didn't have any booze in the apartment, hadn't gone away in a year and wasn't in a relationship.

He'd have to settle for his hand and porn later. *Damn it.*

Then there was his muse…the uncooperative asshole. The muse wasn't talking to him, which meant the characters weren't either. Once he went down the rabbit hole of thinking about his inspiration, or lack thereof… That was when he got himself into trouble. If he didn't write the next big thing, he'd have to dip into his trust fund to finance his career. He snorted. Most people wouldn't think twice. If they were in his shoes, they'd use the money his parents had set aside for him and have a life. Not him. He'd prefer not to touch the surplus he'd saved up until it was necessary. But if he didn't bring in cash soon, he'd have no choice.

Dennis strolled into the room and nodded. "Yes, sir." He placed a stack of letters onto the desk, then clasped his hands together. "Did you need me?" If nothing else, his butler had great timing. Another minute longer and

Tristan would've given in to another bout of depression.

"Thank you." Tristan flipped through his correspondence. Dennis had been the father-figure Tristan hadn't had often as a teenager. He knew Tristan better than anyone and tended to keep him on course. "Denny, I don't know what to do about this writer's block." He scanned the return addresses on the letters. One from his publisher, one from a former boyfriend and three bills. He sighed. Bills sucked. He noticed the blank space on one of the envelopes. His address had been typed. "What's this?" He turned the letter around. "I don't remember signing up for mailing lists or anything that wouldn't put a return address on it."

"I saw that. Perhaps it's one of the letters from a neighbor for one of the local fundraising groups." Dennis cleared the empty takeout boxes from the coffee table. "I'll be right back."

Tristan waited for his butler to leave the room, then opened the odd letter. His chest tightened as he read the words. He should've guessed the plain envelope would contain a letter from his stalker-slash-fan.

Write about my town – Lewiston. I'm waiting.

He sank back in his seat and tossed the letter onto the desk. All of his stories were based in small towns. He'd picked the states at random and made up the names of his towns, but each was based on little burgs and crossroads he'd passed through during his various travels. He stated in the acknowledgments of each novel that the towns were fictitious representations of many places...never anywhere in particular.

He should turn the damn letter over to the police. But what would they do? He hadn't been threatened. He'd been asked rather bluntly, yes. Threats? No. And he had no idea who the letter-writer was. How could he inform the cops if he had no leads?

Tristan closed his laptop, then scrubbed the back of his hand across his mouth. He couldn't seem to put a foot right of late. Everything seemed to be disastrous — he'd lost his last boyfriend to another man, he couldn't write for shit, if he didn't write he'd be dropped, he had a bitching fan...what else could go wrong?

"Sir?" Dennis returned to the room. "This letter just arrived certified. I believe it's from a lawyer. A Jamie Meyer. According to the accompanying letter, it concerns your Uncle Al." He offered up the thick envelope.

"Uncle Al? Jamie Meyer?" He hadn't heard from his mother's brother in ages. "Hang on, I don't know what this is about." He opened the envelope, then withdrew the stack of pages. He barely read the words beyond the first two sentences. His uncle, his last link to his mother's side of the family, had died and Tristan needed to collect his inheritance. *Died. Uncle Al? The man might have been in his early eighties, but he was strong and healthy...wasn't he?* He turned back to his laptop and searched online for the lawyer. After the directive from the reader to write about a specific town, would that person be devious enough to cook up a false letter to get him to come to...? *Nah.* Sullavan wasn't called Lewiston — that he knew. His thoughts were running away with him. Still, he wanted to make sure the lawyer was real.

The website for Jamie Meyer came up in the search. He clicked on the page. The photo stopped him short.

Jamie Meyer was a darn good-looking man. Perfect hair, perfect teeth…a perfect suit based on what he could see from the shoulders-up pose. Tristan wondered what his voice was like. *Christ.* He needed to get laid so he'd stop wasting time with pictures on the screen and considering the guys as possible dates.

"Sir?"

He glanced up at Dennis. *Shit.* He needed direction. "My uncle has passed. I've got an inheritance coming and I need to sort it out with the lawyer."

"Mr. Meyer?"

"Yes." He opened a new tab on his internet browser. He had to get his act together and plan his last-minute trip. *Well, fuck.* "I'll need changes of clothes for at least a week. I doubt this will be a quick process." Maybe he'd get a story out of the situation and a better understanding of the uncle he hadn't seen in forever. The last thing he needed was to get mixed up with the lawyer handling his uncle's estate.

"Do you want me to secure flights and accommodation?" Dennis asked. "I can look in to renting a private jet. I know how you hate crowds."

"You're right, I hate going out into crowds." But he had to do this himself. He couldn't rely on servants forever. "Just give me an hour and I'll have you help me pack."

"I see." Dennis didn't sound convinced.

Tristan logged in to his email, then paused. "If my agent calls, I'm writing. I'm going to email her in a moment, but she can be persistent. If Jordan calls, just take a message. We're not together, but he doesn't seem to know that." His ex had been the one to call off the relationship, yet he'd show up when he wanted something—a place to crash, money, sex… Tristan didn't have the time for him any longer. "If any more of those strange letters come without a return address, just put them aside. I don't want to be bothered."

"Why? Is that reader still writing to you?" Dennis folded his arms. For a man of sixty, he didn't look his age. He kept his salt-and-pepper hair trimmed and stayed in shape. If the age gap hadn't been so wide, Tristan might have made a play for him.

"Yeah. I'm not scared, but I don't trust him or her."

"There wasn't a signature on this letter?"

"No," Tristan said. "Nothing. Not even an initial. The writer simply wants me to create a town based on Lewiston. I have no idea where that place is."

"I've never heard of it."

"Me either."

"I'll be careful, sir, and I think you should, too. I've got some laundry to finish. When you need me, let me know." Dennis turned on his heel and strode out of the room, leaving Tristan with his thoughts.

Tristan cracked his knuckles, then placed his hands on the keyboard. He hadn't been to his uncle's home in years. Was Sullavan, Ohio, still on the map? He brought up the street map, then located the town. Not any bigger than he'd remembered, but still in existence. If he wasn't mistaken, the small town was about an hour's drive from Cleveland. Not great, but it'd give him time to plot a new story. Besides, Sullavan would be good fodder for his trademark small-town setting. His spirits brightened. He had no idea what he'd inherited, but if he could use the situation to plot his next book, he'd be golden.

Half an hour later, Tristan had the plane tickets purchased and a rental car secured for when he arrived in Cleveland. He'd emailed his editor and explained the situation—he had an outline started and would be getting her up to speed within the next week, but after he spoke to the lawyer about his uncle's will. He shut down his laptop and placed the three memory sticks in his messenger bag. He'd finish gathering his writing things together once he'd packed.

Tristan headed down the hallway to his bedroom. Dennis had left his open suitcase on the bed. Instead of thinking too hard about what he had to do, Tristan set about putting his bathroom essentials into his bag.

Dennis strode into the bedroom with a basket of clean clothes. "What should I do if your Aunt Salina calls? Should I tell her where you'll be?"

Tristan zipped his bag. "No. I'm not on her social calendar unless she wants something. She's obsessed with her step-daughter's wedding and I, the son of her only brother, don't matter. Babsy is much more important than I ever will be." Not that he cared. He hadn't been particularly close to his father's side of the family and they only liked him when they wanted to flaunt his status in the book world or to bolster their place on the social registry.

"Don't refer to your cousin Jean as Babsy." Dennis tucked the bag into the suitcase. "It's her mother's right to want to spoil her."

"Whatever." He didn't fault his aunt for the spoiling part, just the lack of interest.

"*You* could have a wedding," Dennis said. "It's not illegal."

"Ah, but no one wants to marry me." He pulled a stack of T-shirts out of the dresser. He laughed, despite not finding the situation amusing. He'd like to be with a man who craved him, not one who wanted his money. "I can't seem to keep a relationship going. That doesn't sound like the right start for a marriage." He paused. "I should probably find a man before I get too deep into planning the wedding, too."

Dennis took the shirts from him. "Alec wasn't too bad. He seemed sweet."

"Anyone's sweet when they see dollar signs."

"What about Cody? You liked him. I believe you were going to have him move in with you." Dennis packed the T-shirts, then opened the closet. "What about pants? Are you wearing jeans or do you need something dressier?"

"Denim." He counted out seven pairs of jeans, then offered them up to Dennis. "Cody was a good man, but I couldn't compete with him. Every time I turned around, he'd be checking himself out in the mirror. I know I'm not perfect, but I'm not awful. When I stood beside him, I felt so...ugly." He turned his back on Dennis. Truth be told, whenever he looked at his reflection, he saw the chunky kid he had been in junior high. Growing twenty years older hadn't changed his body image problems. He'd worked out, lost the weight and ate much better than during his school years, but his inner chubby kid lingered. He closed his eyes. Now wasn't the right time to let himself think about his inadequacies.

"And Justin was bad, how?"

"He wasn't." Justin hadn't been the issue. "We clicked in bed, but there wasn't anything otherwise." Tristan had gotten himself so wrapped up in his own self-esteem problems, he hadn't given Justin enough of a chance. But that was in the past. He needed to move forward.

"Uh-huh." Dennis nodded once. "This trip is about the will and research, isn't it? You'll get a book out of the situation if it kills you, won't you?"

"That's the plan." He tossed underwear and socks into the suitcase. "My career is off track. This will be the push to get it righted." He hoped. "Where are my notebooks?"

"In your office," Dennis said. "I'll get them and your fountain pen set."

"Thanks." Tristan walked into his closet and appraised his collection of shoes. *Christ.* He had money. He didn't have to work. Using the trust fund cash wasn't horrible. Lots of others lived perfectly happy lives paid for by the money from someone else's hard work. Why couldn't he do the same? His parents had given him the cash without question. He grabbed his running shoes and a pair of casual ones, then closed the door.

He'd built his career as a writer. Constant funding and huge paychecks weren't guaranteed. He'd lived on less and done just fine. He could do so again—especially if the story panned out and he found his muse. *Who knew a will could hold so many possibilities for creativity?*

* * * *

One day he'd have a decent office… Michael Kane sat on the floor of the shed next to the Sullavan library and flipped through the box of books. His ass ached. He'd been in a folded-up position on the plywood floor for too long, but he didn't have a desk. He counted the remaining boxes of donated books. If each of the six boxes had twenty or so books… He closed his eyes. A dull ache formed in his sinuses. He'd never get out of the shed.

No, he had to finish sorting. The little library box in the center of town needed more books and the ladies from the Friends of the Sullavan Library would want more novels for the used book sale.

Maybe he should've brought a folding chair along for this task. At least then he'd be off the floor. He would've rather been in the main library building, but then he'd never finish sorting. He scanned the titles of the books in the box—all popular paperbacks bought at the Sullavan general store. He wished the library were bigger. If it was, then he'd be able to put a few more of the hardly used books on the shelves. But Sullavan wasn't big enough as a town to handle a full library. The former one-room schoolhouse sufficed. Everything within the building had been repurposed or donated and most of it had started out in the shed. The other workers at the library were all volunteers. He brought in a paycheck, but it didn't cover his monthly costs.

He kept telling himself he'd look for another job in a larger town so he could have a proper office. The head librarian needed a space to deal with the inevitable paperwork, to sort through donations and to eat his lunch in peace. Not in his case. He shared his space with the circulation desk. Wouldn't his buddies from college laugh? They'd all gone on to bigger, better libraries. Not him. He moved to Sullavan.

So he liked being approachable... If a patron had a problem, he was easy to find. Plus, the open floorplan of the library gave him a better vantage point to keep an eye on the bank of three computers and to watch for possible thefts. He wasn't sure what the thrill of stealing a thesaurus was, but at least one managed to walk out of the library per month.

He picked up his clipboard and resumed sorting through the donated books. If he didn't increase his pace, he'd never get done.

"Hey, you." Dicey, one of his volunteers, knocked on the shed door. "Are you hiding?"

"No. I'm sorting." He plunked a worn copy of a recent crime thriller into the book sale box. "I'm hoping there are some classics in here. That department is rather thin and the high-school students keep using them for reports. It'd be nice to have more than three copies of *Wuthering Heights* and *Jane Eyre*. I know many of the students can't afford to buy their own books. Having them here helps out everyone."

"Is *Jane Eyre* the current book being used for projects?" Dicey asked. She puffed a lock of hair out of her eyes.

"Yes. Why?" What had he missed this time?

"Then that explains why we had to order a bunch in and the ones we should've had are missing. Not checked out. Missing." She folded her arms. "I hate to admit it, but we've got tons of heart in Sullavan, but no money."

"I know. Having a lot of heart is a good thing, though." *Just bad for funding.* He sighed. "I wish I could get a grant to buy more books or some wealthy patron would magically show up and donate whatever we wanted...but that won't happen."

"I've tried to conjure up money, but my spells don't work."

He stared at her. Dicey Smith embodied eccentricity. Her hair was never the same color for more than a week. She wore long dresses and, depending on the day, claimed to be a witch or a fortune teller. But she entertained him. She was loyal, sweet and didn't expect payment for the hours she spent at the library.

"I'll bite," Dicey said. "If you can get a grant, where does the money come from? The state won't cough up more and the town can't carry it. I know what you make and it's not much. The Joneses and the Martins have already donated their fair share."

"I know." He relied on the generosity of the Friends of the Sullavan Library and both wealthy families to help make ends meet, but even with the help from the state, he managed to fall short.

"We need fresh blood." Dicey tapped on the door.

"Yeah."

"In Sullavan?" He abandoned his clipboard and the box of books. "I can't tell you the last time someone new moved in." He left the shed, then locked the door. "I'm the last individual to buy a house in a twenty-mile radius."

"Don't remind me." She fell into step beside him. "Then Al died and the population went down." She swatted Michael's arm. "Did you know I dated him in school? We were sweethearts."

"I remember you mentioning something about that." He nodded, then held the door for her to enter the building first. She'd been crushed when she'd first found out Al had passed.

"Anyway, we need new blood in town. Something to jazz the place up." She pointed to Michael. "Right?"

"You're old enough to be my mother and I'm gay," Michael said.

"Which is why we're perfect for each other." Dicey rounded the counter and plopped onto the chair. "If all else fails, we're a match."

He rolled his eyes. "I doubt it."

"We both like…" She dropped her voice to a whisper and glanced around the nearly empty building. "Dicks."

"Dicey, please." He didn't mind her feeling comfortable enough in his presence to be blunt, but what if a patron heard her?

"Oh, okay." Dicey leaned on the counter. "Lauren, did you hear what I said?"

Lauren poked her head out from between the shelves in the children's section. "There's no one here but the three of us and yes, I caught every word."

"Drat." Dicey glared at Michael. "Oh well."

"Just be glad there aren't patrons here." Michael took his post at the other end of the circulation desk. "Count your blessings."

"Speaking of blessings, I'm lucking out on the man front. How about Lauren and I find you one?" Dicey grinned. "I could conjure one."

"No." Dating never worked for him—not that he'd tell her that. "No conjuring or otherwise. I'm good on my own." He wasn't sure why he'd been honest. Once she got an idea, she didn't let go until she saw it through. He'd be her next mission.

"I'll wear you down one day at a time." She sighed. "You know, I went out there to ask you to come in here because we needed help, but that didn't bring in patrons."

"Why'd you think it would? School isn't out yet and story time was this morning. Everyone in town is either at work or not coming here. We aren't exactly a hotspot." Michael tapped the keys on his laptop. He looked over his email, then paused. Most of it was nothing but interoffice memos from the main branch of the library system or from a patron requesting a hold. "Why am I getting notifications from the senior center regarding donating used books?"

Dicey blushed. "What do you mean?"

He knew that tone of voice. He bit back a grumble. "Why is someone named JK asking if we have extra books? You're the secretary for the Friends. Why didn't you answer this?"

She averted her gaze. "Because JK is cute and he's single. He's also young."

"Don't try to fix me up."

"He's right out of college and, according to his aunt, he's gay." She batted her lashes. "Someone in this library needs to get some. Why can't it be you?"

"Dicey." He blew out a ragged breath to steady his nerves. She knew how to hit the right buttons to drive him crazy. He wasn't in the market for a relationship, and not one with a guy ten years younger than him. He wasn't in the mood to train a lover. Besides, how could he be sure this JK would stick around? He might have told himself he'd put himself on the market for a new job, but the truth was, he liked Sullavan and wasn't leaving any time soon. He typed out a reply, then hit send.

Michael massaged his temples. He loved Dicey and Lauren. Most days they were great. Today? Not so much. Lauren was fine, but Dicey… She'd drive him nuts before she gave up volunteering for good.

He spent the next two hours behind the circulation desk and dealt with the after-school rush. During the lull at six, he re-shelved the returned books and neatened up the children's section. When the bell dinged, he didn't bother to look up. Dicey and Lauren were behind the desk and could handle the patron if there was a problem.

"Hi, I'm here on the hunt for books about Sullavan. Can you help me?"

Michael froze. He hadn't heard that particular warm baritone voice in the library before. The speaker was forthright, but polite. A shiver ran the length of his spine. He glanced over the display of early reading books to appraise the man at the counter. His jaw nearly dropped and his nerve endings sizzled. He'd never seen the man before—not in the library or Sullavan, Ohio.

The gentleman, tall with black hair and five o'clock shadow darkening his cheeks, stood with his thumbs hooked into the belt loops of his jeans. The tailored shirt clung to his slender body. When he followed Dicey to the local color section, Michael noticed the man's toned legs and his feet. He wore socks with the casual shoes. Such a small detail shouldn't have pleased Michael, but he preferred men who bothered to wear socks instead of going barefoot. Maybe he'd found a kindred sock spirit.

He paused. What was he doing? A kindred sock spirit? He'd heard the guy speak and given him the visual once-over, but he'd built up a connection to him in his mind. *Jesus.* Dicey was right. He needed sex—at least a fuck to clear his head. He needed to hide, but there weren't many places in the building to keep out of sight. If he could return to the desk without incident, he'd be able to duck behind the bookcase of DVDs. Maybe then the hunk wouldn't see him.

"I'm not sure we have much," Dicey said. "There are a few books about the subdividing of Sullavan land and one about Edgar Sullavan. Is that what you want?"

Whatever the man said, Michael couldn't understand.

"Our head librarian, Michael, would know more." Dicey met Michael's gaze. "There you are. I've got a job for you." She turned her attention back to the hottie in the button-down. "Are you here doing a term paper? College paper?"

The man smiled and his blue eyes sparkled. "Research, yes. Paper, no. I wanted to learn about Sullavan and was told to come here."

"Oh." She frowned. "Michael."

He sighed, then headed over to the research desks. "Hi. I'm Michael. All of our books based on, involving or written about Sullavan and our founder, Edgar Sullavan, are here." He pointed to the lone shelf. "You're welcome to peruse any of the titles, but because they're reference, we can't loan them out. What kind of research are you doing? I know a few of the older folks in town might be good references."

"Thank you." He smiled again. "I'm working on a book."

"Are you an author?" Dicey asked. She pushed in beside Michael.

"I am," the man said. "History is my passion."

"You're not from around here." Dicey laughed. "I like you."

"I like you, too." The man took one of the books from the shelf. "I'm researching my family and I traced them to Sullavan. I thought I'd see what else I could find...for my book."

"Oh. You're a writer?" Michael's ears perked. Sullavan tended not to have the money to draw in writers for talks. Even if this guy wasn't a big-name author, maybe he'd be willing to have a coffee time chat or something. "What do you write?"

"Novels."

"Nice." The guy wasn't terribly forthcoming. *Rats.*

"I'm Tristan." He stuck out his hand. "I'm researching the McCartney side of my family. Al was my uncle."

Michael nodded and shook hands with Tristan. "I knew Al well. He liked to browse the westerns section. I think he read every one we have. He was a great man and I'll miss him."

Tristan's eyes widened. "It's nice to know someone who knew him."

"I've got a few stories about him, but not many." Michael sighed. "You're welcome to whatever information you can find in the books we have. If you find things you want to take, you'll have to make copies, which are a nickel each." He'd given that speech so many times, he'd memorized the words.

"Copies?" Tristan tipped his head. "Those still exist?"

"Yes." *Who is this guy?* "We're a tad backwater, here in Sullavan. We haven't branched out into all forms of technology."

"Copies," Tristan said. "Huh."

"Yes." Michael fought the urge to roll his eyes. "I'll leave you alone to your research. If you have any questions or need help, just ask. One of us will do our best to assist you."

"Of course."

Michael turned on his heel and left Tristan alone. Having new people coming to town wasn't completely bizarre, but he wasn't sure if he could trust Tristan. Al McCartney had been a fine, upstanding citizen. He'd never mentioned having a nephew and Tristan didn't look a bit like Al. The story about doing genealogy work could be true, or a scam. He narrowed his eyes and kept his attention on Tristan. He didn't trust the strange but handsome man. Not a bit.

Chapter Two

Tristan picked up two of the books, then settled at the large oak table. He tugged his tablet from his messenger bag. Copies? Who made those any longer when photos could be taken on the tablet or a phone? He chuckled. Sullavan was in a whole different time. He rifled through to a section on the McCartneys and snapped photos with his tablet. *Why waste trees by making copies?*

He couldn't focus. Despite finding some of the information he wanted, he couldn't settle down. His story made partial sense, but if Michael had half a brain, he'd question the tale. Looking up family history…he hadn't set foot in Sullavan in more than twenty years. No one who'd been in town back then would be around now. It wasn't possible.

He should apologize to Michael and the other workers. He sat back in his chair. Why did the name Michael send a shiver along his spine? Why did he want to speak to the librarian again? He stole a glance over at the desk workers. Michael stood with the older lady. He tickled Tristan's fancy. He was cute in a geeky way. Tristan liked Michael's glasses and the air of intelligence swirling around him. Michael could've used a proper haircut or at least a decent one. The just-out-of-bed look did work for him, though. If he were with Michael, he'd neaten up the style a bit. Maybe he could show Tristan what actual bedhead looked like. Tristan chuckled again. Mr. Geek Chic Michael probably had a sweet little woman at home and two kids playing in the yard.

He crinkled his nose. He wasn't a kid person. No way, no how. A dog kind of guy, yes, but kids... *Not going to happen.* Crying annoyed him and the sheer number of germs involved unnerved him.

Tristan stared at the pages but didn't read any of them. He wasn't learning a damn thing. He wasn't paying attention to the words...just Michael. If he wanted to write his next small-town novel and base it on Sullavan, he'd have to read the books. But he'd also need experience in the area.

"Finding anything?" Michael asked.

"Yes." He closed the hardcover. "I did."

"Are you sure?" Michael tapped the cover. "You're flipping through the pages of the thesaurus. You pulled it from the wrong section when you got the other tomes."

He focused on the title. Of course, he'd picked up the wrong volume. He hadn't been paying attention to what he'd done. If Michael hadn't questioned his story so far, this maneuver would clue him in that Tristan didn't belong in Sullavan.

"Are you okay?" Michael stood tall. "Do you need help?"

"I needed a word." He rubbed the cover of the thesaurus. "Yes."

"Which one?"

"Lascivious."

"Really? For your family history?" Michael frowned. "Uncle Al wasn't a man about town."

"Right, but my other family members got around." Oh boy, he needed to shut his mouth. He'd dug himself in deep. "I'm stuck, so I'll gather up my notes and get going. Thank you. I'm sure I'll be back."

"Oh, okay," Michael said. "Sure. We're open often and I seem to be here all of the time."

"Great." Tristan shoved his tablet back into his bag, then hurried out of the library. He hoped he hadn't stuffed a library book in with the tablet. Coming back to return what he'd stolen by accident wasn't high on his to-do list. He stopped by his rental car and checked his bag. *No castaways. Good.*

He groaned. He'd made a mess of his initial research session. He'd barely looked at the books and had flipped through the damn thesaurus. *A thesaurus! Jesus.* Then he'd escaped like a thief. He had to get a hold of himself. Yes, Michael was pretty, but with Tristan's luck, he was straight. Besides, he lived in Sullavan. Tristan had no desire to put down roots in the small town. But what was it about the place that had him all turned around? Was Michael the reason? He settled behind the wheel of his car, then whipped out his phone. If he was going to stay in Sullavan, he'd need a room. He hadn't thought of lodging before he'd left New York. He scrolled through the list of hotels, but the closest one was more than twenty miles away. How in the hell would he be able to study Sullavan if he wasn't in town?

He blew out a ragged breath. He needed to get a grip. He should go back into the library and ask about closer hotels, but how would he do that without his tail between his legs?

Tristan returned to his results list. What about a bed and breakfast? Were there any of those in Sullavan? He scrolled down the webpage until he located the Sullavan B&B. Four rooms, vacancies according to the website, and food included in the price. Good enough for him. He dialed the phone number for the establishment. After four rings, someone answered.

"Sullavan B&B. How can I help you?" the woman asked.

"I'd like to rent a room." He willed his heart rate to slow a little and for his nerves to stop buzzing.

"Wonderful. When will you be in?"

"In?" She'd stumped him. Thinking on his feet wasn't his strong point.

"Yes, when will you be arriving?"

Oh! Arriving... "Today."

"And how long will you be staying with us?"

"I'm not sure," he confessed. "How long is the limit?"

"We don't have a restriction. If you're already here in town, why don't you come in and we can get you set up? Won't take long and we can discuss the length of your visit?"

If chatting with her meant time to lick his wounds before he had to see Michael again, then he was game. He could use a night to prep for the meeting with the lawyer in the morning, too. He rolled his eyes. *Licking my wounds...* What had happened to him? He was the one with savvy. He worked people over and got what he wanted. With a few questions and a handful of his trademark smiles, he controlled the situation. Not now.

What was it about the small town and the adorable librarian that had gotten to him? *Adorable...* Nah, Michael was cute, but he wasn't Tristan's style.

"Excuse me. Sir?"

Oh God. He'd forgotten about the woman on the other end of the line. "Sorry. My... I'll be there once I find the place. I haven't been back to Sullavan in a long time and I'm all turned around." Talk about the understatement of the century.

"Absolutely. We're on Main Street next to the Hallsman Used Car lot. Can't miss the house. It's a powder-blue Victorian," she said. "The sign is rather large, too."

"Thank you. I'll be right there." Good God. The place was next to a car lot? What was he doing? He put the phone on the passenger seat, then gripped the steering wheel. He'd lost his damn mind. Getting away from his publisher, avoiding his agent and the emailing fan weren't the best reasons to run to Sullavan. Sure, he was supposed to meet up with the lawyer and discuss his uncle's estate, but still. He had to start the next book and needed a plot. Would he find the start he wanted in Sullavan? He hoped so.

"You can do this," he muttered. "One foot in front of the other. Come on, Tris. You're the man. Act like it." He pulled out of the library lot, then made his way to the center of town. He located the B&B right where the woman had said—next to the car lot. She hadn't been kidding about the blue house sticking out. The sign dominated the front yard.

He parked behind the house and strode around to the front, then drank in the view. A white fence obscured the front of the car lot. Wind rustled down the street and the leaves on the towering maple trees seemed to wave at him. He stuffed his hands into his pockets. A few large houses lined the street for a couple of blocks. From his vantage point, he noticed the manicured lawns and overflowing flower beds. The houses piqued his interest. He'd have to do some exploring.

When he headed up to the front door of the B&B, characters started talking to him in his head. Whoever the characters were, at least one of them lived in a grand old house. He'd have to write his ideas down in his notebook and hope he could keep up.

He strode past the wraparound porch and into the lobby of the B&B. A woman stood behind the desk. When she looked up, her eyes sparkled. "Hello," she called.

"Hi." He folded his hands on the marred wooden counter. "This is the lone hotel in town?"

"Sure is. I'm Molly. My mother owned this grand lady when I was a kid and I took over after she retired. Are you the gentleman I spoke to on the phone?"

"Yes. I'm Tristan." He sighed. "I'm out of sorts and could use a place to stay."

"It's a pleasure to meet you, Tristan." She scribbled something on her tablet, then turned the screen around. "Sign in here and I'll get you a room. We're happy to have you for as long as you'd like to stay. Lord knows we've got plenty of room."

"No guests?" He'd spotted the vacancy notification on the website, but wasn't sure if the icon was a decoration. He signed his name, then nudged the tablet back to her.

"We're empty." She tapped the screen. "I haven't had any guests since the hotel went up over by the freeway. I guess no one wants to come to Sullavan. They'd rather stop just off the main path without venturing south."

She shrugged. "It's not like we have a lot to see. We're a plain town with nice people and we're glad to have you."

"I'm glad to be here." He patted his back pocket. "Do you need my credit card?"

"I trust you." She slid a thick leather fob with two keys attached across the counter. "These are yours. Room three. Get your bags and, if you're hungry, I've got split pea soup on the stove. You parked behind the house, correct? The red car?"

"Thank you and yes, I did. Is that the wrong spot?"

"You're fine. We have camera security, but I wanted to be sure. Hurry up and come back for supper." She winked, then disappeared into a room behind the counter.

"Thank you." Tristan nodded. He hadn't had that kind of soup in years. His stomach growled. Yeah, he needed to slow down, eat and reorganize his life. "I'll be right back." He left the lobby long enough to retrieve his things from the car, then returned to the building. He wandered up to the second floor and located his room with ease. He should've asked about the rates, but did that matter? He'd be staying at least a week. Maybe she'd give him a volume discount.

"Good. You found it." Molly stood in the doorway. "I've got extra towels. Just ask. Also, I forgot to let you know what the rates are. It's a hundred a night, but I'm willing to negotiate. If I think of anything else, I'll let you know. Any questions?"

"Nope. I'm good. I'll see you in a bit for something to eat."

"Perfect." She left him to his thoughts.

Tristan sank onto the bed. Weariness set in bone-deep. A nap would've been nice...but so would food.

He forced himself to get up and unpack. If he didn't set his things out now, he'd never get it done and would spend the week or so living out of the bag. He plunked the tablet and his notebooks on the desk, then dragged his toiletries into the bathroom. For a tiny B&B, the place was nice and clean. He admired the artwork on the walls. Were the people in the photos Molly's family? He stared at a photo of a woman in a hoop skirt. She was frowning at the photographer or something happening behind him. He settled on the edge of the desk and picked up his notebook. What was the woman's name? Why was she upset?

He scrawled down notes. He could see the situation in his mind. She'd just lost her husband and was expected to submit to a photograph to commemorate the date. The reason she was scowling was because her son was racing around behind the camera. She wanted to laugh at his exuberance, but was expected to look stern. Her son would end up being the father of someone important for the book. Tristan grinned. He'd think about her and the son later, but he had a start. *Hell yes.*

He abandoned his things and tucked his notebook into his back pocket. He'd work on the story later — after dinner. Split-pea soup sounded divine. He headed back to the first floor, then stood in the middle of the foyer. *Well…shit. Where's the kitchen?*

"Hello." A man strode through the foyer. "Can I help you?" His eyes sparkled and when he smiled, he showed off his teeth. "I'm Barry. I haven't seen you around before."

Tristan paused. Wasn't Barry quite the forward guy… "I'm staying here for a few days, so yes, I'm new. I'm looking for the kitchen or dining area. Molly told me to meet her for supper."

"Don't get too wound up with Molly. She's sweet, but she'll never settle down." Barry nodded, then pointed to the door to the right. "Dining room is in here. It's an informal setting."

"Great." Did that mean he'd be stuck with Barry? *Oh boy.* He followed Barry into the dining room. He'd expected three or four tables, but instead noticed one gigantic one. Barry hadn't been kidding about the informality. He selected a seat and pulled his notebook from his pocket before he settled on the chair.

"Are you a writer? Or a journaler?" Barry plopped down beside him. His knee brushed Tristan's. "What do you do for a living? What brings you to Sullavan?"

Tristan kept his notebook shut. He tended to be the one asking a hundred questions, but still. "First, I'm a writer, yes. Blogging and journaling was never my strong point. I'd rather put the effort into the story rather than something silly for a webpage, but that's me. I make a decent living from my writing and I'm here because of it." He wasn't ready to mention his uncle to Barry. The nosy bastard probably had a story about them knowing each other or something.

"Nice. I've wanted to write a book for ages, but haven't. I've heard it's not hard to write. I just don't have the time." Barry unfolded his napkin and placed it on his lap. "Molly!"

The door on the far side of the room opened and she stepped into the space. She held a large soup pot. "Dinner's ready. I need to grab the rolls." She placed the pot at the middle of the table on a ceramic warmer. "Bowls, utensils and the silver are all on the sideboard.

Help yourself. Barry, you've done this before. Give me a hand." She disappeared behind the door again.

Barry shrugged. "I come here often for supper. She makes good food." He picked up the bowls and plates. "Can't knock her soup."

"Thanks." Tristan held on to his notebook while he retrieved the silverware. Something about Barry didn't sit right with him. The guy was too pushy. Too nosy. He placed the silverware in front of the two plates, then retrieved a place setting for Molly. "You didn't set one for her."

"Oh." Barry shrugged again, then took his chair. "She works here. She can get her own."

If he'd even been a little attracted to Barry, that sentiment blew his feelings up. He might be a cad himself, but he liked men with manners.

Molly returned with a basket of rolls. "Barry...did you set a place for me?"

Before Barry could say anything, Tristan spoke up. "I did. Thought you might like to take a load off."

"I appreciate it." She grinned, then elbowed Barry. "See? You could take some pointers from him."

"I'd like to do something else," Barry muttered.

Molly sat opposite Tristan. "You'll have to excuse my cousin. He's not used to people with manners." She scooted her chair to the table. "I hear you're a writer." She smiled. "I love to read."

"What genre?" Tristan asked. He waited for her then Barry to fill their bowls.

"Oh...I've got tons of books on my tablet. I like pretty much anything, but old Hollywood biographies are my favorite. There's something exciting about learning about people." She waggled her head. "It's kind of like working here. I see different people each day…well, most of the time, and I get a snapshot of their lives."

"Nice to find someone else who enjoys them." He winked.

"Please." Barry elbowed Tristan. "Who reads?"

"I do." Molly picked up one of the rolls. "Tristan, did you stop by the library? We've got a small one, but Michael keeps the biography section stocked. I'm sure he'd work out something if you found a book while you're here. If nothing else, tell him to put it on my account."

"I'll have to do that." Tristan sighed. He liked the odd family feel to the B&B. Molly intrigued him almost as much as Michael.

"Speaking of the librarian, where is he? I thought he was coming by for dinner." Molly left her seat, then strode up to the window. "Barry, you didn't scare him off again, did you?"

Barry and Michael had a thing? Tristan dipped a piece of his roll into the soup. She wasn't kidding about making good split-pea soup. He hadn't had anything like it ever.

"I left him alone." Barry dropped his voice to a whisper. "Ever since we broke up, he's been bitter." He shook his head. "I guess when you have a taste of Barry and give me up, I'm hard to forget."

"I'm sure." Tristan focused on his soup. Michael didn't seem like the type to pair up with Barry. They were too opposite.

"There he is." Molly rushed out of the room. When she returned, she had her arm around one of Michael's. "We've got a spot for you. Always." She waved her hand. "Michael, I'd like to introduce you to Tristan.

You already know Barry. Tristan, this is our fantastic librarian, Michael."

Tristan met Michael's gaze. The tips of his ears burned. He hadn't expected to run into Michael again or for the temperature to rise so fast. He focused on his soup, but noticed Michael sat beside Molly. Was he with her? Just friends? Why did that matter to him?

"Hi. Good to see you again," Michael said. "I met Tristan over at the library." He filled a bowl with soup. "Barry."

"Nice to see you. I've meant to call you. We should get together again." Barry reached across the table. "We had good times together."

Tristan froze. He'd walked into a strange situation. He switched his gaze between the three people. He could see them as friends, maybe. He should leave them all alone. He didn't belong in the middle of their drama. *God.* He had plenty of his own crap to deal with. Besides, he'd be out of Sullavan once he talked with the attorney and had his story started.

"Did you want any of the books donated to the library for the book sale?" Michael asked. "Maybe for the rooms? I've got a lot of recent bestsellers and those copies on the shelf aren't in bad shape."

Molly nodded. "That'd be nice." She grinned. "Tristan likes to read, too. He's going to come by to check out the biography section."

"More like the Michael's ass section," Barry grumbled. He finished his soup, then stood. "I've already had that ass and it's not...whatever." He stomped out of the room.

Molly closed her eyes. "Well, that was awkward. I'll be right back." She opened her eyes, then abandoned her food. She darted through the door and left Tristan alone with Michael.

"Wow. Who knew it would be so exciting here?" Michael chuckled. "I just wanted supper."

"Do you eat here often?" Tristan stirred the remnants of his soup. "Molly makes good food."

"She does and I do." Michael folded his hands and sighed. "I never learned to cook all that well and since we both live alone, we hang out together." He paused, then waggled his fingers. "There's nothing romantic involved. She was one of the first people to speak to me when I moved here to Sullavan. She's been so nice and I'm grateful to have her as a friend."

"Good to know." He finished his soup, then snatched a roll from the basket. "What about…that?" He nodded to the seat where Barry had been. "He's interesting."

"If you know what's good for you, you won't get involved with him. It's a roller coaster. One minute he's Dr. Jekyll and the next he's Mr. Hyde. He's full of himself and thinks only about how he looks. I can't say he was entirely not worth the time when we were together. I learned a lot about myself. I'm good at being alone and not at being with someone who doesn't care about me."

"I've known a few of those in my time." He pushed the bowl away. He'd been the narcissistic one far too often in his life. "Maybe he sees something in you that he can't let go."

"Who knows?" Michael sat back in his seat. A slow smile curled on his lips. "So, what really brings you to Sullavan? Besides me rambling on about my ex-boyfriend. There has to be something. Is Al really your uncle?"

"He is." He might as well be honest. He couldn't deny the attraction between them. "Al is my uncle. He's my mother's brother. I wasn't close to him in the last few years. I have my career and he lived here. We didn't intersect. But I'm here because I'm supposed to meet with a lawyer about his estate. I'm also working on a book. I like to write about small-town situations and unique characters. I remembered Sullavan and thought it would be nice to turn the somewhat morose vacation into something memorable."

Michael nodded once. "I commend you. When my father passed, I couldn't bring myself to go home. I didn't want it to be real. I waited until long after the funeral before I returned. I'm sure my mother hated me, but she never said anything. My cousin told me I was spoiled."

"Death is hard to deal with. I'm not looking forward to finding out what's involved with the estate." He had no idea what to expect. The note from the attorney hadn't said much.

"I'm sorry for your loss. Like I said, I liked your uncle. He was a good man." Michael stood. "I should go. Good luck with the meeting about the estate and your story. If you need any suggestions or info about Sullavan, come to the library. I'll do my best to help."

"I will. Thanks." He stood and shook hands with Michael. "Night." He waited in the dining room until Michael left. His fingers tingled from Michael's touch. He shook his head. The electricity between him and Michael had to be a result of him wanting anyone since he hadn't had sex in what seemed like forever. Any guy touching him would cause a reaction. *Right?*

He carried the empty bowls and used silver to the kitchen. When he glanced out of the window, he noticed Barry and Molly on the back porch. He couldn't hear what they were saying to each other, but she didn't look happy. Tristan abandoned the dirty dishes in the sink. He refused to get involved.

Tristan went up to his room and locked the door. A hundred thoughts bombarded him now that he was alone. He couldn't get Michael out of his head. The way he spoke, laughed and those eyes... He wanted to kiss the librarian. He flopped onto the bed and rubbed the growing bulge in his pants. Wouldn't his ex be shocked? He hadn't lost his sex drive. It'd just gone into hibernation. He chuckled. He hadn't come to Sullavan for a date, much less a one-night stand. He needed characters and a story. Would Barry be one of the players in Tristan's story? Absolutely. Every tale needed a few foils. What about Michael?

He groaned. His stories tended to feature at least one sexy, brooding man. Michael fit that bill. He wanted to feel the softness of Michael's skin, to kiss him and find out if Michael moaned during sex.

Jesus, he needed help. Tristan rolled over, then snagged his phone from the nightstand. The LED light blinked. *Shit.* He had messages or missed calls. He scrolled through the list. The emails could be handled later and the texts weren't important. Still, he owed his publisher an update.

He typed out a message. *I've got the outline started and am working on character sheets. Should have a draft in six weeks at the earliest. I'm neck-deep in research.*

He hit send and swiped back to the main screen, but a blank message bubble appeared.

Hi.

What the hell? He frowned. No name, no idea who wanted to talk to him. Should he answer? *Nah.* He swiped the bubble away, switched his chat settings to invisible and cleared the open apps, but the bubble came back.

I know you're there.

So? He closed the bubble again, but it popped up a third time.

Stop pushing me away.

He'd had enough. *Who is this?*

☺

What in the hell was going on? *Who are you?*

Stop playing coy. You know.

No, he didn't and he wasn't in the mood for games. *Good night.*

Don't try to hide. I see you. I always see you.

He turned his phone off. He'd had enough creepy for the night. Tristan left the phone on the nightstand again, then switched off the light. At one point, he thought he'd had an email stalker in New York, but the guy had been arrested. Could he be back? Or was this a new one? *Fuck.* If he kept worrying about whoever was messaging him, he'd never get anything done.

Ignoring the person wouldn't help, either, but he had little choice. He had to move on with his life.

He buried his face in the pillow and breathed in the scent of the detergent used on the sheets. He needed a plan for the next day. Something beyond the morning meeting with the attorney. If he took his pens and a notebook along, he could work on the character sketches while he waited. Maybe he could walk around town. There had to be at least three or four old Victorian houses that might work for the story. He should stop at the library, too, and figure out if the attraction to Michael was nothing more than a fluke.

Chapter Three

Tristan woke in the middle of the night in the pitch dark. He needed to see to orient himself. *Holy shit.* He had his story plot. He scrambled over to the desk for his pens and paper. He knew who would be in his story. *The son of the woman in the photo had a child of his own and that little boy has grown up to be a businessman. He has to return to the village in order to get his father's affairs – since he's dying – in order. When he comes back, the entire place finds out the man is gay and that's out of the ordinary. Everyone talks, then tries to get him and other men in the area together. He sees the shops and places of his youth, which makes him realize he likes the small town. Things were so different, but also the same. He prefers the slower tempo of his home.*

Tristan stopped writing. Who was the other hero? He had the businessman, but who would the guy pair up with? He'd have to think about that. A subplot came to mind. *The father of the hero had a tangled life that even the hero doesn't know about. A secret second wife and other children. Father had an affair with the hero's high school girlfriend, too. Hero's got brothers and sisters he never knew.*

While he's sifting through the paperwork and unraveling his father's life, he spends a little too much time with the ridiculously handsome lawyer. He ends up sleeping with the lawyer and that gets the town talking, too. Once the story is untangled, the money is distributed equally around the remaining spouses and children. The hero takes his share and donates it to the local LGBT shelter. Doesn't want anyone to feel alone while trying to figure out who they are.

He sat back in his seat and cracked his knuckles. Now that he had a plan for the story, he could work on the character sketches. He laughed at himself. Unlike some writers, he wasn't big on outlines. Once he started writing, the dialogue would take over and the story would twist in ways he wouldn't expect. Part of him wanted to turn on his laptop and tackle the story. The rest of him needed sleep. He yawned. *Yep, sleep would be best.*

Tristan tossed the pen onto the desk, then stretched. He had a great start and once he went on a walk in the afternoon, he'd tackle writing. He shut the light off, then crawled back into bed. He hadn't bothered to strip out of his clothes from the previous day. *Oh well.* He closed his eyes and thought about Michael.

Christ, he had to get his head cleared. But why? Michael was a handsome man. He had muscle in the right places and those eyes... He'd always been a sucker for men with glasses and the dark-rimmed specs looked hot on the librarian. He wanted to run his fingers through the man's hair and be the recipient of his smile.

He flopped onto his back. Getting caught up in a guy wasn't his style — not this fast. He didn't know Michael other than what he'd learned during their short conversations. But he couldn't deny the physical attraction. There weren't many guys who had him tongue-tied. Yeah, he needed to see Michael and figure out if the connection was one-sided and a result of his loneliness, or if it was something more.

Wouldn't his ex get a kick out of the great Tristan Paulson getting hung up on someone? His last boyfriend swore there was no one who could wrangle Tristan for any length of time. No one was that special. Tristan was the one who steamrolled over people and didn't look back after the end of a relationship. He only got involved when he wanted to and never pined over anyone. Then he'd met Michael. He had to be losing his damn mind.

Tomorrow he'd wander around Sullavan and meet with the lawyer. He'd fill in the blanks concerning the setting of his new novel, then maybe, when he'd finished, he'd detour over to the library. Would Michael want to meet for coffee? He'd never know until he asked. He grinned and settled. A shot of Michael just might do his body and soul a world of good.

* * * *

The next morning, Michael walked the three blocks from his townhome to the library and unlocked the building. He waved to Dicey, who was sitting in her car reading one of her various paperback books. He headed into the building and waited for her to join him. He treasured the few minutes of silence. Dicey was like a mother to him, but she didn't stop talking all that much.

He turned on the computers, then made his way over to the patron ones. He wondered about Tristan. The man intrigued him. Al hadn't been much of a talker until he ventured into the library. Was Tristan a chatterer, too? He seemed so.

Michael opened one of the books he'd referred Tristan to and flipped through the pages. He lingered over images of Sullavan in the 1950s with the neon-lit storefronts and the quirky little shops. Anything could be purchased if one walked up and down the main drag. No need for superstores or leaving the area. He loved the architectural wonders of the town, too. So much art deco still standing and all the beautiful ironworks in the park... He didn't know why anyone would want to live anywhere else. Would Tristan enjoy living in Sullavan? Probably not. He struck Michael as a city slicker who had a ton of hot guys lined up to be with him.

He turned his attention to the books again. He didn't have guys crawling out of the woodwork to find him. Thinking about men and Tristan, in particular, wouldn't do him any good right now. He busied himself with paperwork and logging in the inter-library transfer books. Dicey joined him at the counter, but once patrons came in, she paid him little mind.

The door opened and the squeak garnered Michael's attention. When he looked up, Tristan stood in front of him. "Hi," Tristan said. "I need assistance."

Michael's breath caught. He'd noticed just how handsome Tristan was yesterday, but today in a pressed button-down and his hair combed, he blew Michael's mind. A hint of Tristan's cologne wrapped around him. He suppressed a shiver. Would he smell so woodsy on a date?

"I've rendered you speechless?" Tristan laughed. "Molly said I might."

"I...sorry." Michael cleared his throat and regained his poise. He was there to do a job, not ogle a patron. "How are you?"

"I'm great, but I do need assistance. My lawyer is busy until tomorrow. I guess he's in court. So, I can't meet with him. I've got the rest of the day free and I thought I'd work on my research. Which books did you say I needed to use?" Tristan's eyes sparkled.

"Sure." He rounded the counter and escorted Tristan to the rack of books once more. "Whatever you need, this is what we have. There are some records on the computer, but I see we don't have any open." He nodded to the larger table of computers. "If you can wait, you're welcome to one."

"I'll do this first." Tristan smiled. He stepped forward and lowered his voice to a whisper. "It's Wednesday and I see the open hours end at one. Would you like to come with me on a walk around Sullavan and dinner this afternoon?"

Michael stared at him for a moment. He didn't know what to say. "Yeah," he managed. "I would."

"Perfect." Tristan settled onto the chair and opened his notebook.

Michael hesitated, then returned to his post behind the desk. A walk and dinner. It'd been two years since he'd gone out on a proper date. When he'd been with Barry, their time together had consisted of hook-ups and the occasional pizza and beer night. He longed for a solid relationship with a decent guy, but this was Tristan. He'd sort out the details with the lawyer and leave town. Why would he want to keep seeing Michael? He probably had a guy wherever he was from.

Michael massaged his forehead and stifled his groan. He could just hear Barry telling him to stop overthinking and that his need for organization would drive every man away. He couldn't help his quirks.

"I am so hitting that." Lauren sidled up to Michael. "He's hot."

"He is," Michael said. Christ. He needed to get a grip. He had no ties to Tristan. Shouldn't. "You'd be good together."

"I know, right?" she said and her voice rose an octave. "I bet he'd make gorgeous babies."

He wouldn't know about that.

Dicey strode up to the counter. "What are you blabbing about?"

"I'm asking that patron out." Lauren wriggled her eyebrows and nodded to Tristan. "He doesn't know it yet, but he's about to meet his soul mate. I know I've met mine."

Dicey rolled her eyes. "He's gay." She flattened her palms on the counter. "I know because I saw him this morning at the diner with Barry. Barry kissed him and he didn't appear to be pulling away."

Michael's heart sank. *Kissing Barry. Damn.* He should've known his ex-boyfriend couldn't keep his hands off the newcomer to town. Not that Michael could do much about the situation or change it. If they were attracted to each other, then that was that. Besides, Tristan wasn't obliged to him or anyone else and Michael would have to keep that in mind when they went to dinner later. Better to keep his heart locked away rather than consider pairing up with the handsome writer.

"Oh well," she said. "It's five minutes to one. We're free."

He shook his head. "No, we're not." He hadn't realized the hours had passed. He'd been too engrossed in his work and he hadn't gone out to the shed to sort books. *Damn.* He focused on Dicey. "Hon, we have to wait until it's actually five after one and all of the patrons are out."

"We've only got one left and that's Tristan. He doesn't really count." She stuck out her bottom lip. For being in her sixties, she could sure act like a belligerent teenager. "Come on. You know you want to go on that walk with him."

"That's not the point." He had a duty to the people of Sullavan and himself. If he started cutting corners in one place, he'd do it in others and that wouldn't work with his inner idiosyncrasies. "Shut the computers down, but don't you dare lock that door until the stroke of one."

"I knew you'd see things my way." She bounced over to the row of computers and touched Tristan's shoulder along the way. He glanced up, then over at Michael. His mouth curled in a half-smile.

Oh boy. Michael logged out of his computer, then shut it down. Once the clock hit one-oh-five, he locked the doors. No one could get in, but the three of them could leave. He put the last of the checked-in books on the cart to be shelved, then gathered his tablet and phone into his messenger bag. "Ready?"

Dicey nodded. "Just got to get my purse." She grinned, then sashayed around him. "Have a good afternoon, gentlemen. Don't do anything I wouldn't do." She laughed. "Nah, do whatever you want. It's your life." She left the library and continued to chuckle while the door shut.

Michael puffed out a long breath. "So."

Tristan shut the book he'd had open, then turned to Michael. "So."

"I'm ready whenever you are." Michael slung his bag across his body. "Lights off and we're out of here."

"Great." Tristan left the library first and waited on the sidewalk.

Michael checked the doors, then did his quick jaunt around the building to ensure everything was okay from the outside. He joined Tristan by the book drop. Instead of leaving, he stayed put. "I need to level with you."

"You're straight?" Tristan's eyebrows rose. "Right? You and Molly have a thing going?"

"Ah...no?" He frowned. Molly was his friend. Besides, hadn't he made it pretty clear he'd been with Barry?

"You're bi. That's cool. I don't mind. I dated this guy in Yonkers who was bi. He had the craziest sex life." Tristan whistled. "Like a new chick every night and had three guys on the side. It didn't last that long, but still."

"Ah. Okay. You know that's a load of bullshit. Just because someone is bi doesn't mean they're any looser than anyone else. You're assuming he is." Tristan would be a handful. "But he's not my business. What I was trying to say was we should discuss the expectations of the walk."

Tristan froze.

Didn't he want to tour the town? Or had he overstepped his boundaries by correcting Tristan? "What did you want from me?" Michael gripped the strap of his bag. "I'm not the guy who does everyone who passes through Sullavan. If you want that, then find Barry. He'll kneel for anyone. I'm game for dinner and to be friends, but I have this distinct feeling you're going to fly by next week, so I'd rather not get hyper-involved. But while we're on the subject, yes, I'm gay. Not bi, not confused. Gay and I'm out. I'm one of the few guys in this town who is."

"That's great to know."

He expected Tristan to walk then and there. Instead, Tristan rocked on his heels. "I'm gay, too. I don't want a fly-by-night affair." He chuckled. "I just wanted a friend and someone who knows Sullavan to guide me. I wouldn't turn down a kiss or two, but I don't expect you to run off to New York with me. Yeah, I'm not sticking around. You got me there."

At least he knew the truth. He sighed. "That's settled. Where do you want to go and what do you want to know?"

"Anything and everything. I set my books in small towns and this one has been an inspiration, but I'm thinking there's more to Sullavan than meets the eye." Tristan fell into step beside Michael. "I'm not talking backdoor abortions or illegal gambling houses. Just…the cool things about town that are fascinating."

Cool and interesting were his specialties. Michael nodded toward the main road. "When Sullavan was founded…rather, before it was founded, the three-hundred-fifty acres belonged to Edgar Sullavan. He'd purchased it in 1800. He'd inherited money from his mother's side of the family and used it to buy the land." He pointed to the town square. "When we get up to the square, you can see the outline in the grass as to where his house stood. It burned down in 1810. In 1803, when Ohio became a state, people were encouraged to settle here, but the Sullavan area had a lot of poverty. Since he had the land and wasn't really using it — he wasn't farming or anything — he sold off two-acre parcels. But since he was selling his property off, he decided to turn it into a town." He stopped at the square with Tristan. "See, there's the foundation of the house."

Tristan snapped a few pictures, then crouched to touch the remaining stones. "This was a big house."

"For one guy, even, yeah. He had four servants and their families living with him." Michael leaned on the bench in front of where the house had stood. "He might have seemed stingy, making those people pay for the land, but he wasn't. He charged a whole dollar for each parcel." He pointed to the north, then south. "This road isn't Church Street for nothing. Every church in the village is on this street. Three to the north and four to the south. That was part of Sullavan's plan. He wanted the shops on Main Street and the churches on Church Street."

"Handy." Tristan stood, then stretched. "Makes sense then, why the B&B and car dealership are next to each other."

"There aren't any businesses in town that aren't on Main Street." He turned around. "North end of this circle is the school quadrant. The school house that was on that property was moved to where it is now so the larger elementary building could take its place."

"Which is why the library is in the old school house," Tristan said. "Nice."

"Exactly. Why ruin a perfectly good old building just because it's not big enough? So it was moved and the new school was built. When students are ready for junior and high school, they go over to Black River. Sullavan, Western Reserve, Shiloh and Camden all feed into Black River. The actual school is in Camden."

Tristan nodded. "Smart."

"So, we've got the businesses right on the main drag and the churches on the other. The southern quadrant of the town square is for the park and playground. We have fireworks there every tenth of July." Michael gestured to the sidewalk. "There are more trees over there. We can take a break."

Tristan followed him across the street, then sat beside him on the other bench. "Now wait. Why on the tenth?"

"Financial reasons. It's cheaper to have the festivities on an off day versus the main one." Michael shrugged. "We still have a festival for the Fourth of July, but it's more like a weeklong carnival that culminates in the fireworks show on the tenth."

"I've never heard of that."

"All the villages around here do it. No one can afford the rates for the guys who set off the fireworks to do it on the fourth." He rested his arm on the back of the bench, then turned to Tristan. "The park was originally Edgar's back yard...kind of. He made sure there was a place for the children in the area to play. Turned out he was a big kid and liked kids, but never had any of his own." He paused. Most of the townsfolk assumed Edgar hadn't found the right woman to marry. Through his research, Michael had figured out the real reason he hadn't paired up—Edgar was gay and preferred to play the stately gentleman role rather than out himself. The people wouldn't have liked him back then if they'd known the truth, which saddened Michael.

"Edgar is an interesting fellow." Tristan pulled his notebook out and scrawled on the pages. "Just a moment. I'm taking notes and working out something."

"Take your time." He gazed around the park and drank in the beauty of the space. He'd forgotten how nice the area was. Wonderful landscaping, lush flowers and plenty of room for recreation. He could see a wedding being held there.

"I'm impressed." Tristan bumped shoulders with him. "The guy loved his plans, didn't he?"

"Order." Michael nodded. "He wanted things a certain way. When he planned Sullavan, he wasn't naming it after him and it was much smaller. He kept the ownership of the outlying areas, but yeah, the town was dinky."

"It's not that big now." Tristan chuckled. He draped his arm across the back of the bench. "But it's quaint."

"I agree."

"When did the name change? What was it originally?"

"Moreland. I don't know why. Maybe he liked it a lot. But it was Moreland for twenty years, then in 1825 he passed away and the people in charge decided to rename it for him." He grinned. "It's a boring little place, but it's home."

"What's there to do other than walk around and learn about the place?" Tristan asked.

"Not much. We had a bowling alley, but it closed. Had a bistro, but that went under when someone burned it to the ground. There's the diner and two bars, but I don't go to those often."

"No? Where do you go?"

"There's a bookstore and it has a coffee shop. I go there. I spend a lot of time with Molly because she's alone at the B&B. Her last boyfriend was a real peach and when he left, he screwed her over. Stole her money, wrecked her car...so she's kind of touchy." He stretched his legs. "Otherwise I do my own thing. I spend a lot of time at the library and working with the ladies group who helps the library."

"No boyfriend?"

Isn't he full of questions again? "No."

"Me either." Tristan blew out a long breath. "Why don't we go down to the diner? I'm starving and...why not?"

"Sure." He eyeballed Tristan. The guy wasn't asking him to come home with him. Just a meal together. Why did this feel like more? Because he wanted more? Christ, he hadn't gone out with anyone since Barry and even then, the connection wasn't strong. He stood and stretched, then settled next to Tristan. He could be crazy, but he'd like to find out more about Tristan.

Tristan remained beside Michael as they walked to the diner. He could get used to being with Michael. He'd only been in town for twenty-four hours and he couldn't fathom not having Michael in his life. As friends? Absolutely. As lovers? If he had his way, then yes. He admired the different buildings along the route.

Many of the storefronts bore art deco influence. He stopped in front of an abandoned former appliance store. "What happened here?"

"It went under. People wanted cheaper prices." Michael shrugged. "I think it would make a great store for something else." He cupped his hands against the glass and peered through the window. "It's got a second floor and a lot of the neon still works."

"Yeah?" He shielded his eyes and peeked through the glass. Sure enough, he noticed the second floor and the raised areas of the first floor. "Has anyone tried to resurrect it?"

"No." Michael strode away from the building.

Sadness settled deep in Tristan's bones. Where he lived in New York, shops sprang up and collapsed yearly. A few went the distance, but most didn't. He missed the fun of record shopping for vinyl and second-hand books at another store. He saw so much potential in Sullavan, but he also understood the reality of keeping a business alive. He paused.

The characters spoke to him. One of them wanted to keep a struggling business going. One that was started by the father of the lawyer, but was now that he was ready for retirement. Tristan nodded. He'd have to jot that notation down once they got to the diner.

"Are you okay?" Michael stopped. "Tristan?"

Hearing his name on Michael's lips shouldn't have turned him on, but it did. His nerve endings sizzled and his heartbeat sped up. He longed to touch Michael again. The stolen moments back at the park weren't enough. He'd gotten an erection just from sitting beside him.

"Well?" Michael frowned. "What's up?"

"I had a piece of the story fall into place and am trying to remember it." He hurried up to Michael and fell back into step with him. "I'll write it down when we get a table."

"Well, you won't have to wait long. We're here." Michael pointed to a building laden with shiny metal and lots of glass.

Tristan stepped back and admired the diner. If he'd chosen anywhere to house a diner, this wouldn't have been it. The façade reminded him more of a factory than an eatery. "This is it?"

"Yeah." Michael held the door for him. "Carl and Jenny bought the office space from the steelworks and turned it into a diner."

He strode into the foyer, then stopped. The inside wasn't anything like he'd expected, either. A long counter stretched most of the length of one side of the room. Shiny chrome stools lined the front of the counter. Booths comprised the rest of the room, but those featured chrome tubing and reminded him more of bus seats than regular booths.

"They upcycled and recycled pieces from the steelworks as well as the bus depot that used to stand beside the building." Michael led him to one of the booths. "Make yourself at home. One of the servers will be by. Here's the menu." He offered up a single laminated sheet. "There isn't much variety, but the food Carl and Jenny make is awesome."

"Nice." He pulled his notebook from his bag and scrawled his notes into it. He'd worry about the characters later, but the name Jenny sparked his imagination. He added that to the list, then tucked the notebook away.

Michael said nothing and toyed with the menu. He tapped one side with his fingers.

Tristan stilled Michael's hands — to stop the nervous gesture and to hold Michael's hand. He understood what Michael wanted out of the pairing. He needed to know he wouldn't be used and he had good reasons for it. Tristan wouldn't be in town long and getting involved wasn't smart. But that didn't stop him from wondering. Michael was sweet, sexy in a geeky way and everything Tristan didn't look for in a man.

He scanned the menu and decided on his lunch, then focused on Michael again. "Why'd you come to Sullavan? What was the draw?"

"A job." Michael sat back in his seat, but didn't pull away from Tristan. "I was fresh out of college and needed a source of income to pay back my student loans. I applied at over two dozen libraries. Sullavan was the only one to call me back and that was through the parent Black River Library system. They seemed to like me and I got the job. Thirteen years later and I'm still here. I made learning about Sullavan my personal goal because I thought it was important. If someone comes to town, then they'll start here. We have people come back often for genealogical searches."

"Neat." He rubbed the top of Michael's hand. "I can't say I'm that important. I'm not vital to much."

"I'm sure you are. Al thought a lot of you. He spoke about you once or twice."

"He did?" He hadn't thought about his uncle much in the last year. "So, you know me?"

"I know of you. He said he had a nephew who wrote books and was in New York. I assumed the state and that you did what he claimed, but I never asked your name." Michael shrugged. "Al was quiet, but he'd speak to me. I think he felt lonely and coming to the library was a comfort."

The more Michael spoke, the more Tristan saw his uncle in a different light. He'd barely thought about the man, but knowing Al had been proud of him enough to mention him... That was big.

"Then what do you do? Write books?" Michael's eyes flashed. "Anything good? I heard you say something to Dicey about being an author. We're always looking for anyone who's written a book and is willing to impart information to the writers' group. They can use the guidance. I'm no help. I have no desire to pen anything but the daily logs."

He'd have to tell his story. He owed Michael that much. But he wanted to keep his secret a little while longer.

Chapter Four

Michael stared at Tristan. He'd asked something too personal. He hadn't thought chatting about Tristan's writing was off limits, but now? He wished he could take the question back. "Never mind. It's not important."

Tristan smiled. "Just a couple of novels."

"Oh." Novels? *Holy shit.* A couple of three-hundred-page books were nothing? *Jesus.* He glanced down at Tristan's hand. He should put space between them, but couldn't. He liked the way Tristan touched him. The simple gesture offered a bit of comfort, but from what? He wasn't sure. "When do you meet with the lawyer?" He didn't know what else to ask and fumbled for the question. "I know you said, but I forgot."

"Tomorrow at ten. We're going to go over the will and his estate. Sounds like it's pretty cut and dry. Just show up, listen and sign stuff. He'll give me the keys to my uncle's house and I'll be expected to go through it." Tristan paused. "If there are any books, would you be interested in adding them to the library's collection?"

"I'll do my best to get them added, yes." Michael nodded. Donations were always welcome. Knowing they were from Al's collection was more significant to Michael. He'd both liked and respected the man. He'd be honored to have the volumes.

"I'm assuming I'll have to sell off some of the stuff. Think you might want to help me? I don't know the zoning about having a garage sale or whatnot, donation centers and anywhere else to dispose of the items."

Michael's stomach growled. *Where's the server?* He suppressed a groan. Tristan would have to get rid of some of Al's things, but the very thought saddened him. *Someone's whole life reduced to a garage sale?*

"But I'm not entirely sure what I'm up against, so any help is welcome," Tristan said. "Oh, looks like the server is coming."

Michael welcomed the interruption. Thinking about Al's things and how to deal with them shouldn't be so depressing. He'd known the man, but not all that well. Now he knew Tristan — kind of. He knew part of the story, but not much of it. He placed his order, then pulled his hand away and twiddled with his phone.

"Fuck," Tristan murmured.

"What?" He glanced up from his phone. "Something wrong? Lawyer busy?"

"No." Tristan swiped his fingers across his tablet screen and growled. "I don't know what I ever did to this person, but I swear this creepiness can stop." He turned the device around. "See this?"

Michael read through the words on the screen. Whoever had written the email wasn't happy. "Do you get these often?"

"Fan mail? Yes. This? No." Tristan closed out of the email and shoved his tablet into his bag. "I understand where reading is an escape. It's allowing someone else into a world you've created, but Jesus. This person seems to think they own me or at least have a say in what I write."

"Do you often ask for reader input?" Michael asked. He'd never received fan mail or sent it, so he had no idea what the author of the email was thinking.

"I don't. I release nothing until I have a firm idea of the story and have the contract in hand. No one knows anything until I do." His face brightened as the server approached. Tristan rattled off his order as if he'd eaten at the diner a hundred times.

Michael fumbled through his order, then once the server left, he folded his hands and considered Tristan. He thought about questioning Tristan again. "So, have you always wanted to write?"

"Since I was a kid." Tristan grinned. "I used to love to fill notebooks. My mother would buy all these notebooks with pretty pictures on the front or comic book heroes and give them to me to write whatever I wanted. The early stuff made no sense, I'm sure. I never found the old notebooks, but I remember some of what I wrote. I'd jot down all kinds of things. I think it made her happy to see me doing something that wasn't destructive. What about you? Have you always wanted to be a librarian?"

Michael chuckled. "Well…not really. I love books and learning. I want to know things and make discoveries. I love the smell of the ink and paper, the sound of the pages turning and to be surrounded by books." The tips of his ears burned. He wasn't embarrassed by his love of the written word. Hell, he owned his desire. But did Tristan care?

"You speak so lyrically about it." Tristan toyed with his napkin.

Michael considered saying more, but their order arrived along with their drinks. Instead of conversation, he busied himself with eating. One thing that drove him nuts was when people spoke while they ate. One or the other, he liked to say. Never both. Plus, he rather liked the silence between them. He and Tristan seemed to have developed a rapport. They understood each other.

Michael finished his sandwich and green beans, then polished off his glass of water. He sat back in his seat. "That was fantastic."

"It was." Tristan blotted his mouth. "Best grilled cheese I've had in forever." When the server brought the check, Tristan grabbed the piece of paper first. "My treat."

"Oh. Thank you." He hated to sound inconsiderate. "You didn't have to."

"I asked you out. I should pay." Tristan folded the receipt. "Next time you're welcome to get the check."

"Deal." Michael placed a five-dollar bill on the table, then followed Tristan to the register. He didn't stay with Tristan and instead went out to the sidewalk. He needed a minute to breathe. He'd learned a little, but not enough about Tristan. *Christ, what is happening to me?* A couple of days, he felt comfortable with the man? He'd lost his mind. Hadn't he learned from his time with Barry that trust was earned, not given? Damn. He glanced over his shoulder. Besides, he couldn't help feeling hurt. Tristan had kissed Barry. Didn't the kiss mean anything? And if he kissed Tristan, would that be a hollow gesture, too?

Tristan emerged from the diner. "I thought you left."

"Nah. Just needed to be outside. It's a beautiful day."
He stuffed his hands into his pockets. "Thanks again
for lunch—er, supper? Lupper?" He laughed at his
confusion. "Whatever it was, I enjoyed it."

"My pleasure."

Michael hesitated, then collided with Tristan.
"Sorry."

"Don't be." Tristan's eyes sparkled and he mashed his
mouth down on Michael's.

Michael swore he saw stars and his brain misfired.
He'd been kissed before, but not like this. He bit back a
groan. The kiss was good and hot. Perfect. He couldn't
close his eyes. He needed to know this moment was
real, despite trying to convince himself not to get
attached to Tristan.

Tristan broke the connection first and licked his lips.
"I'm not supposed to do that."

"What?" He'd been knocked off-kilter. He needed to
regain his bearings. "Lick your lips? Or kiss me?"

"Both." Tristan slid his hand around to the back of
Michael's neck. He rested his forehead against
Michael's and traced circles with his thumb on
Michael's skin. "You said to keep my distance."

"I did." His voice sounded huskier than he'd thought
possible.

"But I don't want to."

"You're leaving soon," Michael mumbled.

"I know." Tristan brushed his nose along Michael's.
"This feels like a dream."

"Uh-huh."

"Don't want it to end." Tristan feathered his lips over
Michael's and kissed him again. "But I know the score.
You're right."

"About?" He didn't know up from down, right from wrong. Tristan had him all turned around.

"Us being together. It's doomed," Tristan murmured. "But I don't care. I like challenges and doing this with you seems like a worthy challenge."

Michael couldn't speak. He should argue or at least stick up for himself, but he couldn't form sentences.

"Come back to the B&B with me," Tristan said. "I want you." He kissed Michael a fourth time. "Please?"

For a long second, Michael considered going with Tristan. His body craved the attention and his dick throbbed. He could use the release. He wanted so badly to lose himself in Tristan and ignore the ramifications. But he couldn't. "No."

Tristan pulled away a bit. "No?"

He shook his head. Maybe Tristan wasn't used to hearing the word no, but he had no choice. "I'm sticking around Sullavan. I don't want to be your man of the evening. I'd rather go home with a hard-on than be with you and regret it." *Shit.* He hadn't thought he could push Tristan away, but being honest might as well have sent him packing back to wherever he was from.

"Understood." Tristan let go. "I wish you didn't make such good sense."

"It's a fault of mine." He struggled to keep from going after Tristan, or at least pleading for Tristan to stay. "I can't be a sometime guy. I'm the boyfriend type. You're passing through. We won't mesh."

"But that doesn't mean I'll stop trying to get with you." Tristan grinned. "I like you, Michael, and I meant what I said when I asked for your help." He paused. "I meant what I said about being with you, too."

Michael stared at him. *Really?*

"I'll come by the library after my meeting with the lawyer. Yes?" Tristan touched Michael's shoulder. "We'll do this."

"You're free to visit the building whenever you want." *What a ridiculous answer.*

"And I want you."

"It's a fool's mission." He wanted to say he wasn't interested, but he knew it was a lie.

"Good thing I love missions." Tristan let go of Michael and waved. "See you tomorrow."

"Sounds good." He waved and watched Tristan jaunt down the sidewalk. Michael sighed. He'd lost his touch. Liking a man who'd leave was silly. They could have a sweltering affair, right? A few days of the perfect relationship because it wouldn't have strings...right? He groaned. He had a feeling he wouldn't be the same once he got involved with Tristan. He needed to get his head out of his ass and keep plugging along with his life. The library needed him—not Tristan. He wished convincing his heart what his head already knew didn't seem so impossible. After Tristan, he'd never be the same. But could he move on without him?

* * * *

Tristan spent the night tossing and turning. He kept thinking about Michael and the kisses. Instead of pushing Michael away with his boldness, he'd created a bizarre connection between them. Michael hadn't come home with him, but he'd certainly considered it. He could've had Michael in his bed. Michael.

But as much as he thought about the sexy librarian, the emails came to mind. The fan wasn't quitting.

Tristan was the first to admit he lived his life on the edge. He chased crazy leads for his books and didn't settle—except with men. So why did the latest email and Michael both have him out of sorts? Because the fan hadn't given up and Michael was different from Tristan's type. He forced Tristan to behave and use his manners. Michael expected Tristan to be the real man, not the full-of-shit author persona. That had to count for something, right?

He wasn't sure.

Then there was the fan. Who had such a deep desire to have their book written? Who would keep contacting him? Did other authors have this problem? Were they pestered until they wrote for the fans, not for the characters? Or did they ignore the outside influences?

Although he could've sworn he stayed up all night, he finally fell asleep. The alarm clock buzzed at seven in the morning and roused him. He groaned and stretched. The bed was fine, but the rest sucked. He could use a hearty breakfast and good conversation. He showered, dressed then headed downstairs in search of Molly and food.

Instead of Molly, he located a basket of muffins and two pitchers on the table. A note accompanied the mini feast.

Had to run to the store and dentist. Will be back soon. Enjoy breakfast.
Molly

The dentist at seven in the morning? He glanced down at the time on his phone. Okay, so it was closer to eight, but still. He snatched a muffin from the basket, then poured himself a cup of coffee. If he'd written the note into one of his books, the readers would laugh and claim no one wrote such a thing. Then again, he would've followed up with a snarky line from a secondary character. *The dentist? Must be a thorough kind of dentist.* He snorted. Yeah, he'd have to add her note into his book somehow.

He carried the muffin and coffee back to his room. Once he'd put the food down, he sat at the little writing desk and read through the paper on his tablet app. A new gallery exhibit had opened in the studio near his apartment. The chamber orchestra had a concert scheduled for that weekend and a fellow author was lecturing at three of the local library branches. The baseball teams were both on hot streaks and the football teams were in talks to sign players before the draft.

He leaned back in his seat. For all the stuff going on, there wasn't much happening. Part of him missed the excitement of the city. He could be at the lecture, opening or concert within an hour and there was always something to do. But he kind of liked the laid-back quality of Sullavan. There were things to do in town, but not the rush. He'd get bored if he stuck around.

Or would he?

Why was he even considering it?

Being in Sullavan would mean fewer interruptions for his writing, and the story of the town captivated him. He'd be able to use many of the pieces in later tales. But was the quiet enough to make him stay? Would Michael want him if he did?

He needed to stop thinking about the what-ifs and live. He had time to write and a place to do it. He checked the clock. Almost nine in the morning. He should finish up his muffin and head down to the lawyer's office. He read and reread the name on the paperwork. Jamie Meyer, esquire. Was he the only lawyer in Sullavan? If so, then it was no wonder the guy was busy.

He sighed. Uncle Al would give him hell for not settling down or at least being respectable. Was passing down the estate and whatever else was involved his uncle's way of putting up speed bumps in order to make Tristan smell the roses, so to speak?

Probably.

Tristan abandoned his coffee cup and the paper from the muffin, then tucked his things into his messenger bag and headed down to the front door. He should stop obsessing about what others wanted for him and embrace his life. Obsessing about Michael wasn't smart, either.

He wandered down the street to the square, then checked the street signs. According to the paperwork, the office was on North Main. He kept going until he found the right building. He stepped into the foyer. A pretty blonde woman sat behind the desk.

"Hi, I'm Tristan Paulson, and I'm here to see Mr. Meyer." Tristan grasped the handle of his bag. "I have an appointment for nine."

"I know who you are." She slid a book across her desk. "I've been expecting you. I'm a huge fan. I've read all of your books and this is my favorite one." She paused. "Would you autograph it?"

"Sure. Should I put your name or just my scrawl?"

"Oh. My name. I'm Sallie." She smiled and fluttered her lashes. "Thank you."

"No problem." He wrote a quick note thanking her for being a reader, then added one of his quirky smiley faces below his autograph. "Enjoy."

"I will." She caressed the cover. "You know, you should write about Sullavan."

"Oh?" For half a moment, he wondered if Sallie was the emailer. *Nah.* He'd just met her.

"We're quirky enough." She tapped the top of her desk, then caught him watching her. She grinned. "Invisible keyboard."

"Nice." *High tech...* "Well, I'm ready when he is."

"Jamie will be ready in about ten minutes. He's dealing with another client. You're welcome to wait here and have a cup of coffee. We've got cream, three kinds of sugar and hot cocoa, if that's your preference." She resumed typing on the desk. "Just be a few."

"Thanks." Tristan considered the coffee, then decided against a cup. Too much more and he'd float away. He strode over to the picture window and watched the scant traffic on the street. At home, the line of cars up and down the block never seemed to stop. Here, maybe two or three vehicles cruised the boulevard. Not fancy cars, either. Plain, dependable vehicles meant to get the passenger from point A to point B.

"Mr. Paulson?"

When Tristan turned, a man in his mid-thirties, with blond hair and dark eyes, smiled. His suit fit like a second skin and the scent of his cologne swirled around Tristan. He offered his hand. "I'm Jamie Meyer. Your uncle entrusted me with his estate planning."

"Ah. It's a pleasure to meet you." He shook hands with Jamie. *Firm grip.* When he met Jamie's eyes, a shiver ran the length of his spine. Now Jamie was his type of guy — polished, proper and damn sexy. The opposite of Michael. He paused. *Michael.* Fuck. He'd been making eyes at Michael, but now that he'd seen Jamie, he wasn't sure about his stance. What the hell was wrong with him? He'd gone right back to his old ways, that was what. Tristan regained his composure and followed Jamie into the second room.

"The documents are fairly simple." Jamie sat behind his desk, then pushed papers toward Tristan. He read through the will. "Does that make sense? You've been given the house, property and everything contained within."

Tristan glanced over the documents. Although he'd listened to everything Jamie had said, he still couldn't believe it. His uncle had three hundred thousand dollars? He'd never imagined Al had kept such a stash of money.

"Per his wishes, he's donated one-third to the school system, one-third to the library and the remaining third is to be used to found an LGBT center for Sullavan." Jamie tapped the pages together. "Just sign and we're set."

"He wants me to found an LGBT center?" He didn't know the first thing about founding a center. He knew how to balance his writing budget, but not well.

"Aldon thought it would be nice to have one here in town. He mentored some of the youth. You don't understand how lonely it can be when you're coming out and you're not sure if your family will accept you," Jamie said. "I know. I'm not from here. I came out to my parents and was thrown out of the house. I put myself through college and went to law school to help others."

"Noble." He sagged in his chair. Talking with Jamie brought up so many emotions. He'd been pushed aside by his family until his mother realized having a gay son made her more socially acceptable in her circles. Then he'd been included back into the will. Wouldn't she have blown a gasket if she knew Al was working with the LGBT community in Sullavan? She'd have been here in a heartbeat to help — and get the publicity.

"We don't have a huge LGBT community in Sullavan, but I'm sure there are plenty of kids in the cracks. That's who Al tried to help. People thought he was cranky and reclusive. He wasn't. He worked at the community center quite often." Jamie closed the folder. "He worked closely with the library, too."

"So I've heard." Michael hadn't told him about that. He'd have to make a point to discuss his uncle a second time.

"I'm willing to help you get the center up and running. I've got the addresses of a few buildings that would fit the requirements." Jamie smiled and folded his hands. His tan looked even darker against his crisp white shirt cuffs.

"Thanks." He could use all the help he could get. Michael would be a good resource, too. He'd have great insight and could give Tristan some direction.

"I see you're a writer." Jamie turned a copy of *Springdale* around. "My secretary got me hooked on your work."

Jamie didn't strike him as a reader of his books. "Thank you." He wasn't sure what else to say. If the lawyer had the novel in hand, then why would he ask? Tristan's picture was on the back.

"Is it hard? You know, writing a book? I draft legal documents all the time, but never books. I've thought about penning a novel." Jamie stuck his hands in his pockets. "I've always wanted to pick the brain of an author."

"Well, writing isn't easy. It takes time, devotion and commitment. If the characters and plot are working and grooving, then you've got a good start. I have character sheets for each book and detailed plot points. But if that's not working, then I end up spending a lot of time on social media or goofing off." Usually fucking his boyfriend of the moment, too.

"Understood."

He half expected Jamie to say he had an idea for a book and would Tristan give him pointers or his thoughts.

"Well, we're done here. All you've got to do is sign the papers and you're done. I've got the keys to the house and everything else. Here's the bank information. It wasn't stipulated whether you can keep the proceeds from the sale of his property. It's yours to handle the way you choose. I'll assume you'll want to do a sale." Jamie rocked on his heels. "Garage sales do well around here. Price stuff too high and people won't bite."

"Ah. I'll look the items and property over before I decide, but I'll probably have to get rid of some of it. I can't use the woodworking tools in New York." He scrawled his name on the pages, then pushed the document back to Jamie. "I don't have the room, either."

"I don't suppose you do." Jamie laughed, and the deep, throaty sound echoed in the room. "If you need help, I'm available most weekends."

"Oh." He hadn't expected that. "Uh, I'll let you know." Why was he tongue-tied around Jamie? He thought this only happened with Michael. Maybe he wasn't as attracted to Michael as he'd assumed? Or was he all-around nervous? Who knew? He wondered if he touched Jamie, would there be the same sizzle? He could test the theory, but not now. Doing so would be unprofessional. Besides...he wasn't in Sullavan to find a man. He was there for his Uncle Al and the book.

"Great." Jamie tucked the papers into the folder and pushed the ring of keys across the desk. "You're set."

"Thanks." He tucked the documents and keys into his bag. "I should get going. I want to see the house. I haven't been there in ages."

Jamie rounded the desk and offered his hand to Tristan again. His eyes smoldered. "My numbers are in the folder. Don't hesitate to contact me." He held onto Tristan's fingers for a long moment. Electricity sparked between him and Tristan.

"I won't." Tristan raked his gaze over Jamie. The man was handsome in a polished way. Not a blond hair out of place. No scruff and his skin glowed. He reminded Tristan of a model. His eyes sparkled and his smile came easy. He fit Tristan's usual preferences for a guy — tall and lean and well-spoken. But he came off a little too polished. Then again, he could be hot in a T-shirt and jeans combo. If he cut loose on the weekends, he could be right up Tristan's alley.

"Jamie, you have your next appointment here," Sallie said. "How much longer will you be?"

Tristan froze. Where was she? Probably behind him.

"Not long," Tristan said. He let go of Jamie's hand. "I should go. I need to see the house and Michael."

"Michael?" Jamie said. He frowned. "The librarian?"

"Yes." What was wrong with Michael?

"Oh. I didn't think you knew him." Jamie shrugged.

Was that a bit of his polish cracking? The careful façade slipping? Tristan bit back a snort. "I do."

"Well, I look forward to your call." Jamie rounded his desk and pressed a button on the little panel. "Give me five minutes, Sallie."

Tristan gathered up his bag and nodded to Jamie. He waved, then left the office. His brain ached. He had too much to think about and even more to do. He needed a plan. Instead of running straight back to the B&B, he stopped at the first bench.

He needed at least a solid twenty-four hours to work on the outline for his book. He had character sheets to finish and the setting to flesh out. If he had forty-eight hours, he could knock the outline out. But would he?

Christ. If he worked at the house in the morning and sorted through his uncle's stuff, then used the afternoon and night to write, he might be able to meet his deadlines. He still had to sort out the trust money and other parts of the estate. His better judgment stated he'd need at least a week for to settle things. Then there was the LGBT center. He had no idea how to set such a thing up.

He rested his head in his hands. His heart raced and his stomach lurched. Anxiety hit hard. Could he accomplish everything his uncle wanted *and* get the book done? He wasn't sure. He gasped for air and sat back in his seat. If he was going to even consider all his tasks, he needed silence and strong coffee.

Tristan left the bench and marched straight to the B&B to drop off the folder and pick up his car. Once he'd made the switch, he headed to the bookstore for the coffee. He could conquer his to-do list with the right amount of help and caffeine. He paid for the tart brew and hustled back to the car. *Next stop, Al's house.* But first…he wanted to see Michael.

Chapter Five

Michael rifled through the box of books one more time, then leaned back on the stool. His muscles ached from sitting in the same position. He'd never finish sorting the books in the shed if he didn't keep pushing forward. Half of the contents of the box could go into the library's permanent collection and the other half would be great for the system-wide bookmobile. He'd have to weed out some of the older, worn titles from the library's inventory, but maybe if he re-shelved, he could save as many books as possible from being removed.

One of the books caught his attention. The romance bore a simple title. *Tristan.* He snorted. No matter where he turned, he kept being reminded of the man who seemed to take up his thoughts. Tristan, despite his pushiness, was a nice guy. He was handsome and his kisses warmed Michael's blood. His lips still tingled. But what was he doing? Tristan would leave.

He sagged in his chair. Would a short affair do him that much damage? No. He'd survive. He might even have a nice time. Something simple, hot and unforgettable. A quickie relationship with Tristan could be just the thing he needed. A good time with no regrets.

He picked up the last book in the box. The name caught his attention. *Another Tristan book?* He flipped the novel over and his breath lodged in his throat. *Tristan Paulson.* Other people in the world could have the same name. Just because Tristan said he was a writer didn't mean he was published. He hadn't crowed about having books in circulation.

Michael spied the photo. His friend stared back at him from the professional image. *Holy shit.* The moment he saw the picture, he knew. Tristan. How'd he miss this? Yes, he'd been told Tristan was a writer, but he hadn't been given a rundown of Tristan's work. Most writers he'd met wanted to give him their entire backlist and biography. Tristan claimed he was in Sullavan doing research. Why hadn't Michael done research on him? He should've put the facts together and realized he had an actual published novelist in his midst.

Well, fuck. Had he been too dazzled by Tristan? Stunned? No. He hadn't used his damn head to learn more about the new guy in town.

Michael flipped through the novel. Although he'd once heard of Tristan's work, he'd never read any of it. He shuffled the pages, but saw nothing. He shook his head and closed the book. He didn't need to read Tristan. What he wanted was answers. If Tristan wasn't talking about his life, then what was holding him back? Didn't he trust Michael? And why did that possible lack of trust bother Michael to his core?

Dicey appeared at the door. "Hey. Have you gotten anywhere?"

"I did." He tossed Tristan's book into the box meant for the collection. "I'm almost done."

"Good, but don't toss books." She grinned. "You have a visitor." She drummed her fingers on the doorframe. "For a guy who isn't planning on being here long, Tristan keeps showing up."

Michael paused. Dicey liked everyone, but her tone wasn't upbeat. If she saw something in Tristan she didn't like, she needed to tell him. What had she noticed that wasn't right? "You don't like him."

"I never said that," she said and blushed. "Now…"

"Now what?" He leveled his gaze at her. "Tell me."

She shrugged. "He shows up a lot."

"And?" Lots of people visited the library on a daily basis. Most came to read the papers or use the computers. Tristan being there wasn't out of the ordinary — except he wasn't from Sullavan.

"I don't know," she said. She wouldn't look at him. "I'm concerned."

"About? Tell me so, if I'm needed inside, I can get going or steel myself for what I might see." He hadn't wanted to vocalize that last bit. *Damn.*

Dicey toyed with the peeling paint on the wooden frame. "I'm concerned. He shows up and he's nice, but he knows he's going. Since he's started coming around, you've been happier than I thought was possible. I don't want to see you get hurt. I know you're careful, but you're like a son to me. Family anyway. I'm protective of you. I don't mind him visiting, but his sweet act is almost just that…an act."

He wasn't sure what to say. Yes, Tristan seemed too good to be true and Michael had decided to err on the side of caution, but...he liked Tristan—not just as a boyfriend but as a friend, too. Was his radar off? Normally he could spot fakers. Not with Tristan. Or was he seeing only what he wanted because he was lonely?

"Just be careful." She patted Michael's arm. "If you think he's good people, then do what you see fit. If you're even a little concerned, then use your common sense."

"Thanks, Dicey." He abandoned the box. He could sort books later. He followed her out of the shed, then locked up and headed into the main building. Tristan sat at the middle study table. He had his head down and was scrawling something in a notebook.

Michael hesitated. He didn't want to look too eager, since he didn't know what to think about Tristan at the moment.

Tristan glanced up and stopped writing. His face brightened. "Hi."

"Hi." He smiled. He couldn't ignore the sizzle in the pit of his stomach or the rush of heat below his belt. "How'd it go with the lawyer?"

"Good. I've got lots of new information, keys and checks. Jamie was thorough. I swear, I learned too much. My brain will explode." Tristan stood. "I didn't know my uncle well in the last few years, but I'm glad you were tight with him."

Michael tensed. He'd have to open up about how well he knew Al sooner rather than later. But not now. "He came in for books. I got the westerns in that he liked and he borrowed them." Better than telling the whole truth.

"Yeah, I remember you saying so." Tristan pulled a piece of paper from his bag. "My uncle bequeathed all of his books to the library. I bet you didn't know that."

"I didn't." Michael's knees buckled. If he'd thought he had too many hardbacks to deal with in the shed, he could only imagine how many Tristan would be donating. Al had been a voracious reader and at Michael's last count, Al had over three hundred books. Where in the hell would he put all the new additions? He didn't have much room.

"Well, he did. I'll need you to help me box and move them here." Tristan opened the folded page. "This is for you."

"Huh?" He glanced down at the item. A check. *Wait.* "What's this?"

"The last time I looked, it was a check made out to you for the library." Tristan grinned. "Now you can add onto the building or whatever the library needs— especially since now you're housing what I assume will be a whole lot more books."

Michael nudged Tristan's hands away and didn't take the check. He needed to talk to Tristan in private. "Dicey? Hold down the fort." He ushered Tristan into the men's room and locked the door. "I know this isn't the greatest place to talk, but it'll have to do."

"If you wanted a quickie to thank me for the money, you don't have to. I'd rather we have that quickie in my room at the B&B. It's more fun there and less...conspicuous. I'm sure your co-workers all know what we're about to do." Tristan snagged Michael in his embrace. "But I'm game."

He nudged Tristan away. "Jesus. No." His head ached. "I'm not coming on to you." *Not here and not right now.*

"Oh." Tristan bristled. "Sorry."

"I need honesty." He folded his arms and leaned against the bathroom door. "What's going on?"

"I gave you a check for a hundred grand, courtesy of my uncle. He wanted the library to have the money and his books to go here for others to enjoy." Tristan matched Michael's stance. "Why?"

"You're a writer. Why wouldn't he give the books to you?" Someone he loved, not someone he dealt with after the temporary love went away.

"No room," Tristan said.

"When were you going to tell me you're a bestselling published author? You're famous. I blathered on about having you come talk to the writers' group and you said nothing. You acted like you weren't anyone exciting." He tensed and his headache increased.

Tristan sighed. "I'm sorry."

"Me too." He shook his head. "I can't accept that money."

"Why?"

"I just can't." Not with the memories attached. Not when he knew how Tristan would react once he found out Michael's truth.

"Don't be ridiculous. I'm not the one coughing up this cash. My uncle wanted you to have it. So far, I'm not seeing an issue."

Other than him finally having to admit he'd been Al's lover for a summer and that he'd thought for those three months that he was in love...*yeah, no problems at all.* Then Al's nephew came to town and dredged up Michael's history. No sweat. He bit back a chuckle. No wonder he had trust issues. He couldn't even trust himself. "Why not tell me who you were from the beginning—not Al's nephew but the famous part?"

"What? I've written books and made a career of it. I have a trust fund because my mother married into a wealthy family. No one believes I'm the actual author of my books. The critics think I've had them ghostwritten since they believe I can buy anyone off. I haven't. Those are my words and my blood, sweat and tears in those novels. Now you know. I'm not ashamed for keeping quiet. What I wanted was to be accepted for me, Tristan. Not some figment of me that you and everyone else have created. Is that wrong? Too fucking bad."

"No," Michael murmured. "It's not wrong."

"I've got a goddamn stalker who keeps emailing me suggestions to write about a town called Lewiston. I have no fucking idea where that is and I haven't tried to look. On top of that, I'm supposed to be plotting my next book. Instead of writing, I'm trying to keep my sanity. I want to be safe and live my life. Right now, I don't know if I can."

Michael stared at Tristan. God. He'd gotten upset for mostly nothing. Yes, Tristan hadn't told him everything, but was his life story Michael's business? *Who am I protecting myself from? Me?* "I'm sorry."

Tristan shifted his weight from his left to his right foot and leaned against the wall of the bathroom stall. "You didn't know."

"Still…" He couldn't hide his shame.

"Michael." Tristan reached for him, then pulled back. "You gave me boundaries and I tried to stay within them, but I lied by omission. I get it. You need trust, but so do I."

"So, what do we do?" He hated being so angsty.

"First, you accept that check. It's for the library and made out to you or the system. I don't know. I just know I was supposed to give it to you. Al loved this place and he wanted to help it grow." Tristan inched toward Michael.

Michael nodded.

"Second, allow me to donate his books. Again, it's in the will. I have to comply. Besides, I don't even know what books he has to donate," Tristan said. He crept closer to Michael. "I'll cough up whatever you need to shelve, preserve and store them until you have space. I'll gladly dip into my trust for this." He smoothed the wrinkles in Michael's shirt. "I spent four summers in Sullavan and I had no idea we had a library. I never knew anything about this town."

And he knew nothing about his uncle. "You missed out." Michael allowed himself to relax. He liked when Tristan touched him. The ache in his lower belly grew and he longed to press himself against Tristan.

"Third, I like spending time with you. You're one of the good ones. You held me accountable when I wasn't ready to fess up. Not many people challenge me." Tristan wound his arms around Michael. "I'm intrigued and turned on by you." He paused and his eyes widened. "Based on that rod in your pants, I'm guessing you're pretty turned on, too."

"I am." He cleared his throat. This was so not the time or place to have a damn erection. "How do you know I'm not being nice so you won't think I'm your stalker? Or so I can get my hands on your money…that I didn't know you had?" *Jesus.* He needed to stop talking. He'd dug himself a deep hole.

"Do you know anything about Lewiston?" Tristan asked. He swayed with Michael.

"Which one? There isn't a Lewiston around here, but I'm sure there are at least two towns by that name in the surrounding five-state area." Michael shrugged. "But those towns are at least two hundred miles away."

"Exactly."

"I'm confused." He wanted to melt against Tristan. The warmth of Tristan's breath seeped to his core. He could get lost in Tristan's eyes and be happy never to find his way back out.

"The stalker wants me to write about Lewiston. No state or particulars given. Just write about this town." Tristan brushed his nose along Michael's. "If you have no idea, then the writer can't be you. You're too honest."

Don't be so sure about that. "Oh." He fumbled for words. With Tristan so close, his brain misfired. "I could be playing the fool."

"Nah." Tristan feathered a kiss over Michael's lips. "You don't trust me, but I trusted you from the start."

He had no words. Nothing. Besides, he couldn't shy away from Tristan. He'd have to tell him the truth, but the magnetism between him and Tristan was too much to fight.

"Would you take my check?" Tristan's voice came out husky. "And my books?"

"Yeah." Right now, he'd take anything Tristan would give him.

"How about going to my uncle's place tonight and we'll order pizza? We can sort and talk." Tristan cupped Michael's jaw in both hands. "Or do something else."

Fucking balls, he was in over his head. He had to gather his bearings. "How about we deposit that check first and figure out later…later? I'll tell Dicey and Cilla where I'm going. I'll count it as my lunch break and eat later." Maybe by then he'd have his head cleared.

"You're sure? You should eat."

"I'll be fine. I'd rather not have that check in the open." He wriggled free of Tristan and missed his warmth. He sighed, then unlocked the door. He almost collided with Dicey. "Hi."

"I wasn't listening," she said, then looked away. "Promise."

"Right." He stood tall. "I'll make an announcement later, but Al McCartney donated money to the library. I'm going with Tristan to the bank. I'll be back in half an hour, tops. Hold down the fort, okay? I'll have my phone and will run if you need me." He nodded once. "Okay?"

"Sure." Dicey stared at him. "Uh-huh."

Michael shifted into business mode. He had to think straight if he was going to the bank. Love-sickness and erections weren't welcome, no matter how sexy Tristan might be. He retrieved his phone and keys.

Dicey darted behind the counter and gestured to Tristan. She said something to him in low tones. When Michael approached, she scurried away.

"Everything okay?" Michael asked.

"Couldn't be better." Tristan held the door for Michael. "I'll bring him back in one piece."

Michael groaned. Dicey had probably given Tristan advice or asked about what they'd done in the bathroom. After that comment, she'd tell everyone he'd had sex in the men's room. He shoved the keys into his front pocket and his phone into his shirt pocket.

"She tried to warn me." Tristan fell into step beside Michael. "Told me if I hurt you, she'd hurt me."

"She would."

"I know," Tristan said. "She likes you."

"She's mentioned that a few times."

"What is it about you that's so irresistible?"

"Don't ask me. I have no clue." He focused on the sidewalk before him and kept moving forward. He had to change the subject. "I like that you're writing about Sullavan. Are you doing the research for that next book?"

"Sort of. I'd planned on writing another novel, but had no inspiration. I was going to throw a dart at a map and go wherever the dart landed, but I got the call from Jamie first." Tristan shrugged. "Divine intervention, I guess."

Michael cringed and hoped Tristan didn't notice. He had nothing against Jamie Meyers other than the guy was sexy and had money. He'd be more compatible with Tristan. Plus, Tristan wouldn't want to be with the man who'd once been with his uncle. It wasn't right.

"I lied to my publisher and said I had an idea." Tristan shrugged. "When I got here, I went right to the B&B. I saw this photo on the wall and my imagination went berserk. The characters started talking to me and I got part of the outline jotted down that night."

"Good job." Michael nodded. "We turn here. There are three banks in Sullavan. First National, First County and Bank of Sullavan. Each one is owned by a different board of trustees. They're pretty much interchangeable except for the buildings. I love the architecture. All columns and marble façades. Here's our bank. First County." He opened the door for Tristan. "The ironwork around the teller windows is original. The marble is, too. County's the oldest bank in town." He approached the available teller and, within fifteen minutes, the check was deposited and the deal sealed. The manager said he would call the financial officer for the library. At least the check wasn't in the open.

Walking around with a hundred grand, even just written down, seemed impossible to Michael.

Tristan remained beside Michael and left the bank. "That was simple." He laughed. "I thought donations were difficult. You smiled, I signed stuff and we're done."

"I never helped handle a donation that big." Other than second-hand clothes, old textbooks and Christmas donations, he'd never done anything so expensive.

Tristan didn't say anything until he and Michael were in front of the library. "I should ask you to lunch since I used your lunch hour."

"It's fine." He had stuff he could eat on the go. Besides, he spent more lunch hours working than he spent them relaxing. "I won't have time anyway. Cilla leaves at two, then Dicey at six. Lauren will be in at three, but still. I don't like leaving the place understaffed."

"Understandable. When are *you* done?"

"At eight. We close on Wednesdays and Saturdays at one. We're closed on Sunday and the rest of the week we're open until eight. I'm the only full-time librarian, so I have to be here when most everyone else isn't."

Tristan pulled a pen from his bag. He grabbed Michael's hand and wrote numbers on Michael's skin. "Call me. I want to get together and not just for the books."

"You haven't seen them." He pressed his hand against his thigh and hoped the ink wouldn't smear.

"No."

"Give yourself time to go through the books and Al's things. Wander down memory lane. He'd want you to." Michael sighed. "Then worry about me."

"Why don't you call me anyway?" Tristan wriggled his eyebrows. "Please?"

"I will." He should've kept his distance, but Tristan was too tempting.

Tristan started away, then strode back to Michael. Instead of speaking, he kissed Michael hard on the mouth. A rough, claiming kiss …and it worked. Michael moaned into the kiss. Anyone could see him and Tristan. Did he care? Part of him did, but the rest didn't.

Tristan rested his forehead on Michael's. "Don't forget."

"I won't." He couldn't if he'd tried. He watched Tristan climb behind the wheel of his car and drive off. Dicey's words came back to him in a flood. She wanted him to be careful. But Tristan was so enticing. He wanted to dip his toe into the dating pool once more, even if it meant a fling with a guy he'd never see again. He touched his lips. The tingle was still there. He shouldn't have been attracted to Tristan, but whatever. *I could live a little, right?*

Christ. He needed aspirin. His headache wasn't going away and he had the feeling it wouldn't until Tristan Paulson left town.

Tristan drove away from the library, his heart hammering. Seeing Michael was a good jolt to his system. Michael reenergized him. He liked the way Michael felt in his arms, too. But then there was Jamie. Okay, so the lawyer hadn't come on to him, but the vibe was there. Was he callous enough to think he could juggle two men in one small town? Then have the balls to leave them both high and dry?

Instead of stopping at the B&B for food, he drove straight to his uncle's home. He should've grabbed something to eat, but the desire to get the hell away from his problems overruled his hunger pangs. He motored to the edge of town, then turned onto the gravel drive leading to his uncle's farmhouse. Technically, the property was in the village limits, but to the outside observer the place looked like a farm. He parked by the house and turned the car off. The silence enveloped him and he appreciated the calm.

He breathed in the fresh air. For a split second, he could see himself living here. Would the silence be deafening to his writing career? Or just what he needed to stay on task? He left the vehicle and wandered around the front yard. Despite some overgrowth, the flower beds were still lush with vibrant color. He could only imagine the number of hours his uncle had spent out here. He'd forgotten just how picturesque the property was and how much he enjoyed being there.

Tristan fished in his pocket for his keys, then made his way to the front of the house. He glanced down at the ring. Five keys and no labels. *Drat.* He tried each one in the lock until the mechanism opened. He'd have to put a mark on that key to remind him that it went in the front door. Once he stepped into the house, memories rushed back to him. He'd spent four summers on this property. Each time he'd arrived, he'd pretended not to be a child of wealth, but a regular kid. He'd learned how to fish, camp, start fires, shoot and cook so he could take care of himself. He'd never used any of the outdoors experience in his current life, but he still remembered what was important. *Crazy.* Why had he buried all those memories? Because once he went home, his parents had demanded he play a part in their spoiled situation. He'd acted like a playboy brat, but no one had corrected him—except his uncle. At one time, he'd hated his uncle for requiring more from him. Now he wished he'd had more opportunities to get to know his mother's brother.

Now that Tristan was back in Sullavan, the real man—not the asshole—had come out. The muted version, the one with sentimentality and heart, showed up. Which side did he like better? The quieter one. He strode into the kitchen. Tears burned at the corners of his eyes. He should've spent more time with his uncle. He'd forgotten Al's love of art and books. He spotted the library. His heart lodged in his throat.

Tristan ventured into the dark room and flicked the switch. The walls were lined with shelves and every available space featured books. He leaned against the Queen Anne chair and sighed. So many books... *What in the hell?* Panic set in. His heart hammered again and he wiped his clammy hands on his pant legs. The sheer volume of stuff in the house overwhelmed him. He had so much to clean out and not enough time. Then there was the book he should've been working on. His legs trembled and he swayed. He needed to sit down.

He collapsed on the chair and sucked in a ragged breath. No amount of panic would help. He had to meet this challenge head-on. No matter how much he didn't want to face his problems, they wouldn't be gone because he flipped out. He willed himself to calm down. He had a few contacts for help and could get through this.

He pulled his phone from his pocket, then paused. *I'll call Michael.* Wait, no he wouldn't. He didn't have Michael's number. *Shit.* He sighed, then turned the ringer on in case Michael happened to call him. He grinned. Yeah, he'd grown fond of the librarian.

Tristan glanced around the room again and gripped the arms of the chair. He'd have to treat his next few weeks as an adventure. Writing at night and working during the day. The longer he stared at the books, the more the characters spoke to him. Calm settled around him and he nodded. The library was his redemption. The characters needed the books to spur his imagination and he had to hang on for the ride…maybe bring Michael along.

Chapter Six

Tristan smoothed out the piece of paper and looked over his notes. His hand ached from writing so much, but he liked what he had written down. Not only did he have the character names, but the outline was complete and he knew how the first scene would play out. Writing longhand wasn't his usual, but of late he'd done a lot of stepping outside of his norm. Not jumping on Michael from day one, not trying to screw the next available guy...he'd even gotten some writing accomplished.

What time is it? He fumbled on the desk for his phone.

Using the first available paper for his notes hadn't been the best idea, but he had to go with the flow. When the words came, he followed. Where in the hell was the phone? Under more papers. He moved the sheets out of the way and turned the device over. As if on cue, the phone lit up.

Tristan swiped to retrieve the call and switched to the speaker setting. "Hello?"

"Hi, it's Jamie."

He paused. *Jamie?* Realization dawned on him. *The lawyer.* "Oh, hey."

"Thought I'd check on you," Jamie said. "Everything okay?"

"Yeah, I'm pretty good. It's been a day, though. I dropped the check off with Michael. I had planned on calling the school, but I got lost in my writing."

"I spoke to the superintendent and explained the situation. He's expecting to hear from you in the next few days."

"Oh, thanks." Rather forward, but Jamie was a lawyer and knew how to get business accomplished, he supposed. He flipped through the handwritten pages. As much as he wanted to get back to his story, he needed a break...but not with Jamie.

"You're quiet," Jamie said. "Need help? It's after six and I've got everything in hand for tomorrow. I'm available."

After six? Shit. He hadn't even checked the time. His phone had rung too fast for him to notice. Did he want to meet up with Jamie?

"Tristan? I can be there in ten minutes or can pick up food and be there in half an hour."

What does he want? "Nah, you've got to work tomorrow and I'm still up to my neck in stuff here. I haven't even scoped out the rest of the house. We should plan on something this weekend."

"Are you sure you don't want me to bring you food? It's been three weeks since Al's passing. I have no idea if anyone bothered to clean out the kitchen. Either way, you'll need food."

"Thanks, but I'll be okay. I had the utilities turned back on once I found out I owned the house, so the fridge is running." He hadn't thought about the state of the kitchen other than there was power. The idea of cleaning up rancid food churned his stomach. But…if it had to be done, then he had no choice. "You should get your rest so you can be all important and legal-y tomorrow."

"Nonsense."

"I'll be fine. Really." He pinched the bridge of his nose. Jamie wasn't getting his hint.

"All right, but I'm coming over around eight to check on you. No arguments," Jamie said. Before Tristan could say anything, Jamie hung up.

Tristan stared at the phone. Normally, he was the pushy one, expecting to be dealt with and loved. Being on the other end felt kind of odd. He sighed. He'd lost a lot of control by coming back to Sullavan. Part of him didn't mind, but the rest of him wasn't sure that not having everything in order was a good thing.

He left the phone on the table and considered his options. He had the house and could save a little cash by staying there versus at the B&B, but if Michael came over for dinner with Molly… He wandered out to the garage. His uncle still had the '72 Chevy in the garage. If the truck worked, then he could ditch the rental car, too. The truck would be better for hauling. If he knew his uncle, the truck was still in great condition and gassed up for the next drive. When he checked the gauges, his instincts were proven correct. He tested the keys he hadn't marked and when he slid the last one into the ignition, it fit. He left the keys in the truck and stuffed his hands into his pockets. He might as well use what he'd inherited.

He headed back into the study and phoned the rental car company. Within fifteen minutes, he'd set up a time for the company to retrieve the vehicle. His stomach growled. Time to head into town for food, then back to the house to write...but with a pit stop at the B&B. He removed the keys from the truck ignition, then went back into the house to lock up. Collecting his things from his room shouldn't take long and if he called one of the pizza joints on the main drag, he could have the pie waiting for him when he finished.

Tristan slid behind the wheel of the rental car, then called in his pizza order. Once finished, he drove straight to the B&B. Molly stood at the counter.

"Hi, you." She smiled. "I haven't seen you around. How are you?"

"I'm good. I got the keys to Al's place and have been not going through his things." He drummed his fingers on the counter. "I need to settle up my bill. Since I have the house, I should probably stay there."

"Won't there be too many memories?" She opened her laptop. "I'm sorry. That's none of my business."

"No, it's a good question. I hadn't thought about it. The thing is, I haven't been there since I was fourteen. I have memories, but it's not the earth-shattering grief kind. It's like coming back to a warm spot and feeling safe—that sort of feeling."

"So, you're Al's nephew?" She pressed a button and a piece of paper slid out of the printer. "Here's the bill."

"Double it." He didn't even look at the figure. "Whatever it is, double it."

"Tristan."

"Consider it a gratuity for your time and patience with me." He pulled out his credit card. "I insist."

"But—"

He read through the charges, then nodded. "Yes, this isn't nearly enough. I realize you've got to stay competitive for the area, but I insist on overpaying." He winked.

"Uh…sure." She turned her attention to the laptop. "You're a strange man."

"It's a writer thing. Yes, I'm an author and my uncle really is Al." He slid the paper back to her and placed four twenty-dollar bills on the counter. "I inherited his house and estate."

"Big job." She didn't take the slip or the money. "What are you going to do?"

"According to his wishes, there's a cash donation set up for the school system and one for the library. The rest…I'm not sure. Does Sullavan have restrictions on garage or yard sales?"

She tensed. "We have a garage sale week." She spread her fingers on the counter. "It's not for another month, but the people in town have one gigantic sale. Folks come from all over to shop the deals. There's nothing that says you can't have a garage sale at any other time, though."

"Good. I'm going to have to sell some of Al's stuff." He didn't want to sell anything, but if he still wanted to return to New York, he'd have to lighten his load.

"I'm sorry you have to do that, but I understand." She handed him his copy of the receipt. "I'm sorry to see you go, too. Feel free to come back whenever you're hungry. The kitchen is always open."

"I will. Thank you."

"You can leave the keys on the counter when you're done." She paused. "Michael is here on the weekends after the library closes so he can have supper." She winked, then left him alone.

He didn't know what to say. He shook his head and made his way upstairs. Cleaning up his things and packing only took a few minutes. He stuffed everything into his bag, then double-checked he'd picked up after himself. Tristan checked under the bed, in the sheets, then in the bathroom. Knowing him, he'd leave something behind. Once satisfied, he zipped his bag and tucked his laptop away, then paused. He hadn't spent much time in the room, but the place felt more like a home than his apartment in New York. Why? He wasn't sure. Because he'd let his guard down once he came to Sullavan.

Still, leaving saddened him. His phone buzzed in his pocket. Tristan put his bags on the unmade bed and answered the call. "Hello?"

"Hi, it's Michael."

He brightened and sank onto the mattress. "Hey, you."

"What's happening?"

He could be wrong, but did Michael sound nervous? "I'm picking up my stuff from Molly's, then going to Pandy's for my pizza so I've got supper when I go back to my uncle's place. I got absolutely nothing sorted out, but a lot of writing done."

"Well, good on the writing and boo on the sorting."

He laughed. "Do you want to share the pizza?" No hesitation. He knew exactly who he wanted to spend the evening with, but he had to convince Michael to stay.

"I'm here until eight. It's only half past six. By the time I get there, the pizza will be cold," Michael said.

"I'll reheat it." *Please? I want to see you.*

"I'll try to get over there."

"Don't try. Do." He hefted his bags onto his shoulder, then checked the room over one last time. He'd never get what he wanted if he didn't beg. "Please?"

Michael didn't respond right away. "Yeah."

Is that agreement? "I'll take that as a yes. You know where the house is, right?"

"I do," Michael replied, his voice quiet.

Excitement rippled through him. "I'll have dinner waiting. See you in a little bit."

"Yeah. See you." Michael disconnected the call.

Tristan slid his phone into the front pocket of his bag, then locked up the room and strode straight downstairs. He couldn't wait to see Michael. Was it possible that he'd fallen for the quirky librarian? Yeah, and he had. When he reached the counter, Molly wasn't around. He grabbed a piece of paper and left her a note.

You rock. Thanks for everything. Put in a good word for me with Michael.
XOXO,
Tristan

He left the key in the folded page, then headed back out to the car. He deposited his bags into the trunk, then hurried down the street to Pandy's and retrieved the pizza. He bought two large bottles of soda and paid the bill, then carried everything to the car.

He drove home with renewed vigor. Michael would be over soon. Instead of eating, he dragged his things inside and focused on cleaning up the kitchen. He located the garbage and tossed the food out of the refrigerator. Wasting the food sucked, but most of it was beyond the expiration dates. He cleaned off a spot on the counter, then located plates and cups. He wanted to make the right impression.

Tristan paused. *Fuck.* What was he doing in the kitchen when he should be upstairs settling in? He abandoned the food and took his bags to the second floor. For a moment, he considered using Al's room. Something in the back of his mind dictated he use the guest space. He ducked into the smaller of the two rooms and paused. A wave of nostalgia hit him hard. He'd spent four summers here and few of the furnishings were different. In moments, he'd been transported back to when he was fourteen and trying to come to terms with being gay. He left his bags on the floor and sat on the bed.

"Well, Uncle. I'm here." He folded his hands. Speaking to the spirit of his dead uncle soothed him. "I don't know what you expect from me, but I hope I make you happy. I'm overwhelmed and I've never had to sort out someone's life. I feel lost." He bowed his head. "I wish you were still here. I miss you and would love to have gotten to know you better." He wiped tears from his cheeks. *Shit.* He hadn't planned on crying.

The full weight of what he'd been asked to do hit him. Seeing his uncle's things broke his heart. He'd let time and distance get between them. He'd looked up to Al. Yes, the man could grumble and argue, but he'd had a big heart. Tristan picked at the ring on his middle finger. He'd never be able to talk to his uncle, save for essentially talking to himself, ever again.

Tristan blew out a long breath and forced himself to stand. Instead of focusing on what he couldn't change, he worked on settling in. He carried his toiletries to the bathroom, then wished he'd brought a box. His uncle's razor was still on the sink and his toothbrush was in the holder. He wasn't ready to pitch anything yet. Being here would take some getting used to. He put the razor and toothbrush in the cabinet over the sink. If he didn't keep moving forward, he'd never leave the room.

He returned to the guest room and unpacked his clothes. He arranged his jeans and shirts on the dresser. Putting the garments into the bureau wasn't bad, but he wasn't ready to disturb his uncle's stuff—not upstairs anyway. He'd get there later.

The doorbell rang and Tristan froze. The bell toned again, but this time he realized what the sound was. He hurried to the first floor and skidded to a stop at the door. Michael stood on the porch and waved.

"Come in." He unlocked the main door and pushed open the screen door. "Excuse the stuffiness. I should crack a few windows."

"Al would hate it smelling musty." Michael inched into the house, but didn't venture far from Tristan.

"Probably." He laughed, then tucked Michael into his embrace. "I'm so happy to see you." He kissed Michael's cheeks. "You smell good...and you're here early."

"Cilla and Dicey conned me into leaving early. They said they'd close. I'll check the building before I go home, but I'm sure it's fine." Michael stayed in Tristan's arms and rested his hands on Tristan's hips. "You sounded so insistent."

"I need you." He liked the way Michael felt against him. If nothing else was right in his world, Michael was, and he wanted to keep the good feelings going. "I have pizza and soda. Haven't even opened the box." He kissed Michael on the lips.

"How can I say no?"

"Uh...really easily." He slipped his hands into Michael's back pockets. God, the man had a nice ass. Squeezable and taut. "I'm glad you came."

"Not yet." Michael wriggled his eyebrows.

Tristan paused for a beat as he caught on to the joke. "Cute. Do you want to come?"

"Not until after our second date." Michael smiled. "I'm not that easy."

"I'll remember that." How fast could they get to date number two? He dragged Michael to the kitchen. "I even remembered to get the cups and plates out."

"I'm impressed."

He let go of Michael, then opened the pizza box. Despite the bit of tension, Tristan relaxed. He handed Michael the first piece of the pie. "This is the start of something awesome. I just know it." Down to his soul, he knew. "You and I are going to be epic."

Michael hesitated before accepting the slice of pizza. He'd forgotten how many memories were in the kitchen and the house. He'd only been with Al for three months and had never lived at the farmhouse, but if he didn't give Tristan an explanation, he'd burst. He ate in silence and considered his options. He wasn't sure how to broach the topic. *Oh hey, I was lovers with your uncle.* No, too pushy. *Your uncle and I had something I thought was special, but wasn't just friendship.* Too vague. *I was in love with your uncle for three months, but he never loved me.* Ugh.

"You're a hundred miles away." Tristan put his plate down, then stalked over to Michael. "I'm that boring?"

"No." Far from that. Tristan excited him and made him want to open his heart.

Tristan took the plate from Michael. "I've been thinking about you all day." He licked his lips and caged Michael between his body and the counter. He rubbed the bulge in his jeans against the one in Michael's pants, sending shimmers of heat through

Michael's body. Michael fought his better judgment and slid his fingers into Tristan's front pockets. Tristan dragged his nose along Michael's. "Yeah." He shifted his hips. "I can't lie. I want you."

"Yeah." He had no other words. His regret and confusion melted away. He was drawn to Tristan. The man didn't care who Michael was or what he'd done. Tristan wanted to be with him.

Tristan turned with Michael in his arms and leaned against the counter. He tucked his hands beneath the waistband of Michael's jeans to cup Michael's ass.

Michael groaned. He liked take-charge men. When Tristan cupped the back of Michael's neck with his free hand, Michael didn't fight the delicious feeling. He kissed Tristan and savored his tanginess.

Tristan pushed the kiss. He turned the connection feral in an instant. He consumed Michael with the heat of the kiss. Michael couldn't drag air into his lungs fast enough, but he didn't mind. He liked the way Tristan held him.

Michael straddled Tristan's thigh and rode his leg. He groaned. Tristan tasted good — sinful. Michael smoothed his palms over Tristan's chest. Christ, the man was all hard muscle and strength. He wanted to unwrap him and learn every inch of Tristan.

"Yeah, babe." Tristan ground against Michael, then sucked on his tongue.

Michael broke away and panted. Desire flowed through him. He could've sworn the temperature rose a few hundred degrees.

Tristan licked along Michael's throat and his teeth scraped Michael's skin. Another groan ripped from Michael.

"You're a talker. I like it," Tristan said. The scruff on his cheeks abraded Michael's. He tugged Michael's shirt from his pants, then slid his hands over Michael's belly. "I want to strip you down," Tristan said between nips. "Want to explore you."

Fuck...he'd just been thinking that about Tristan. He gritted his teeth. "Yeah." He wanted to get the hell out of the kitchen in favor of somewhere softer and horizontal—like the bed.

Tristan stopped kissing him, then rested his forehead on Michael's. "I need you."

"You do." It wasn't a question. He wanted Tristan, too.

"Crave you." Tristan dropped to his knees and opened Michael's pants. When he glanced up at Michael, he grinned. "Need you." He rubbed his face against the crotch of Michael's jeans and marked himself.

Michael threaded his fingers into Tristan's hair. Being this bold was out of his comfort zone, but it felt right because he was with Tristan. He rocked against him and closed his eyes. Heat centered in his dick and he moaned. "Yes."

"Oh, wow. I didn't think I'd see this."

Michael froze. He knew that voice. Jamie. He should've known the lawyer would be involved somehow. He opened his eyes and focused on Tristan.

Tristan sat back on his heels. "Oh, hi."

Jamie strode up to Tristan. "I didn't think you two were a twosome. Guess you are." He turned on his heel and walked out of the room.

"So?" Tristan scrambled to his feet. "Jamie. Fuck." He splayed his hand on Michael's chest. "Sorry. I'll be right back." He chased Jamie.

Michael buttoned his jeans, then righted his shirt. He had no claim to Tristan. He couldn't blame Tristan for wanting to sample the goods of Sullavan. But Tristan trying others on for size didn't mean Michael had to stick around to watch. He finished his glass of soda, then wiped his mouth with the back of his hand. His body still hummed from Tristan's touch. It wasn't fair. He hadn't been this affected by anyone…ever. Tristan seemed to be different.

Michael squared his shoulders. He didn't know what was going on, but he wanted to get out of there. He made his way through the living room to the front porch. Tristan and Jamie stood just outside the door.

"You don't understand," Tristan said.

"Right. Just stop." Jamie glared at him. "I thought… I don't know what I thought."

Michael rattled the door to let them know he was on his way out. He stopped for a moment. "I'm heading out. I have to work in the morning." He hurried down the steps and around the flower beds to his car. He shouldn't have been retreating, but he couldn't compete with Jamie. Christ. Jamie was everything he wasn't—rich, handsome and sophisticated. He wasn't damaged goods, either.

"Michael." Tristan caught up with him beside his car. "Don't go."

"You've got company. I'll go." Michael fiddled with his keys. "It's cool."

"Jamie isn't *company*." Tristan scrubbed both hands over his face. "He is, but it's complicated."

"I understand. He's your lawyer and you've got papers or whatnot to discuss." He had to sound as level as possible. Tristan deserved someone with a calm demeanor, not angst and too much emotion.

"No." He touched Michael's arm. "Wait. When does the library open on Saturday?"

Michael frowned. "Ten. Why?"

"Come over tomorrow night. Please?"

"Tristan." Why did Tristan insist on wanting him there? Things were already awkward with Jamie waiting on the porch. He didn't have to make it worse.

"I'm not with Jamie and, if it wasn't pretty clear before, I like you." He hooked his fingers in Michael's belt loops. "I like you *a lot*."

"You don't know me." And once he found out, he'd run the other way.

"I know enough." Tristan crowded Michael against the side of his car. "You're a good guy. You're sweet and don't expect anything from me. I want to be with you. I want to talk about books and writing, then maybe finish what was started in the kitchen. You have no idea how refreshing it is to find someone who doesn't care about my money."

His money? "Tristan." Part of him wanted to stay, but his common sense won out. He had to get the hell out of there.

"Give me tomorrow night. Yes? I'll cook and we'll have a good night together," Tristan said. He kissed Michael. "I can't get enough of you."

He paused. Someone liked him. A guy. A hot one. Why was he second-guessing the attraction? Because he had secrets. "I'm not a good guy."

"You're a great one." Tristan grinned.

"Tristan." He'd never get through to Tristan without telling the truth.

"You can't say anything that'll make me like you less."

Want to bet? "I slept with Al." He hadn't meant to let that slip, but now that he had, he couldn't take the words back. He hated to admit he felt relieved, too.

Tristan let go of Michael. His eyes widened and his lips parted. "What?"

"I did. The first summer I came to Sullavan. I met him in May and by September it was over, but we were together." He met Tristan's gaze. "You're right. I don't want anything from you. No money or whatever. I like you and I hope you can like me again sometime, but I understand if you don't. I'm pretty sure you deserve better than me, too. That's why I didn't want to get involved in the first place. I had a feeling you'd be disgusted by me in the end."

Tristan didn't speak. He balled his hands and swept his gaze over Michael.

"I'll go," Michael whispered. He'd done enough damage. He left Tristan and zipped down the driveway. His heart broke. Yes, he didn't know Tristan well, but he liked him so much. No guy would ever want to be with a man who'd also been with a member of the guy's family—especially with a forty-year age difference. He drove away from the house and didn't look back. He couldn't. His stomach churned. His truth kept coming back to bite him in the ass. First Barry hated that he'd been with someone so old and now Tristan would be disgusted because of who Michael's lover had been.

He'd be better off if he stopped trying to find someone. He swung by the library long enough to ensure the doors were locked, then headed home. Once he reached his ranch house, he turned off his phone. He parked in the garage and went inside. He flopped onto the bed and stared at the ceiling. *Christ.* He was acting like an angst-ridden twenty-something. Why hadn't he seen the potential problems and done something about them? Why hadn't he stopped things with Tristan before everything had gone out of control? *Because I like Tristan.*

Now he had no choice but to accept his fate and lose his chance with Tristan. *Damn it.*

Chapter Seven

Tristan stared at the place where Michael's car had been long after Michael left. Michael had slept with Al. Not once. Not twice. For three months. *Holy shit.* He didn't know how to feel. Not only had he not known his uncle was gay, but sleeping with Michael... *Jesus.* The age gap between them was huge.

He wandered back to the porch and settled on the steps. He couldn't hate Michael. He'd dated a couple of twenty-year-olds two years ago and when he was eighteen he'd been with a guy in his forties. He'd been looking for every possible way to rebel and get sex. He hadn't cared who he slept with as long as he got off. Michael wasn't much different — probably.

So why did the truth hurt? Because he wanted Michael. Now he wasn't so sure.

"Are you okay?" Jamie sat beside him. He plunked his hand onto Tristan's thigh. "What'd Michael say? You're pale."

"Nothing." What had happened with Michael was none of Jamie's business. He still wasn't thrilled about Jamie busting in on them.

"Oh? Did he tell you he can't see you?"

"No." He stared at the flowers, then the stones making up the walkway. "I think he's jealous of you." He had seen the pain in Michael's eyes. He understood the truth even more. Michael felt less than acceptable because he had a past. Sure, Tristan was angry. Michael hadn't been honest. But he couldn't stay mad. Michael had a right to his history. He must've had a good reason to be with Al. Loneliness? Wanting to learn from a man with experience? A true attraction? He wasn't sure and couldn't help his jealousy. Michael knew a whole different side to Al that he'd never see.

"I don't believe that," Jamie said. "He's a decent guy."

"You think?"

"He's quiet and mousy for a guy but he's harmless." Jamie shrugged. "I heard he dated your uncle. Guess he's into older men." He bumped shoulders with Tristan. "The whole town knew."

"I see." He folded his hands and rested his elbows on his knees, then his chin on his knuckles. "Did my uncle or Michael ever make a play for you?"

"Al never really talked to anyone and Michael isn't my type."

"Why not? What's wrong with Michael?" Other than he'd slept with Tristan's uncle.

"I like a guy with a career," Jamie said. "Someone with drive and a competitive spirit. I can't be with a guy who isn't bringing in his own paycheck."

"Michael has a job." *What the hell?*

"He dated Barry, too."

"So?"

"Barry's just... He could do better." Jamie stood, then held his hands out to Tristan. "I'm not working tomorrow. You've got me all night. Let's tackle some of this house." He tugged Tristan to his feet. "You've got gorgeous eyes."

"Thanks." His heart sank. He'd learned so much about Michael, yet knew nothing. "But I've got the house thing... I'll be fine. I know what I need to do." *Sort of.* "Thanks for offering to help and I'll call if I need you or if I've got a problem. I need to spend some time alone." He had to think fast. The way Jamie shook his head made Tristan wonder if he'd go. Tristan sighed. "I need to write tonight. If I don't get twenty-five pages done, I'll never be able to live with myself."

"Are you sure?" Jamie stuck out his bottom lip. "I'm available."

"I know and I appreciate it." He clapped Jamie on the shoulder. "But I don't write well with company."

"Not even Michael?"

"Nope." He had no clue if he could write with Michael in the house and tonight he wouldn't find out. He needed separation from the problem and time to sort out how he felt. "Thanks, but I have a deadline. I'll talk to you later."

"Sure." Jamie kissed Tristan on the cheek. "You've got my number." He strolled away from Tristan, leaving him alone on the porch.

Tristan waited until Jamie's car was gone before he went inside. He had too many things to think about. Once he'd locked the doors, he opened the rest of the windows. The musty smell, along with the aroma of stale pizza, dissipated. He didn't know what to do, but Christ, he couldn't calm down enough to write. Doing most anything while emotional never worked, but he didn't have a whole lot of choices. Either he could plow through the outline and start some semblance of the story or sort items.

He wandered into the library and shuffled through the notes he'd created. The story made sense and had a few decent plot twists, but he couldn't concentrate long enough to put pen to paper or even type out what he'd jotted into the notebook.

"Damn it." Tristan shoved the pages off the desk. Paper fluttered through the air and landed on the carpet. He paced the length of the room to work off his energy. "Why does the guy I like have to be the one who slept with my uncle? Why can't he be normal? Why'd the one who should be a good match have to be so damn irritating?"

Tristan blew out a long breath and stopped walking. He'd never get answers by talking to himself. Then again, he'd never get the story straightened out if his notes were in disarray on the floor.

He knelt and picked up the pages. Although he hadn't numbered anything, he had a faint memory of the plot line. He read through one of the sheets. The writing wasn't familiar, but when he got into his work, his normal scrawl became sheer scribbles. But this didn't look like *his* scribbling.

"I realize it's hard to understand how I feel," Tristan read out loud. Yeah, not his words at all. "But you won't. I barely know myself."

What? Who wrote this? Tristan sat on his butt and tilted the page toward the light to better read it.

You'll never see this. I won't let you. I have to hope instead that you believed what I said. I'm doing this for your own good. We're not a match. Us being an us was a mistake. Michael, I don't love you and never will.

Holy fuck. He dropped the page. Was his uncle writing an anti-love letter to Michael? He didn't understand. *Why would Al do this?* Tristan shook his head. If he wanted any kind of answers, he'd have to rip open the wounds within Michael. If Michael wanted closure, he'd have to see the letter — after Tristan finished reading it.

You're young, cute and fuck like a dream. You don't belong with me. Stop being quiet and accepting low standards.

Damn. His heart bled for his uncle and Michael. He still didn't know his uncle the way he'd thought, but the agony in his words was palpable. The man didn't want to let Michael go, but he had because he thought Michael should aim higher. Then there was Michael. He must've confessed his love to Al. A declaration of affection would bring out this kind of rebuke. He'd probably poured out his soul only to be pushed away. No wonder being in the house seemed to make Michael tense.

One day you'll see I'm not the asshole. I'm someone who cares about you. Sullavan needs a man who can help others. I'm not him. You are. I'll always be your friend, but no longer your lover.

Tristan turned the page over, but, instead of more letter, all he found were his notes. He shoved the extra stack of pages into a neat pile, then arranged them with his notes on top. The pages weren't in order, but he turned them over anyhow. He separated the notations out. Within minutes, he found the remainder of the letter.

I can't be the man you need, but he's out there. I'm not your great love. Keep looking. You'll find him the way I found Emerson.

Al

Emerson? Who is that? He'd have to find out. He'd also have to do some work to get Michael to speak to him, but he'd worry about that detail in the morning. Tonight, he'd sleep. Fuck it. He'd rub one off—then sleep. He deserved a good orgasm after the day he'd had.

Tristan turned off the lights and headed upstairs. Along the way, he stripped out of his clothes and left a trail behind him. He ended up in the bedroom in nothing but his boxer shorts. He stretched out on the bed. The chilly night air swept over him and his nipples beaded. He closed his eyes and slid both hands into his boxers.

He needed a fantasy before he could get off. He stroked his flaccid cock. Who could he focus on? His ex, Jordan? No. The man had been fun for the first few weeks, but then his desire for money and fame had taken over. Jordan had turned out to be just another fake wanting to latch on to the Paulson money.

What about Jamie? There were possibilities with him. At least he was hot, but controlling in bed. Two dominant personalities in the bedroom weren't a good start for hot times and he'd bet Jamie knew what he wanted from his playmate.

Michael. *No.* That was a road he couldn't travel yet.

Tristan forced himself to think about Jamie. He freed his dick from his boxers, then wriggled the underwear down his thighs. In his fantasy, he'd meet Jamie in his office after hours. This time he found no one there, except the lawyer.

"Hey, you." Tristan stretched out on Jamie's desk, buck naked, and cupped his balls. "Need you."

Jamie rounded his desk, but as he moved, his features changed. His hair darkened and his brown eyes turned green. Tristan rolled onto his side, then switched to stroking his erection. "Michael?"

Michael nodded. "I liked what we started in the kitchen. Thought we could take things to the next level." He stripped out of his clothes until he stood nude before Tristan. "Join me."

"No." He shook his head to emphasize his point, then increased the pulls on his dick. "I can't."

"Why not?" Michael climbed onto the desk and settled between Tristan's knees. "Are you afraid of me?"

"No." He spread his legs even more and focused on Michael. He had plenty he wanted to say but his mouth refused to cooperate. Instead, he rocked his hips and fucked his hand.

"Pretty." Michael crawled over Tristan until he had him pinned down. "Come apart. Stroke that fine cock and fucking jizz all over me."

Tristan paused. *Michael talked dirty like that?*

"Do it." Michael's eyes blazed. He licked his lips. "I'm waiting."

Tristan abandoned his restraint. This was his fantasy and he needed the orgasm. He planted his feet on the bed, then gritted his teeth. His movements turned feral as heat engulfed him. A moan vibrated in his throat. He tipped his head back. The pressure from the day, from learning the truth about his uncle and Michael as well as the stress from not working on his book, flowed out of him with the climax.

"Fuck me, Michael," he shouted. Cum spurted onto Tristan's belly in a warm streak. He opened his eyes and panted. His muscles slackened from head to toe. He stared at the bedroom ceiling. Good thing he didn't have close neighbors.

Tristan sagged against the sheets. He needed to move, but wanted to stay put. The cum dried and chilled him to the bone. He wriggled the rest of the way out of his boxers and cleaned himself off, then scurried under the sheets. Right now, he'd sleep. He'd worry about why he'd conjured up Michael, as well as his feelings for the man…in the morning. Everything would sort itself out with a little sleep.

* * * *

The next evening, Michael sat behind the counter at the library. He'd shelved everything he could find, redecorated the bulletin board and tidied up the magazine rack. He'd even managed to finish sorting the books in the shed. Despite staying busy for the lion's share of the day, he couldn't forget Tristan. The words he'd said to Tristan rang in his memory. What had he been thinking? He hadn't. He'd seen Jamie there and knew he'd been outclassed. Instead of fighting for the man he liked, he'd blurted out the truth and bolted.

Although he'd tried to keep up cheery appearances, he noticed Dicey and Cilla were giving him a wide berth. Neither spoke to him except to ask for help with the computer or to let him know they'd returned from break.

"Dicey? Why are you avoiding me?" He pulled the stack of returned books from the bin and proceeded to scan each book back into the system. "I won't bite your head off."

"Promise?" She plunked the newly scanned books onto the rolling cart. "You're a bear today. You think you're being sweet, but you're cranky. Everyone sees it." She lowered her voice. "Had a falling out with Tristan, didn't you?"

"Am I that obvious?" He sank onto the nearest stool. "Sorry."

"And you're going to hide at Molly's, aren't you?" She folded her arms. "Michael."

"What?" He knew the argument was coming. She'd nail him with sixteen good reasons why he should stop avoiding Tristan. He should say something, but why bother? She was right. He needed to talk to the man and get their issues into the open...again. His head ached. He didn't regret what had happened between him and Tristan...he just wished the situation had been smoother.

"You need a date." She leaned on the cart. "But not Tristan."

He froze. "What?"

"Yeah. Someone who won't jerk you around. I like Tristan. He's funny and cute, but I'm still not sure he's the one you should be seeing. I have this feeling you're going to get your heart broken," Dicey said.

"What if I already did?" he murmured. "I told him about Al...and me."

"I see." She bowed her head. "And he said?"

"Nothing." He sighed. "He stared at me, but kept his mouth shut."

"Then there you go." She patted his arm. "That tells you everything, but I doubt you're going to listen because it's ten minutes to eight and he just showed up in a truck."

"What?" He peeked out of the window. Sure enough, Tristan, in a form-fitting T-shirt and painted-on jeans, exited the truck. Michael bit back a groan. The outfit worked too well for Tristan. He was probably getting ready for a date with Jamie.

"Act cool." Dicey gripped Michael's shoulders. "Don't let him see you sweat. You're a good guy and he's not worthy of you if he can't see the man inside."

"I don't understand you." He turned away from the door. "Dice, one minute you're warning me against him and then the next you're all but encouraging me to go for him."

"I'm... Just be careful. I know how you got all wrapped up in Al, then Darren and Barry. You want someone to complete you, but you're good enough on your own. Find that guy who makes you better, but isn't the other half." She shook her head and walked away.

He blew out a ragged breath. She had a point. He'd hung his hopes on finding a partner, but hadn't bothered to just date.

The bell over the door pinged and Michael faced the counter. Tristan strode into the library. He grinned. "Just the man I'm looking for."

"We're closing soon. If you need any materials, grab them now." Michael busied himself with straightening the papers on the counter. He couldn't look at Tristan, but he could smell him. Damn. His knees quaked. Tristan's scent reminded him of sin—if it was possible for sin to have an aroma.

"We need to talk," Tristan said.

"No." He wasn't there for conversation.

"It's important."

"Why?" He met Tristan's gaze. Frustration he hadn't realized he was holding came rushing out. "So you can soothe your conscience with Jamie? You're free. Have a ball with him. I don't care."

"No." Tristan rounded the desk and grasped Michael's wrist. "Girls, I'll have him back in ten minutes. No hanky-panky in the bathroom, I promise, but I am taking him outside." He hustled Michael from his hiding spot and walked him out under the awning in front of the library. Rain streaked across the transparent sheets of plastic surrounding walkway.

"Is he in the truck?" Michael asked. "Are you doing this to make him jealous?"

"No."

"Then what?" His voice cracked. *God damn it.* He hated when his fucking voice failed him.

"I didn't invite Jamie over," Tristan said. He let go of Michael. "I had the night planned for us. He said he wanted to stop by, but I'd hoped it was an empty promise. I was wrong."

"I'm sure my admission didn't help." He paused. "Or did it?" He'd encourage them to get together.

"It did."

Like he'd thought. "So, you and Jamie will be happy together. I'm sure he's a nice guy. Congratulations."

"You're hurting." Tristan gripped Michael's shoulders. "Look at me."

"No." He didn't want Tristan to see him fall apart.

"You are and I am, too," Tristan whispered.

"Tell Jamie." He shouldn't have snapped at Tristan, but he couldn't stop himself. The pain was too engrained in him.

"No." Tristan tightened his grasp. "You're missing something here. Yeah, I don't know what you saw in my uncle, but I believe you loved him."

Great. Now everyone would know...not that they didn't already, but still. "Okay."

"He cared about you."

"He *cared* about himself and his damn books."

"He..." Tristan tipped his head. "He wrote you a letter. I want you to see it. Once you've read it, I have a question."

"Wonderful." *Damn. That was supposed to be an internal retort.* "Sorry."

"You're fine." Tristan rubbed Michael's shoulders. "Who was Emerson?"

Oh fuck. He hadn't thought he'd be talking about his former flame's partner. "He and Al were together for a long time after we split. He was Al's soul mate. He died two years ago from complications from AIDS. He was a decent guy and liked to read. He and Al went through my biography section together book by book for an entire year."

"Sounds like you got along with him."

"I did." How could he not? Emerson hadn't done anything wrong. He'd just been the right man for Al when Michael wasn't.

"Was he young?" Tristan asked.

"Forty-five." Compared to Al's age then of sixty-eight...

"So, my uncle liked younger men."

Michael sighed. "He had a type." At least twenty years his junior and always with a ripped bod and tight ass.

"Let me show you the letter. I think you'll get closure." Tristan inched up to Michael. "I know you will."

"I had it. He left me and we remained friends. He died and I'm still here. Done. Boom. Nothing more to say." Christ. Why did this hurt so much? The pain he'd buried for so long welled to the surface. He hadn't wanted to talk about Emerson or Al. Hadn't wanted to see Tristan and face up to his past. *Fuck.*

"You're wrong." Tristan curled his fingers under Michael's chin. "You're fooling yourself."

"You're so sure?" *Is he a damn psychiatrist?*

"You wouldn't be so pissed if you had embraced the closure you swear you have." Michael's hands shook and his headache increased. Tears threatened behind his eyes and his throat closed. His heart pounded.

"You're a self-help book, aren't you? Wrapped up in butter-soft jeans...right?"

"I'm trying to get you to calm down and be rational. I understand. You have every right to be mad. You loved him and he found someone else. I've been there, but I'm usually the dump-er, not the dump-ee." Tristan brushed his thumb across Michael's bottom lip. "No matter what, the end of relationships always sucks."

"Poetic and true." He needed to reel in his sarcasm.

"I owe you dinner. A nice one. I'll bring it over to your place. You can kick me out when we're done eating and cleaned up. We could eat and talk or at least share a nice meal together. Please?" The muscle in Tristan's jaw tensed. "I'm begging."

"Why?" He didn't need to beg. Michael wanted Tristan in his home. That had to be fucked up, but it was the truth. He liked Tristan and even if the man was sure to leave him, he wanted one more shot at a decent relationship.

"As much as you're trying to push me away, I don't want to go." Tristan crowded Michael against the hard plastic. "I want to be right here with you."

"You're crazy."

"Probably. I'm a writer. It's expected." Tristan shrugged.

"Shouldn't you be writing? Not here with me?"

"I've got plenty of things I could be doing." Tristan placed his finger over Michael's lips. "But settling this with you and moving forward is more important. The story can wait one more day."

"Tristan." He wanted to push. To shove Tristan into the rain and out of his life. But he couldn't.

"Well? I'm not giving up. I've got the food in my truck. Molly set me up in style. She said she wanted you to be taken care of." Tristan grinned. "See, when I told her I was trying to win you over, she jumped at the idea of helping."

"Molly," he muttered. She'd be the death of him.

"She knows you and she cares. So do I. You don't understand." Tristan toyed with the collar of Michael's button-down. "I'm not thrilled about you and Al, but I can't fault you. I'm more jealous than anything. You know a side of my uncle that I can only wonder about. I never knew he was gay. Trust me. If I had known, it would've made my coming out a little easier." Tristan brushed his nose along Michael's. "I want to know more about him through you, but it's more about knowing you. He saw something in you. Something special. I'm drawn to you—not because of him, but because of you."

Chapter Eight

Michael had no fight left in him. Tristan's words struck a chord deep in his soul. He needed to come clean with Tristan. The only way healing would take place was if he talked about the summer with Al. "Fine."

"Yes?" Tristan tipped his head again and met Michael's gaze. "You're sure?"

"Yes." A chuckle bubbled in Michael's throat. He wasn't happy, but he'd finally accepted his fate. He'd talk about his past.

"Good." Tristan snagged Michael in his arms and kissed him. "Besides...that tingle between you and me isn't fake."

"But—" It had to be. He couldn't be so excited to see Tristan. Couldn't lose his heart to someone who'd leave. It wasn't possible.

"No buts...except mine." Tristan's eyes sparkled. His breath warmed Michael's cheeks. "I want you in my ass."

"Even after—" *Holy fuck.*

"Yeah." Tristan kissed him again. "I'm tired of over-thinking. I know who I want and I'm willing to risk temporary heartbreak in order to get the prize at the end."

Michael shook his head. He had no words. Nothing to combat Tristan's tangy sweetness.

"I'll be out in the truck. Want to follow me home or are you allowing me to come over?" Tristan slid his hands down Michael's sides to his hips, then back to his ass. "I don't know where you live."

"Let me close the library, lock up and then you can follow me." Michael licked his lips. He wasn't sure what he was getting into, but he couldn't see another way out.

"Deal." Tristan squeezed Michael's ass. "I said we'd be epic. I wasn't kidding."

"I know." Michael lingered another minute in Tristan's arms, then wriggled free. He didn't understand what had just happened, but he wasn't arguing. He went into the library and stopped short.

Dicey folded her arms. "Well?" She cornered him. "You're going out with him, right?"

"We're taking things slow." He ducked out from around her and did a quick walk-through to ensure there weren't any lingering patrons. The computers were already turned off. He checked the bathrooms were empty then closed the doors. He keyed the security code into the keypad, then switched off most of the lights. "If you're ready... I am."

Dicey didn't move. "Only if you're going to go with him." She poked him in the chest. "I know I'm being wishy-washy about him. I'm just... I worry about you, but listening to you out there..." She sighed. "You need to stop thinking about the past and go forward. You deserve a break. A catch. Don't let him get away because you think you're unworthy. You're very worthy. He might not be the one I'd pick for you, but that doesn't mean he isn't good enough."

"Message received." Michael rounded the counter and retrieved his bag. "You're right."

"Good. Let's go. I heard him say he had dinner for you." She winked. "I hope there's actual food involved." Without another word, she left the library.

Michael sighed. He seemed to be doing that a lot of late, but he wasn't sure how else to handle Dicey and Tristan, among others. He turned the rest of the lights off, then locked the doors. He started toward his car, but paused. Tristan sat in the rain on the hood of the truck. *Jesus.* Michael's heart hammered and his dick hardened. Tristan, slick with rain, could be a model. He knew how to work his assets.

"There you are." Tristan sat up. "Sexy as ever."

He should've told Tristan to keep his voice down, but kept quiet instead. Michael strode over to his car. "I can't get too far. You'll catch a cold."

"I won't, but if I do you'll make sure I get better." Tristan slid off the hood and waved. "Bye, ladies."

Dicey laughed and the sound rang out in the silence. Cilla waved, then left.

Michael shook his head. He'd never live any of this down. He wasn't a showy person, but Tristan was and he kept forcing Michael out of his comfort zone. Michael slid his gaze over to Tristan. "Are you sure you're not going into politics? Running for mayor? Maybe you're trying to encourage reading in Sullavan. Something."

"I'm only trying to sway one voter. You. Is it working?"

"Could be," Michael confessed. He leaned against the fender of his car. The rain had stopped, but water splotched all over his hood. "I'm just a couple of blocks from here."

Tristan crowded him, pushing his damp crotch against Michael's hip. "I really want to kiss you again."

"I can tell." *Damn.* Was that his dick shoving into Michael's thigh?

"You don't want me to." Tristan splayed his hand on Michael's chest. "You're fighting me."

"I'd rather have privacy."

"Smart."

"Your food is probably cold. We should get moving." Michael didn't move from Tristan's embrace. "Right?"

"Molly packed it in these crocheted things. I doubt there's any heat loss." Tristan pressed a kiss to Michael's lips. "Unless you mean in me. I'm burning up."

"You're corny." Michael held his keys tight. "If you follow me to the house, I'll help you carry the food in. Then you can kiss me all you want." All Tristan wanted—fuck, Michael wanted to be kissed senseless. To be consumed and adored.

"I like that deal." Tristan wriggled his eyebrows, then kissed Michael once more. "I'm a horrible thief."

"I can tell."

Tristan abandoned him beside his vehicle and climbed behind the wheel of the truck. If Michael thought Tristan looked sexy *on* the truck, he looked even better *in* it. Michael shivered. A thought crossed his mind. He'd love to stretch Tristan out across the front of the truck. Christ, the fucking they could do against that vehicle.

Michael adjusted his pants to relieve the pressure on his erection, then forced himself to settle behind the wheel of his car. He drove home and along the way he kept checking that Tristan was behind him. *Fuck.* Would Tristan stretch out naked on the truck? If they had privacy he might. Michael tried to focus on the road, but the idea of Tristan naked in any way possible corrupted his thoughts. Tristan seemed way too cozy in the truck and Sullavan.

Would he stick around?

Michael pressed the button to open his garage, then turned onto his meager driveway. He parked in the bay, then waited for Tristan. For a moment, he swore Tristan had abandoned him. Michael left his car and hefted his bag onto his shoulder. He froze. Did he want Tristan to see his house? Christ. He had a tiny house. Tristan was used to big places and luxury.

Tristan left the truck. "This is your place?" He smiled. "I like it. It's quaint."

"Tiny." Michael strode up to him. "What do you need from the truck?"

"If you grab my bag and the basket, I'll get the dish and the bottle of wine." Tristan offered up a messenger bag and a wicker basket. "I can heft the rest. Molly said we needed everything she packed. I haven't looked so I don't know what's there."

"She's thorough." He carried his bag plus the extra things into the house. Tristan kept up behind Michael until everything was in the kitchen. Michael pointed to the main door leading to the garage. "Lock your truck. The neighborhood isn't bad, but the kids get...silly every so often. If there's anything in there they want and it's unlocked, they'll snatch."

"I'm sorry to hear that." Tristan walked out of the kitchen and disappeared into the garage. Moments later, he returned. "This button closes the main door?"

"Garage?" Michael asked. "Yes."

"Then I'm locked up and so is your garage. We're safe." Tristan closed the main door. "Now, about dinner."

"What'd she make?" Michael unfastened the ties on the cover. Whatever Molly had packed, it smelled wonderful. "Pasta?"

"Stuffed shells with a special sauce. I can't remember what she called it." Tristan settled beside Michael. "She says you're a sucker for pasta. I am, too."

"Nice to know." He patted his belly. "I shouldn't have the carbs. I haven't had much time to run." Not since Tristan had come to town. He pulled two plates from the cupboard.

"You're a runner?" Tristan took the plates from Michael. "I am, too. I used to run marathons. I used the time to work out plot points. People thought I loved running. I do, but it's a great time to think." He dished two of the large shells onto the first plate. "Lately, my running has taken place on the treadmill. Is there anywhere around here to run? Sidewalks?"

"We've got nice trails at the metro parks. There are two-, three- and four-mile paths. A few hills, but some is flat and it's all gravel. I prefer running there instead of on the sidewalks." Michael accepted the plate. "Did you want wine with dinner?"

"One glass." Tristan walked his dinner to the dinette set. "Unless you have beer. I'm more of a beer guy."

"You're in luck. I've got four beers left."

Tristan took Michael's plate from him. "Perfect." He kissed Michael's cheek. "She sent rolls and butter, too. I don't know why she didn't think you'd have butter."

"I do. Just bought the tub." He opened the amber bottles then carried them to the table. "But I'm glad she cared. I'm a horrible cook."

Tristan stood by the table. "Where is the silver? We need forks."

"Shit. In the middle drawer." He'd forgotten all about silverware. He watched Tristan move around his kitchen. Granted, the space wasn't large, but he seemed at ease. When he returned to the table, he sat opposite Michael.

"She thinks the world of you." Tristan shook out a napkin. "I bet she goes out of her way for her guests, but this is pretty over the top."

"Molly?"

"Uh-huh. I hear you two dated." Tristan sliced one of the shells. "Not long."

Embarrassment washed over Michael. Everyone in town knew everyone else's business, but still. He'd never be able to downplay his past. "Yeah, for a few weeks."

"Found out you're better as friends, eh?" Tristan winked. "I've been there. What happened — if you don't mind me asking?"

He minded, but he'd have to talk eventually. "She wanted sex and I couldn't. I love her and I wanted to be with her, but I couldn't...you know." He wanted to hide. He knew his limits and being around Tristan pushed all of them.

"Been there, too." Tristan nodded. "More than once."

Michael ate in silence. He preferred the quiet. Conversation wasn't his strong point and Tristan kept asking things he wanted to ignore. He'd dug himself a huge hole at Al's place and couldn't see a way out.

Tristan finished eating first and sat back in his seat. "Damn. She is a good cook."

"Uh-huh."

Tristan dragged his bag over to the table, then withdrew an envelope. "You eat. I'll talk. I can see you're all tense."

Gee whiz. Thanks.

"My uncle wrote you at least two letters. I found these on his desk. I thought they were scratch paper and scribbled notes for my story on the back. According to Al's words, you weren't supposed to read them." He opened the envelope. "I think you should."

"Tristan." He nearly choked on the pasta. "If he said no, then no."

"You'll understand him better."

"Just tell me what they say. I can't read them." He didn't want to. He'd break down and he refused to do so in front of Tristan.

"It's not as bad as you think."

"I doubt that." He rested his fork on the remainder of his dinner. "Al didn't want me and pushed me away when I was dumb enough to tell him I loved him." *There. Now he knows. Fuck.* Michael blinked back tears. He'd thought he could handle the split, but even fifteen years on, the break-up still bothered him.

"Just read it." Tristan shoved the envelope over to Michael. "I understand how he felt. Part of me wants to be upset with you. I can't imagine you were with him. But the rest of me isn't mad. I see in you what he did. He loved you, but his version of love was to let you go. He seemed to think you were meant for something more."

Michael downed half the bottle of beer to fortify his nerves. He didn't want to know, but he needed closure. He pushed his half-eaten plate of pasta away and opened the envelope. "Here goes nothing."

Tristan swirled his beer around in the bottle. He wasn't sure how Michael would react to the letters. If he were in Michael's shoes, he had no idea how he'd feel. If he had a clue that the man he loved wasn't pushing him away for purely selfish reasons, he might have felt different. But he wasn't Michael. For all he knew, Michael would be destroyed.

Michael pushed the letters away and rested his elbows on the table. He pinched the bridge of his nose.

"What are you thinking?" Tristan whispered. "Michael?"

"I'm numb."

Now there was an emotion Tristan could understand.

"He loved me, but hated me. I don't get it." Michael stared at Tristan. "He hated me."

"He didn't *hate* you. What bothered him was your youth and freedom. It's not the same." Tristan downed more of the beer. "You're not the object of his fury."

"Feels like it." Michael toyed with his silverware. "Why couldn't he tell me? That's the other part I'm struggling with. I kind of understand his dislike for youth and freedom. He's from a different era than we are and it wasn't easy for him to come out. That makes sense, but I didn't set the rules. I mean, okay, hate me for what I can't control, but why let me think he just plain hated me? We were friends. I supported him when he met Emerson. Hell, I encouraged them to get married. He didn't listen, but I tried."

Tristan sighed. Michael was so much more than Al had given him credit for in the letters. Michael was a special man. Tristan leaned forward in his seat and folded his hands on his lap. "I don't have all the answers. I don't even have half of them. What I do know is that he was a complex man."

"How do you remember him?" Michael asked. He reached for Tristan. "I mean, when you think of your uncle, what comes to mind?"

He laced his fingers with Michael's and marveled for a moment at the tiny gesture. Michael—a man who could be so closed and cautious—trusted him. He'd reached for Tristan. Had Tristan worn him down that much? Or was this how things were meant to be? He and Michael were meant to go through this experience together. He swiped his thumb across Michael's knuckles. "Al was my uncle. He didn't care about the money my parents had and he didn't want it. He could be grouchy and coarse, but he insisted on taking care of himself. He planted things, kept himself in shape and expected me to be self-sufficient. I used to think he was a jerk for pushing me to experience life without money. Then I grew up. I understood. I had to stumble a lot and sow my share of wild oats, but I saw how he wanted me to be more. The same goes for how he treated you."

"You think?" Michael crinkled his nose, but didn't pull away.

"I do. We've both grown some, but then he came into our lives. He was there for most of mine, but a summer of yours. He saw potential. I'm sure some of how he felt about you was clouded by his own experiences. He must've felt strange about coming out. Then you showed up. Being gay was acceptable. You could be liberated and he didn't see how."

Michael sighed again, but said nothing.

"Then there's me. I'm the child of wealth. My mother married into it. If my mother had her way, I'd be in a posh penthouse in New York, allowing everyone to wait on me and living it up. I'd be seen and decadent. I'd be an asshole and I certainly wouldn't be happy." Tristan rounded the table and knelt beside Michael. He grasped Michael's hand again. "I don't understand how he knew, but throwing us together like this seems fated. I keep telling you we'd be epic."

"You're missing screws." Michael half-laughed. "But I can't argue."

"So, what do we do?" Tristan crawled between Michael's knees. "I've got a whole slew of ideas."

"Stay tonight." Michael cupped Tristan's jaw in both hands. "Stay with me."

"Yes." He nodded. He couldn't think of anywhere else he wanted to be. Tristan settled in the vee of Michael's legs and kissed him. The more he touched and learned about Michael, the more he wanted him. He nibbled on Michael's bottom lip, then licked the seam of his mouth. He bumped noses with Michael and embraced the immediacy of being with him.

"Tristan." Michael smoothed his palms over Tristan's shoulders. "You're sure?"

"I am." He slid his hands under Michael's shirt. Damn. The man wasn't lacking in the strength department. He couldn't wait to unwrap his new toy. A moan erupted from his throat. He ground his belly against the bulge in Michael's pants. He resumed kissing Michael. Their teeth clashed a couple of times, but he didn't care. He swallowed Michael's groan.

"Damn." Michael pushed him away for a moment. "I need to catch my breath. You stole it."

"I wanted it more." He rubbed his nose along Michael's. "I want you." He opened Michael's pants. "Like now."

"Fuck." Michael shifted his hips. He planted his back against the chair long enough for Tristan to shove the jeans and boxer shorts down his thighs.

Tristan licked his lips. Michael wasn't hurting in the dick department, either. He couldn't wait to taste him. Instead of plunging in, he paused. "Have you been tested lately?" He'd picked a silly time to ask that, but the words tumbled out faster than he could think about what was going on. "Sorry." He curled his fingers around Michael's shaft and stroked. "Bad timing, but... Are you?"

"You've...yeah." Michael blew out a long breath. "Neither of us will be clean in a moment when I blow." He gripped the arms of the chair. "Yeah, I've been tested. Being single for the last year tends to help. Anything else you want to know while you're jerking me off?"

"Nah. I'm good. Clean, too. Just wanted to be safe." He wanted to devour Michael, too. Seeing him there, so loose and happy, pleased Tristan.

"I have rubbers." Michael slid down in the seat and moaned. "Keep stroking. It's good."

"I can be better than good." He dragged his tongue down the underside of Michael's shaft. The man had a beautiful dick. Thick enough to make an impression and with just enough curve to touch him in the right spots. He flicked his tongue across the knobby head.

"Jesus." Michael threaded his fingers into Tristan's hair. He didn't push or force. He rocked his hips. "Yes. Feels good."

Perfect. He bobbed his head, taking Michael to the back of his throat before pulling most of the way back. He buried his nose in Michael's pubic hair. The tangy scent of Michael wrapped around him. He'd never get enough of the librarian.

"That's hot." Michael spread his legs, despite the pants and underwear tangled up around his ankles.

Tristan caressed Michael's sac. Michael jerked forward and rammed his dick down Tristan's throat. He froze, then pulled free from Tristan. "Sorry," Michael whispered. "Got carried away."

He let go of the tip of Michael's erection with a pop. "You're fine." He rose on his knees and kissed Michael. "I like an eager lover. Then I know I'm pleasing him."

"You are." Michael's voice came out ragged. His breathing turned shallow and pre-cum shimmered on the tip of his dick. "More?"

The pleading in Michael's words rang straight through to Tristan's soul. He had to put him out of his misery. Tristan resumed bobbing his head and increased his speed. He curled his tongue along Michael's shaft. Each moan from Michael and tug on Tristan's hair spurred Tristan on. He swallowed Michael deep.

"Tristan." Michael tensed and rocked his hips. His movements turned feral. He hissed. "Can't. Hold. Back."

"Then don't." Tristan nuzzled Michael's dick. He met Michael's gaze. "Now," he said around Michael's cock.

Michael moaned and shoved his shaft down Tristan's throat once more. Hot cum filled Tristan's mouth. Instead of pulling back, he held fast. He wanted everything Michael could give him.

"Tristan." Michael panted and sagged in the chair. "Damn."

Tristan chuckled to himself, then licked Michael clean. He sat back on his heels. "Good?"

"I can't move." Michael scrubbed both hands over his face. "I don't think my knees will work."

"I bet they do." Tristan wiped his mouth, then sat fully on his butt. "You're dying to be inside me."

"What if I am?" Michael's eyes flashed. "Since the day we met. Hell, I want you in me, too."

"Kinky." He winked. "I'm game."

"What about your writing?"

"If the sex is hot and I'm relaxed, the story will flow." He helped Michael get free of the wadded-up clothing. "I'm better when I'm happy. Being with you makes me happy."

Michael kicked his jeans and underwear out from under his feet. He grasped Tristan's hand. "Come with me." He led Tristan to the bedroom. His heart hammered and his palms were clammy. The last time he'd brought someone home seemed like forever ago. He flipped the light on.

"I love it." Tristan collided with Michael. He wound his arms around Michael. "You're so sexy."

"Me?" He still didn't see himself as sexy.

"Yeah, you." He turned Michael around and feathered kisses over his face. He caressed Michael's chest. "I'm so glad I found you."

Fire licked Michael from within. He moaned and grabbed Tristan's ass. He needed to lose himself. To stop thinking and take what he wanted for a change.

"I want you." Tristan's eyes flashed. He walked Michael backward until he collided with the bed. He tumbled onto the mattress. Tristan grinned. "Damn." He yanked his shirt off, then shoved his pants down around his ankles. Once naked, he pinned Michael beneath him.

Michael ignored his insecurities. *Fuck them.* He feasted on Tristan's mouth and basked in Tristan's taste. Getting Tristan out of his system would be tough. Just about impossible. He didn't care. He ground his crotch against Tristan's.

"Get the rest of the way naked," Tristan said between kisses. He raked his nails down Michael's sides. "Want you to fuck me."

He wanted to be inside Tristan, too. Blood coursed through his veins and he gasped for air.

"Where are the condoms? Lube?" Tristan sat up and flexed his upper body. "Or aren't you interested?"

"I want you." Michael moaned. He wrapped his fingers around Tristan's cock. "Tristan."

"Yeah?" Tristan rocked into Michael's hand. "That's so hot."

"Let's get hotter. Condoms and lube are in the nightstand." He wasn't sure how he sounded so coherent.

Tristan whistled and nodded once. "Good." He crawled off Michael and stood beside the bed. He rifled through the drawer until he held up the needed supplies. "I won't need much prep. I'm so ready."

Michael sat up long enough to remove his shirt, then stretched out on the bed. He'd never thought of himself as handsome and compared to Tristan, he was a pale second place.

"You're over-thinking again." Tristan tore the condom wrapper open. "I'm not working hard enough." He settled between Michael's knees and sheathed him. He stroked Michael's dick four times. "You're hard as hell, though." He leaned over Michael and sucked on his nipple.

Michael threaded his fingers into Tristan's hair. His nerve endings sizzled. He puffed for air and rubbed his hard dick on Tristan's thigh.

Tristan let go of Michael's chest. "Better." He sat back on his heels and dumped lube over Michael's cock. "I can't wait for this to be inside me."

"Yeah." Michael held out his hands for Tristan, not that Tristan needed his help. He met Tristan's gaze. He loved the fire and passion burning in the blue depths. The breath wrenched from him. Tristan was too pretty for words.

Tristan straddled Michael's thighs. He reached around and toyed with his own asshole. "Won't take long." He lined Michael's dick up with his hole. "Oh fuck." As he lowered himself onto Michael's shaft, his eyes rolled back. He whimpered. "Damn."

Once he had Michael fully within his body, he flexed his asshole. The sensation knocked Michael for a loop. Michael couldn't think straight. The only thing he could do was experience Tristan.

"You fit so well in me." A lazy smile curled on Tristan's lips. "You're stretching me, but I'm digging the burn."

"You're tight." He palmed Tristan's ass. "Ride me. Get yourself off on my dick." He planted his feet to give himself better leverage. The change shoved his cock deeper into Tristan.

"Yes." Tristan writhed and rocked on Michael's erection. Sweat glistened on his chest. His nipples peaked. He tipped his head back and groaned. "I'm not gonna last." He shuddered.

Michael stilled Tristan. He needed just a little more from him.

"What?" Tristan's eyes widened. His chest heaved and his lips parted.

"Trade me positions." He patted Tristan's leg. "Let me set the pace."

Tristan slid off him and spread out on the bed. He tucked his knees to his chest. "Do it."

Michael propped himself up on his knees. He stuffed his dick back into Tristan's ass. Being inside Tristan was like coming home. It felt perfect. He held on to Tristan's thighs. The change in position gave him better leverage. He pushed balls deep, then pulled most of the way out again.

Michael increased his speed. He dug his fingers into Tristan's legs. When Tristan shuddered again, Michael groaned. Christ, he was close.

"Let me come," Tristan pleaded. His legs twitched. "I need to."

"Do it." Michael pushed harder. He focused on the connection. He'd never be the same.

"Come with me," Tristan said. He fisted his cock. "Oh Jesus."

"Tristan." Michael gazed down at Tristan. The orgasm built low in his stomach. His resistance shattered. "Fuck."

"Michael." Tristan tensed. Cum spurted across Michael's chest, then landed on Tristan's belly. His eyebrows pinched together, but the look in his face turned serene.

Seeing Tristan come and feeling the warmth of Tristan's climax on his body pushed Michael over the edge. He jerked forward and his cock throbbed within Tristan's ass as he came.

"Holy hell." The lazy smile returned to Tristan's face. "Love that."

Michael slumped forward and rested his weight on his hands and knees. He added a few extra thrusts as the orgasm washed over him. "You say *love* a lot."

"I do." Tristan's voice came out low. "I'm an all-in kind of guy."

"I see." Michael withdrew his dick from Tristan's hole and crawled out of bed. Tristan didn't move other than to stretch out. He watched Michael, but said nothing. Being on the spot unnerved Michael. He ditched the condom and his skin heated. "What?" Michael asked.

"You don't know what to do right now, do you?"

"What?"

"You'd be tossing the guy out at this point." Tristan tucked his hands beneath his cheek. "Correct?"

"I'm usually the one who is expected to leave."

"I'm not going anywhere unless you tell me to, because I don't want to go. I don't want you to go, either." Tristan snuggled up in the sheets. "I came here because I like you. Because I want you."

"Okay." Michael turned on his heel and retrieved a towel from the bathroom. He needed the moment of separation to clear his mind. Tristan liked him. Not just for the sake of the fuck, but really cared about him. *Wow.* He headed back into the bedroom. "Want to clean up?"

"You're such a gentleman." Tristan wiped the cum from his belly and cock. "You're a gem, too."

Michael cleaned the lube from his dick and the jizz from his abs. "I'm just a guy who doesn't like to sleep in the wet spot." He returned to the bathroom long enough to toss the towel over the railing. He strode back to the bed and Tristan patted the bed. Michael climbed in beside him. He turned off the light.

"Do you know why I use the word love so much?" Tristan asked. "Because I was told never to use that word. I'd never know what love is. Not the real kind anyway."

"Who said that?" He faced Tristan. "They were wrong." He couldn't imagine telling someone love didn't exist. Sure, he wasn't close pals with the emotion, but still. Others could have love and one that would last, too.

"Would you believe it was my mother?" Tristan kissed Michael. "I look for the beauty in things. I believe it's possible to love things, people...whatever. I lost that for a while. I got caught up in the fakeness of life, but now I see things clearly."

"You do?" He splayed his hand on Tristan's chest. "Don't say things you don't mean. You don't have to spare my ego. I understand."

"Why would I lie?"

"You'll decide soon enough that you love everything but me." He hated to be so down, but he knew the score and besides, the odds weren't in his favor.

"You might be surprised." Tristan snuggled up tight to Michael. "Good night, hon. Here's to a thousand more nights beside you."

Michael froze. He'd ended the night on a sour note and Tristan still seemed to believe the relationship would work out. *How?* They were total opposites. Tristan would go back to his life in New York. Michael wouldn't follow him. He squeezed his eyes shut. He had to stop being so negative and looking for the awful sides of situations. *Ride this wave. Enjoy Tristan.* He might not have another chance with him.

Michael listened to Tristan's even breaths. If Tristan believed they had a shot, then who was he to argue? The relationship could be a build-up to a disaster or something epic. He wouldn't know until he and Tristan ran their course. His heart lightened. They had right now. That was good enough for him.

Chapter Nine

Michael rolled over and collided with a solid wall of person. *Tristan.* He opened his eyes. Tristan was beside him and still asleep. Michael had known the previous night wasn't a dream, but seeing Tristan there reassured him.

Tristan personified prettiness while he slept. His thick lashes lay against his cheek and pale freckles showed. The beginnings of lines formed at the corners of his eyes, but they gave him a sexy weathered look. Day-old scruff showed on his chin and along his jaw. Michael smoothed his hand over his cock. He could jerk off to the vision of Tristan. Hell, he just might.

"You're staring at me," Tristan murmured.

If his lips hadn't moved, Michael would've sworn he heard Tristan speak in his mind. "Sorry." He paused. "You're awake?"

"I've got a hot guy beside me. It's been hard to sleep." Tristan blinked. "I don't mind you watching me…but I hope you like what you see."

"I do." Embarrassment washed over him. He shouldn't have been staring.

"Good. I hate when I don't measure up." Tristan patted Michael's hip. "You've got to work today, don't you?"

"I have to be there by ten and it only takes me fifteen minutes by foot or ten by bike." He'd have to check the weather radar, but biking would be good for his soul this morning. He needed the extra exercise to wear him out. Maybe if he were tired, he wouldn't think about Tristan all day.

"The idea of you on a bike is so sexy." Tristan moved the sheet, tangled their legs together and brushed his chest against Michael's. "I should write or sort stuff…but first… Shower with me?"

"Sure." Like he would say no?

Tristan laughed. "Listen to us. We're being so polite." He grasped Michael's hand.

"What else should we be?" Tristan's question confused him. He frowned. "I don't understand."

"We should be horny bastards. Should be scrambling to fuck again and leaving a trail of sheets everywhere. Not asking and using niceties. Just raw passion." Tristan dragged Michael flush to him. "Or am I missing something?"

Michael paused. He wasn't sure what to say, but he had to be honest. "I'm not good at this."

"At what? Sex?" Tristan laughed again. "You were fantastic last night."

"I meant relationships. This is new and it's not guaranteed, but I'm bad." No, he was out of practice, scared and nervous.

"You're not bad." Tristan frowned. "You blew my mind."

"I'm jumping the gun." Trying to define what they were to each other before they were anything was crazy. Yet, he wanted a label.

"I've been trying to hook up with you since I got to town. I've practically begged you for a relationship." Tristan grinned. "Stop worrying so much. We've got now and it's better than I ever imagined. You're who I want."

He stared at Tristan. He wasn't *that* great. Average, maybe, but not fantastic.

"Stop worrying." Tristan kissed him. "You're so churned up that you're going to explode."

He didn't answer and wasn't sure what to say again.

"Come shower with me. I'll scrub your back and front." Tristan snuggled up to Michael. "You can tell me all about you...like, where you grew up."

"What?"

"I'm trying to lighten the mood." Tristan let go, then sat up. "Come shower with me." He tugged Michael to his feet.

Michael followed him into the bathroom. His head swam. Tristan changed topics so fast and had him right on the edge. No one had cared about his past. Even Ian, the man he'd lived with for six years, hadn't asked.

Tristan turned the water on. "Towels?"

"Here." He fumbled in the cabinet, then placed two thick towels on the toilet seat.

"So?" Tristan shoved the curtain out of the way. "Did you grow up in Sullavan?"

"No." He stepped into the steam and stood behind Tristan. He leaned against the back of the stall. "I'm from Niles. It's outside of Warren, Ohio. It's a nice place, but I wanted to stretch my wings. I went to college at Kenton, then landed here. I could've worked at the library in my home town, but I wanted new adventures. My mother called it my wanderlust."

As Michael talked, Tristan wetted the washcloth and filled it with suds. He scrubbed Michael's chest and arms, then turned Michael around.

"Whoa." Michael swayed into Tristan. He couldn't remember the last time a lover — or a one-night stand — had taken such care of him. His body tingled and blood rushed to his dick.

Tristan caressed the cloth between Michael's ass cheeks. "Have you found what you were looking for?"

"Huh?" He had to pay attention. *Shit.* "What?"

"Around here. Have you found what you were looking for in Sullavan?" Tristan asked.

"Kind of." He faced Tristan and took the washcloth from him. "I wasn't sure what I wanted. Mom said I'd turn into a girl. I haven't. I don't know. I guess she knew I wasn't happy, but I wish she wouldn't have said that. But I found a home in Sullavan." He wished he could change a few parts of his past, but what was the use? He had a future at the library. He'd been okay in Sullavan and hadn't thought about leaving, even though he was lonely. Christ, he needed to get out of his thoughts.

"Home in Sullavan, eh?" Tristan nodded. "I like it. Could be a book title."

"I suppose." He slid the cloth over Tristan's chest. God, the man was strong. His nipples beaded and the muscles in Tristan's arms flexed. Michael wondered how many arm curls Tristan did. He caught Tristan's gaze and dropped the cloth. "Drat."

"Want me to get it?" Tristan wriggled his eyebrows. "Or was that you trying to be sly?"

"You'll have to wait and see." He knelt in front of Tristan and breathed in his scent — soap and Tristan. He wrapped his fingers around Tristan's shaft.

"Oh, honey." Tristan groaned. He palmed the back of Michael's head. "Michael."

He dragged the top of Tristan's dick over his lips. Salt and soap slid across his tongue. He glanced up at Tristan.

"Yes." Tristan leaned against the wall of the shower and widened his stance.

Michael flicked his tongue across the blunt head of Tristan's erection, then stroked. Power radiated through him. He cupped Tristan's balls.

"Yes. Suck me. Do it." Tristan guided Michael's head. "Take me in."

He hadn't needed any encouragement. He wanted to please Tristan in every way. A groan rumbled in Michael's throat. He swallowed Tristan deep and paused. He hummed.

Michael buried his nose in Tristan's pubic hairs. He curled his tongue around Tristan's shaft, then swallowed. *What'd Tristan think of that?*

"Holy shit." Tristan bucked, jamming his dick deep into Michael's mouth. "Please?"

Michael bobbed his head and, at the same time, stroked Tristan's cock and fondled his balls. Power flowed through him. He enjoyed giving pleasure and loved the taste of Tristan — salty, musky, but with a twist of sin. He hummed again.

Tristan rocked his hips. "Yes. Fuck." He tipped his head back and groaned again. His movements turned jerky. "Michael."

He kept going. Having Tristan on the edge…yeah, no way he'd back out now. He watched Tristan while he continued to suck him off.

"Fuck," Tristan said, drawing out the word. He took over the tempo and fucked Michael's mouth with abandon. A strangled cry erupted from him. Sticky cum spurted down Michael's throat.

Instead of pulling away, Michael rode out Tristan's orgasm. He bobbed his head a few more times and when Tristan finished trembling, Michael licked him clean. Michael sat back on his heels. The shower water stung his shoulders and the back of his neck. For the last few minutes, he'd forgotten he and Tristan were in the shower.

Tristan sagged to the floor of the tub and a lazy smile curled on his lips. "If all your blow jobs are like that, I'm in love."

"Guess you'll have to find out." Michael stood and ignored the word Tristan had used — *love*. What the hell? *He must say that to all the boys.* Michael rinsed. Better to stay busy with something he could control rather than thinking too hard about things he couldn't. He detached the shower head and offered it to Tristan. "Need a hand?"

"Nah. Just a minute or two to recover." Tristan laughed. "You wrung me out." He managed to stand and clutched his ribs. "I haven't had this good a time in forever. Haven't laughed this much in so long."

"I'm happy to provide the service." At least he thought so. He stepped out of the shower and dried off. Tristan had gotten to him. The word 'love' rolled around in his brain, annoying him…but when Tristan said it, Michael believed him. He kind of wanted to hear all sorts of sweet things from Tristan—but he wasn't sure love existed.

Tristan rinsed and turned the water off. Michael offered him the other towel. Tristan paused with the towel in front of his junk. "I could get used to this twosome we've got going. You're too good to be true and I don't know if I want to go back to my other life."

"I'm a regular guy. This is a vacation." Michael laughed, but the amusement didn't show in his voice.

"Well, I got the best blow job on this vacation from you, Mr. Regular Guy." Tristan dropped the towel on the floor. "I need a nap. My knees are shaking." He strolled out of the bathroom, leaving Michael alone.

Michael sighed. If he and Tristan were going to be something more than a quickie, he'd have to train Tristan to pick up after himself. He hated the smell of damp towels after a shower. He fixed the shower curtain, then hung the towels. Running a brush through his hair would be good. He grabbed the brush and headed into the bedroom.

Tristan had stretched out naked on the bed. He held his phone and the light shimmered on his face.

"Already connected to civilization?" Michael asked. "My Shangri-La wasn't enough?"

"The light blinked and I couldn't ignore it. Sorry." Tristan frowned and tapped the screen. "Are you kidding? Fuck me."

"I did that last night and you loved it." Michael eased up beside him and wound his arms around Tristan. "Why? Want round two? I've got an hour before I have to be at work."

"No." Tristan patted Michael's thigh. "Trust me. I want to fuck you. I want you in me again, too. But I meant this." He handed over the phone. "My stalker hasn't taken a holiday like I thought."

Michael frowned, then read the message.

You're not writing. You forgot about Lewiston. No notes. No updates. What's the deal?

"What is Lewiston?" Michael asked. "Another story? Is it one you started and abandoned? Or what?"

"I never start and abandon anything, especially not work." Tristan tossed the phone onto the bed. "All of my notes are in longhand until I begin the actual writing process. It's my thing. I never leak anything unless it's already fully formed and written."

"I guess you can't hack a piece of paper." Michael left the bed and picked up his brush. He stared at his reflection and arranged his hair. He glanced back at Tristan. He wished he looked good right out of the shower like Tristan.

"I normally have a notebook with me everywhere. I left it at the farmhouse last night because I hoped we'd end up the way we did." Tristan stood. He shook out his shirt, then stuck his arms through the sleeves. "I don't know how the stalker knows where I'm at with the story because I'm not writing about Lewiston. I have an outline for the Sullavan one, but nothing in the computer. I haven't had time." He tugged his boxer shorts back on, then stood behind Michael. "Where do we go from here?"

"I don't know." Michael faced Tristan. He smoothed the wrinkles in Tristan's shirt. "Depends on you. I have a house and a life in Sullavan. You're the mobile one."

"Not really," Tristan murmured. "Well, kind of. I should've put down roots a long time ago so I can be more disciplined about my writing. I've got the apartment, but it's just a glorified locker to put my crap in." He flattened his palms on Michael's chest. "I'm better when I'm happy — although I do tend to channel the emotions of my characters. I want to be here with you."

"So, look out for sappy days?" Michael asked. He wished he had something on instead of just a smile.

"When I write gut-wrenching, I tend to absorb it and get melancholy. It's part of me really getting into the character's head." Tristan shrugged.

"It happens."

"Will you come over tonight?"

Michael blinked. He needed time to process Tristan's questions. "You change the subject on a dime." He shrugged out of Tristan's embrace, darted over to the dresser and pulled out a pair of boxers. "Yeah, I'll come over. What about your stalker? What are you going to do with him or her?"

"Well..." Tristan stepped into his jeans. "This individual has been writing me for two years. The cops don't know who it is and since he or she isn't threatening me, they can't do much. It's just correspondence. I usually ignore the letters — which is why I changed the subject." He stood in the middle of the bedroom. "I've never written for anyone but me. This person keeps giving me suggestions, but I don't use them."

"I see." Michael tugged a pair of khakis from the closet. "I'd be scared if I were you."

"That's probably what the writer wants — and for me to write a book about Lewiston. I'm not caving." Tristan took the pants from Michael. "Writing about Sullavan and being here with you is more interesting."

"Until you get bored." Michael took the pants back. He knew guys like Tristan. When the need to move hit, he'd be left in the dust.

"You can't believe that," Tristan said. "You think I'll get bored?"

"Uh-huh." New York would call. The lure of the night life, a party or an ex-boyfriend would call Tristan and buh-bye Sullavan.

"What if I'm busy learning about a certain librarian and don't want to go?" Tristan asked.

"You'll change your mind." He put the khakis on, then selected a maroon button-down shirt. "I've been there, done that and have nothing to show for it but the T-shirt." Being with Al came to mind.

"I'm not my uncle."

"True. You've got more hair."

"Smart ass." Tristan kissed him hard on the lips. "You need to trust me. I know it's not your forte. We've both kept secrets, but I can't do this alone. I can't manage my uncle's stuff, write this book and fall for you all by myself. My last boyfriend would disagree with me, but I'm the boyfriend type. I like being in a relationship. I need the stability and the warm body beside me."

Michael stared at him. Did Tristan realize what he'd said? Stability and a warm body… He made being together sound so…bland. "Then why aren't you in a relationship? Not one with me."

"My last boyfriend was a self-possessed ass?" Tristan laughed, then sobered. "No, that's not fair. My ex believed monogamy was a foul word. He slept with anyone who'd drop their pants for him. He calls me every so often for money."

"Ah." He'd known a few guys like that and had dodged the bullet. He threaded his belt through the loops. "I take it you don't give in to him?" At least he hoped not.

"Nah, I don't. My aunt scared him off. She's more of a social climber than he is and she's got money, too. She married into it." Tristan folded his arms. "Money seems to be the root of the problems in my family. They have it and they want more. They'll lie and cheat to get it, too."

"Then you must live a complicated life." Michael ducked away from Tristan and put his socks on. "My life is so much less complicated. My entanglements involved your uncle, then a man named Kevin, and Barry — whom you met. But not all at the same time and never for money." He scooped his watch up and clicked it around his wrist.

Tristan stilled Michael's hands. "Money won't help everything and speaking of my uncle... He endowed a hundred grand to the school and another hundred grand for the creation of a center for the LGBT community in Sullavan."

Michael froze. "A what?" He'd had no idea. Al hadn't been out and hadn't wanted anyone to even think he might be gay. "How'd he know we needed a center or that there would be enough individuals to support it existing?"

"All I gleaned from the paperwork was that he wanted a place where people could go to feel included. A place to hang out, crash...get help, fed." Tristan shrugged. "I think it's noble."

"It is." Michael swayed into Tristan. "I wonder what possessed him to do it, though."

"No clue." Tristan stuffed his hands into Michael's front pockets. "I don't know how to start something like a center. I know counselors in New York and I can convince at least one to come here for support. But where do I get the stuff or the building? I'm clueless."

"You're not." Michael massaged his temple, but remained close to Tristan. He had to think. "There are a few larger houses on the south end of town that are empty. Old Victorian digs. You could probably rent one or buy it cheap and turn it into a home. Hell, if you get the people staying there to work on rehabbing the house, it'd make it more important to them. I've got a friend who is a contractor and can offer advice."

"Would you help?"

"I'm at the library most of the time." But he'd do what he could. He wanted to spend time with Tristan. "But how are you going to do this? You're going back to New York."

"I'm begging." Tristan tipped his head to the side and grinned. "Pleading."

"I'm only one guy, Tris. I have a full-time job. I want to help you, but I don't know if I can juggle it." Or if he could risk getting his heart broken. *Christ.* Getting involved with Tristan in the first place was bad. Tristan would leave. Men didn't stick around in his life. What would he do when Tristan went back to New York? He'd carry on, sure, but he wouldn't be the same. He'd have to look at yet another reminder of a failed love when he looked at the house...even if the relationship hadn't failed yet. *Fucking balls.*

"Try. For me." Tristan brushed his nose along Michael's. "I wouldn't ask if I didn't think you and I could be dynamic with this."

"But—" *Dynamic? Epic...* Michael's resolve melted a little. He wanted to be loved. Cherished. What Tristan offered was too damn intoxicating.

152

"You called me Tris. No one calls me that—no one except my uncle." Tristan caged Michael in his arms. "I don't understand the connection but I feel it. I'm supposed to be here in Sullavan and with you. We're supposed to do this." He rested his forehead on Michael's. "If we recruit a couple of my New York contacts and get people in to help us on a volunteer basis, you won't be quite so needed at the house...just at my house."

"You've got huge ideas...and a book to write. How are *you* going to manage it all?" Michael asked. "Plus, you have that stalker."

"And a house to sort out, a relationship I'm trying to start..." Tristan sighed. "We'll do it. We're a great team. You sort, shelve and lend the books and I'll write them. We'll make this house thing my uncle wanted a reality and fuck my stalker. I write for me, not him or her."

"Tristan."

His eyes flashed. "Call me Tris. I love it when you say my name."

"Tris." Michael bowed his head. "I can't believe I'm saying this, but okay."

"Yes?" Tristan tipped Michael's gaze. "Really?"

"But if we do all of what you want, I have a condition." He swallowed against the lump in his throat. He had no idea how Tristan would take his request. "I want this—whatever we've started between us—to be just us." He couldn't handle knowing Tristan was seeing Jamie on the side. "Tell me if you don't want to be monogamous. I'm not sleeping with you if you're even thinking of sleeping around."

"Are you getting territorial?" The fire in Tristan's eyes flared and his smile widened. "Twinging with jealousy?"

"Maybe." *Fuck.* "I am a one-man kind of guy."

"Good. I am, too." Tristan dragged Michael to the bed and tumbled backward with Michael on top of him. "I finally wore you down enough to be with me. I'm not planning on screwing that up by splitting my time with someone else."

"And you're not wigged out by my past?" Michael straddled Tristan's legs. "Not a bit?"

"My stalker doesn't scare you?" Tristan threaded his fingers together with Michael's.

"It does. I'm already worried about you and what this person may do," Michael said. "I'm scared of how I feel about you, too."

"Why?"

"You're famous. Well, compared to me and my experiences, you are. It stands to reason someone or someones — plural — would seek you out. It also makes sense you'd decide I'm boring after a while."

"Maybe."

"I've been left a lot. Al, Kevin, Barry…none of them wanted to stick around. I didn't understand Al's reasons, but Kevin and Barry wanted someone flashier. Hotter. Not me." He stared at their interlocked hands. "Just be patient with me. I tend to look for the reasons someone won't be a good fit and try to jump ship before I can get hurt. I'm horrible at it because I have faith in people far beyond when they deserve to be set adrift."

"You're human," Tristan said. "We're both a little damaged, but we'll find a way. Something tells me it's going to be together."

"Okay." He hoped Tristan was right. But the doubt didn't go away.

Tristan winked. "So…who can I talk to about looking at a house?"

Michael sighed then kissed Tristan. Things weren't perfect or even sorted out, but they had a start. He had to stop thinking the worst and aim for the best.

* * * *

Tristan drove back to his uncle's house with his heart light and his outlook positive. He had a good thing going with Michael, even if it was still new and fragile. One way or another, he'd get Michael to see they were best together.

Still, Michael's doubts weren't lost on him. Michael was right—Tristan had a life before Sullavan. He had friends and things he liked to do in New York. But slowing down and enjoying the moment was nice, too. More than nice...the change in pace suited him. Sure, he wasn't writing, but he wasn't fogged by partying and drinking. He had a clear head and an open heart. Not bad for a guy who had been voted most likely to burn out by age thirty-five. He'd made it to thirty-seven, thank you very much. Life was better, now that he had Michael.

He pulled into the driveway and parked in front of the garage. The rental car was gone and an envelope had been stuffed into the space between the screen door and the main one. He scanned the front of the envelope before opening it. Just as he'd expected, the people from the car rental place had left the receipt behind. He tucked the envelope into his bag, then unlocked the house and headed inside.

The musty smell wasn't as pervasive. Another scent, like warm bread, settled around him. He groaned. *Fuck*. He hadn't cleaned out the kitchen yet. He'd never get any writing done at this rate. He put his bag on the chair next to the door, then nodded once. The answer was so plain…he had the voice tech on his laptop. If he hooked it up and turned on the mic, he could relay the story into the program and edit once he'd tackled the kitchen.

Tristan changed his clothes, then checked his phone. No new messages or emails. *Perfect.* He gazed around the guest room. The house was his and paid for. It had once been a mecca for his uncle and could be a fabulous home again. He refused to create a shrine to his uncle. No, this was a place to start over. Hope spread through him as he changed into a sloppy shirt and rumpled board shorts. He could make the house shine. Living in Sullavan wasn't beyond his capacity. He'd always said he wanted a real home and roots. Sullavan was the right place and this was the right time.

With a little help from Michael, he might even be able to create the center like his uncle had wanted, as well as an escape for him and Michael. Anything was possible.

Tristan carried his laptop down to the kitchen, then turned on the machine. He opened the file for his notes. Cleaning wasn't his forte, but he had no choice. If he didn't toss the junk and old food, no one else would. One chunk at a time, one page at a time, he'd tackle the kitchen and his story.

* * * *

Four hours later, Tristan finished scouring the countertops. He'd filled three garbage bags full of recyclable materials, trash and spoiled food. He wished he had a composter. At least then he could've put the food to some use. Once the bags were hauled to the respective garbage and recycling cans, he headed back inside. His back ached, but not only was the room now spotless, he had his first three chapters composed. He hit save on the file, then closed the lid of the laptop. If Michael had been there, they could've celebrated the minor victories by making out in the kitchen.

No Michael. No making out.

Tristan picked his phone up. Not checking it religiously felt odd. Back in New York, he'd used the device to while away too many hours. As he swiped through the screens, a call came through. The photo of his ex-boyfriend smiled back at him.

Tristan cracked his neck, then answered the call. "Hi, Cody."

"Hey, you. Don't you return calls?" Cody asked.

Shit. What'd he do this time and what did he have to sort out? "I do, but I haven't heard from you in six months." He sank onto the closest chair. "What's wrong?"

"Nothing really. I just wanted to talk to you."

"Ah." Tristan shifted in his seat and stared at the living room setup. When Michael arrived, he'd have him help move the sofa against the far wall. There they'd be able to watch thunderstorms through the picture window. He missed watching storms. Would Michael enjoy listening to the thunder and lightning with him? The cuddling under a blanket while snuggling closer each time a loud boom sounded?

"Are you listening?" Cody asked. "Tristan."

"I heard you." Not really. He'd been thinking about anything but the conversation. "Sorry. I don't have much to say."

"Asshole."

"Fuck you very much." *The jerk.*

"What is with you?" Cody asked. "I called the apartment. Like five times I called. Dennis took the messages. He claimed he was letting you know I wanted to talk to you." His voice cracked. "Are you avoiding me?"

"Not exactly." He hadn't heard from Dennis other than two emails, which wasn't out of the ordinary for him, but nothing in the wording had mentioned anything about Cody. "I've been busy." He jotted down a note to call Dennis. He'd been an asshole and hadn't even checked in. For all he knew, Dennis didn't care. But there was a chance he did and he deserved an update. Tristan would call him later.

"Who are you doing?"

"Cody." Jesus, the man drove him crazy.

"You found someone named Cody? I bet that's a lot easier in bed," Cody snapped. "Does he like hearing his name shouted out, too?"

He pinched the bridge of his nose. "No, and his name isn't Cody. Look, my uncle passed away and left his house to me. I'm in charge of going through his stuff and it's taking time."

"Oh? Stuff?"

He should've known Cody's latent weaselness would come out. If the man thought he smelled a chance to make money, he'd pounce. "It's a farmhouse in rural Ohio and there aren't any antiques here. There's really nothing of great monetary value other than the house and I'm not selling it, so don't get any ideas." Truth be told, he had no idea what his uncle had had, but he wasn't giving any of it to a former flame looking to make an easy buck.

"Oh."

Was that Cody's spirit crashing? *Good.* Tristan crossed his ankles. "Cody, I'm up to my eyeballs sorting through stuff, tossing other things and trying to write."

"Dennis never said anything about an uncle. He's not there? He's still at the apartment?"

"Yes, he's at the apartment, so don't try to break in." He bit back a groan. "Look, when I get back to New York, we'll hang out." The key word should've been if. He hadn't planned on staying in the Big Apple. Now that he had an actual house to live in, rather than an apartment, he kind of wanted to put down roots. Why stay somewhere he couldn't keep when he could do whatever his heart desired at the house?

"Yeah? We haven't clubbed in a long time." Cody laughed. "I'm holding you to that. The moment you're back, we're going out. I miss you."

"Sure." Cody missed him? Since when?

"I mean it. I've been lonely without you. No one understands me like you and no one else will give me shit for doing shit," Cody said. "I like when you hold me accountable."

Ah, so Cody wanted a parent-figure. Yeah, fuck no. "I'm sure you'll find someone who can do all of that better than I ever did."

"Maybe." Cody paused. "So where in assfuck Ohio are you?"

Assfuck...wonderful. "Sullavan."

"Never heard of it."

"It's not a very big place. It's interesting, though." He closed his eyes and grinned. Thinking about the town pleased him. The cast of characters would feature in the next two books at least.

"Just stop. I don't want one of your small-town history stories. You get boring and teacher-y. I hate it,"

Cody said. "Stick to writing that shit down instead of telling me."

"Sorry." He sighed, then opened his eyes. "Look, I need to go. I've got a schedule going and I should be writing. I'm already behind."

"Come home."

"What?"

"You heard me," Cody said. "Come home. You don't belong in a hick town. You're the kind of guy who thrives on action. What really happens in Solomon? A car accident? Critters being run over in the street? Flowers growing?"

"Wow. You've never been outside of New York, have you?" He shook his head. "Never mind. The town is Sullavan and yes, it's a slower pace. People can walk from one end of Sullavan to the other. I don't remember seeing any splattered animals or car accidents. It's just a nice, peaceful place to be."

"You'll get bored," Cody said. "I know you."

Funny. He'd just heard that from Michael, too. "You never know."

"How about I come there?"

"Nah. *You'd* be the bored one." Besides, he didn't want his ex anywhere close to Michael. He liked his insulated existence with his new beau.

"Probably. I have the attention span of a gnat." Cody paused again. "Just come home. Please?"

A shadow darkened the kitchen door. Tristan tensed, then sat up straight. "I have to go. Someone's here." He didn't bother to say goodbye. Instead, he hung up and clutched the phone in his hand. Only a few people knew he was there. Who'd be visiting him? He jumped up from his seat. "Hello?"

The door opened and Jamie held onto the handle. "Hi."

Tristan blew out a ragged breath. "Damn it."

Chapter Ten

"What?" Jamie strode across the room. "You're pale. Are you okay? It's hot in here. Turn on a fan or two." He flipped the wall switch. "Sit down."

"I'm fine. I wasn't pale until you showed up." He massaged his forehead, then tossed the phone onto the now empty table. "At least this time you didn't walk right in unannounced. This is my house and I'd like to know who is visiting rather than being surprised."

"Your house?" Jamie's brows rose. "Really? Are you planning on staying?"

"For now, yes." He willed his heart rate to slow to a normal level. "You need something from me? Or are you here for a social reason?"

"Oh, I need something. You." Jamie flattened his hand on Tristan's chest. "I'm thrilled you're sticking around."

"I'm glad to hear that. I'll need your help, I'm sure. My other lawyer is in New York and I have a hard time getting in touch with him."

"Whenever you want me, just call." Jamie pinned Tristan to the doorframe leading to the dining room. "I can't stop thinking about you."

"We need to talk." He nudged Jamie away and put space between them. "Right now."

"After this." Jamie caged him in again, but this time he kissed Tristan.

The rush wasn't there. No tingle or spark. Nothing. Tristan stared at Jamie, then put his hands up. "Stop. I'm seeing someone."

"Someone?" Jamie rolled his eyes. "If you've got a guy back home, he doesn't need to know what we're doing. This is just fun while you're away."

"I'm seeing Michael." Saying the words out loud comforted him. He wanted to shout from the roof that he and Michael were a pair.

"Are you kidding?" Jamie snapped. "Michael?"

"I'm quite serious. Why? What's wrong with Michael?"

"There's nothing wrong with him—if you like boredom," Jamie said.

"Jamie." Some people could be cruel.

"Come on. He's a *librarian*. How exciting can that possibly be?"

"Because law is so exiting?" Tristan asked. "So what?"

"You don't see movies about librarians—not on mainstream television or in theaters—and you sure as hell don't see them in anything that makes them look sexy." Jamie folded his arms. "They're the ones who die in the horror films or suck everyone off in the porn movies."

"I'm not arguing this with you." *Jesus.* Whatever Michael had done to Jamie couldn't be so horrible as to warrant this kind of venom.

"Well, I am. I'm better-looking, make more money by far and have a higher standing in the community. I have the connections to get your center created. I've looked at the suitable buildings in town and the best you're going to get is the abandoned community center. It'll need work, but it's got the facilities you need."

Okay, so Jamie had a point about the building. Still, he didn't have to be such a dick—a hot one, but still a dick—about Michael.

"What do you say? You'll forget Michael and let me help you?" Jamie tipped her head and smiled.

Tristan sighed. He hated being pushed into a corner and Jamie knew where to put his hands to shove the hardest. "I'll helm the project because I know what my uncle wanted." *Liar.* "I'll need your help down the road, but for this to work, we need to work together as a community. Everyone. It won't happen if we're fighting each other over God knows what."

"Sure." Jamie hugged Tristan and lingered too long for Tristan's comfort. "You won't regret it," Jamie said. "Promise."

"Uh-huh." He had too fucking much on his plate and didn't need a diva lawyer added into the mix.

"What do we do?" Jamie clapped his hands. "I'm ready."

"I'm putting you on the community center detail. Prices, permits—whatever information I need…you get it. Don't draw up any paperwork. Just give me the details. You're the man with the contacts, right? Then do that. In the meantime, I'll keep sorting out the house.

Maybe there are a few things here we can sell to help fund the project."

"The house, for one."

Where would he live while he got the center up and running? "Not yet." What if he didn't want to sell? What if the possibility of sticking around kept getting more enticing?

"Think about it. The house would bring a quick influx of cash." Jamie flicked his hair off his forehead. "It's the best move."

"Is anyone in Sullavan buying?" He'd seen plenty of *for sale* signs, but no *sold* ones.

"No, but we can get it listed as a summer hideaway," Jamie said. "People want those. Affluent people trying to flee the city will snap it up."

Christ. He didn't want to hear that information. He massaged his temples. "Just work on the community center. I'll figure out the house."

"Fine." Jamie kissed Tristan. "Then we fuck. Meet me at my condo."

"Uh—I have to take care of here. Let's postpone the victory sex until the end of the journey." Or at least until he had no other options. Sad, but true...he wasn't interested in Jamie.

"No Michael." Jamie shook his head. "It's not going to work."

"I'm currently seeing him, so yeah, he's going to be involved." Tristan's patience was wearing thin.

"We'll see. You may not be together forever."

"Right." He walked Jamie to the door. "Good night. Keep me posted on the community center."

"Will do." Jamie flashed him another smile.

Tristan ducked before Jamie could kiss him again. Once Jamie stepped off the porch, Tristan locked the front door and checked the back one, too. He needed separation. Jamie had given him the keys, but for all Tristan knew, he'd kept a set for himself. Tristan rolled his shoulders. He didn't have time for this crap.

Still, he couldn't stop thinking about what Jamie had said. *Michael isn't good enough? What bullshit.* Jamie wasn't exactly a catch. The man was too full of himself. He'd be a handful in a relationship as well as bed and not in a good way.

Tristan checked the time. Five minutes to five. If he tried to write, he'd lose focus the moment Michael arrived. If he went the speech mode and had the computer transcribe his words, he might get something done. Then again, he might not. He dragged his computer into the study.

Despite opening the program and setting everything up, the story refused to flow. *Damn it.* Tristan stared at the bookshelves. The sheer volume of stuff in the room overwhelmed him.

His phone beeped. He frowned. Hadn't he set the device to silent? He checked the icons. One text. He pulled up the message.

You're not writing. I'm angry.

What the hell? Tristan growled and reread the message. Whoever had sent it hadn't bothered to list their name or their number. *Why...how...fuck.*

"Tristan?"

He jumped and tossed the phone onto the armchair. "Leave me the hell alone." *Shit.* He should at least answer the door before shouting at the person on the other side. He strode out of the study.

"Fine. I'll go." A shadow moved in front of the front door. "Sorry."

Michael. "No, wait." He needed someone familiar — someone named Michael. "Sorry." He unlocked and opened the door. "Hey, you."

Michael shook his head and laughed. "For a guy who likes me, you have a strange way of showing it. I could develop a complex." He stepped into the house and held up a paper bag. "I also brought the fixings for mac and cheese."

"I'm thrilled. I've had a day." He kissed Michael. The tingle was there and if he wasn't mistaken, it had grown stronger. "But the day got a whole lot better now that you're here."

"I'm glad." Michael toyed with the bag. "I wasn't sure if you liked mac and cheese, but it's one of the few things I can cook. Heck, I wasn't even sure you'd want to eat it. You're all into healthy stuff...aren't you?"

"Just because I lived in the city and had a chef doesn't mean I'm a health nut. I can cheat. Besides, I love mac and cheese," Tristan said. "I haven't had it in years."

"Well, then it'll be a cheat day."

"Nah." He took the bag from Michael and clasped Michael's hand. "It'll be perfect." He led Michael into the kitchen. "I haven't got much. Most of the refrigerated stuff had to be tossed and the pantry items won't help make anything with cheese, but I do have a lot of wine. A *lot* of wine."

Michael chuckled. "He did like his different flavors."

"You mean vintages. Wine vintages." He plunked the bag on the counter.

"No." Michael removed the contents from the bag. "Flavors. He loved wine and the different kinds — blueberry, blackberry, rose petals, dandelion... He had to have it. None of it was terribly expensive. Some is, but most isn't. It's homemade stuff."

"Huh." He needed to spend more time with Michael so he could learn more about his uncle. Al had been such an interesting person and he hardly knew him.

"Want me to make this now or wait? I'm here as long as you want." Michael toyed with the bottle of milk. "The library isn't open on Sundays."

"Sweet." He snagged Michael in his arms and kissed him. He'd never get enough of Michael. He caged him between his body and the counter. He wanted to be with Michael again and in every room. How many surfaces could they christen?

"Tristan." Michael groaned. "You blow my mind and you're jamming the drawer knob into my ass cheek."

"Oh?" *Nice.* He dropped to his knees. "Now I'll blow other parts of you." Tristan opened Michael's pants. Instead of going straight for the gusto, he kept himself in check and rubbed his face on Michael's crotch. He loved the way Michael smelled — like old books, paper and sex.

Michael threaded his fingers into Tristan's hair. "You don't have to do this so fast. We've got the rest of the weekend."

And he didn't want to waste a second. He tugged Michael's pants and underwear down. "Briefs?" He hadn't meant to blurt that out. "Sexy." Michael's erection pointed toward him. Thick enough to make an impression, but just right for his mouth. God, he loved his man's dick.

"Got to switch it up every so often." Michael massaged Tristan's head. "Surprise?"

"I love it." Tristan stroked Michael's shaft. He could've stayed on his knees between Michael's legs forever and been happy. Tristan traced the seam of his lips with the head of his cock. When Michael moaned, he spurred Tristan on. Tristan swallowed Michael to the back of his throat and hummed.

"Oh Jesus." Michael tugged on Tristan's hair. "This."

Instead of answering with words, Tristan bobbed his head. He wanted to please Michael. To make him come apart. Nothing else mattered except Michael. He rolled his tongue around Michael's shaft and buried his nose in Michael's pubic hairs. When Michael moaned, he cupped his balls.

Michael rocked his hips and whimpered. "Feels so good, Tris."

He bobbed his head faster. Only Michael could call him Tris. The name felt right on Michael's lips. He caressed his lover's sac. God, the man had soft skin. He nibbled his way to the hairless patch behind his sac.

Michael tensed. "Damn."

Good. He wanted Michael on the edge. He flicked his tongue across Michael's smooth skin, then toyed with Michael's hole.

Michael rubbed his dick on Tristan's forehead, smearing pre-cum in Tristan's hair. *Yes. Mark me.* Tristan closed his eyes. *So good.* He abandoned Michael's balls, then resumed sucking on Michael's cock. He opened his eyes and met Michael's heavy-lidded gaze. When Michael gritted his teeth, Tristan increased his speed.

Another whimper resonated in Michael. "Tris." He met Tristan thrust for thrust and undulated his body. He stuffed his dick balls-deep into Tristan's mouth. He tensed again and shivered. A low growl erupted from him and cum shot down Tristan's throat. He panted.

Tristan bobbed his head a few more times, making sure to clean up every drop of Michael's offering. He licked Michael's shaft, then stopped and sat back on his heels. "Delicious."

"More like delirious." Michael wobbled to the floor and sat opposite Tristan. "You make thinking impossible."

"That's the plan." He crawled between Michael's legs and kissed him. "I want you to be just as addicted as I am."

"I am." Michael stared at him. "I didn't think it was possible."

"What isn't possible?" He folded his legs beneath him. "Tell me." What had he missed?

Michael sighed. He didn't try to cover his nudity. "I didn't think I could fall for anyone. Not again. I've been hosed over so many times and I thought love — even the tiny seed to start it — was gone. Then you showed up. It happened so fast. I swore I wouldn't get close to you. Wouldn't even think about you. I was warned so many times."

"By Dicey?" Tristan yanked his shirt off. If Michael was going to sit there half-naked, then he'd join the party.

"Why…did she talk to you?" Michael frowned. "I should've guessed."

"She told me if I knew what was good for the both of us, I'd stick to myself and leave you be. You'd been through enough. She never said what and I didn't push." He placed his shirt over Michael's crotch. "Sorry. Didn't think you'd want to have a discussion in the near nude."

"I don't mind. I'm not the greatest-looking guy, but I'm not an ogre." Michael shrugged. "But thanks." He met Tristan's gaze. "I'm shocked she didn't tell you everything. She likes to talk." He handed the shirt back to Tristan. "Want this? I need to stand back up or I'll be in this position all night."

"Then stand." He took the garment from Michael. "Smells like your cock."

"That happens. Might be gooey, too." Michael hefted his jeans up over his hips, then zipped and ditched his shirt. "We'll go topless together."

"Sweet." He snagged Michael in his arms again. "I do like your cock and I love the way you smell."

"You're silly." Michael didn't pull away. He laughed. "So, what did Dicey tell you? What exactly? She's protective of me. I love her devotion, but she can be a little too…Dicey."

"She means well." Tristan shrugged. "She said she'd hurt me if I messed with you. It didn't matter who I was or how much money I had, she'd tear me a new one." He laughed. If nothing else, he appreciated Dicey's friendship with Michael. He missed having close compatriots and wished he had more. "I believe her."

"You're better off if you don't discount her, yeah."

"Or you." He curled his fingers under Michael's chin. "I know you're tense. Being here has to have you on edge. I'm guessing there are more memories than you want to deal with."

"It's odd…but it's not. There are reminders here. Lots of them, but it's not the same. His touches are everywhere, but so are yours. I see things and it makes me think. This was his place, but it doesn't have to be just *his*. You rearranged the living room. He refused to do that, even though I mentioned moving the couch would make watching thunderstorms easier."

"You thought of that, too?" If he hadn't started falling for Michael, that comment would've been the kicker to push him over the edge. "If the couch is against the wall, you can sit there, cuddle and watch the rain."

"And the lightning coming from the west." Michael paused. "But like the rearranging, you made the house yours. Not gutting. Just moving things around and changing it up." He smiled. "You're getting used to Sullavan."

"Mostly, but you're the biggest part of it." He kissed Michael. "I'm not the settling down type. I might be the boyfriend one, but I hate being stationary. Home has never been a thing for me."

"Ah. I can't make much, but I'm good with mac and cheese." Michael splayed his hands on Tristan's chest. "Where's the saucepan? If we don't make this, the milk will curdle."

"Huh?" *Milk curdling? Saucepan? Fuck.* He didn't cook. That was Dennis' job. He could, but he hated burned food. Besides, he wasn't sure where the pans were.

"Saucepan? You put water in it. About so big." Michael held out his hands. "Have you seen one?"

"No. I didn't look below the counter. All I cleaned out was the pantry, spice cabinet and fridge."

"Then I'm guessing it's still where Al left it." Michael disengaged from Tristan and pulled the pan from the lower cabinet. He filled the pot with water. "Won't take long."

"I didn't think it would. Mind if I watch?" He sat on the counter. "I like to watch cooks."

"By all means." Michael opened the package of noodles. "I never really learned to cook. Not from my family. Mom didn't think it was something I needed to know. She was wrong, but she had her issues with me. Once I graduated from high school, I got out."

"That sucks."

"It made me self-reliant." Michael shrugged, then sprinkled salt into the water. "Hand me the olive oil. I can't cook very well, but I can take care of myself."

"Sure." He offered up the bottle. "What's that for?"

"To keep the pasta from sticking." Michael grinned, then poured a dollop of oil into the water. "I learned that from one of the cooking demos I saw on television."

"Huh." He watched Michael with awe. He wished he could be like Michael. "I was never self-reliant—not until I got older." He fixed his gaze on Michael. The man moved around the kitchen like a dancer, all grace and fluid gestures. He looked like he should've been there all along. Like he'd fallen into the same routine as before. So comfortable. Tristan grinned. A new feeling washed over him—exciting, bold and a little scary. He and Michael were on the cusp of something fantastic. Not just tall words from him in the hopes he'd get what he wanted, but honest-to-God almost relationship status.

"Why weren't you?" Michael asked.

"Huh?" Shit. He'd forgotten the topic of conversation. "I'm sorry. What?"

"Why weren't you self-reliant?"

Tristan chuckled. He should've shared this before, but he'd worried Michael would run the other way. "I'm a rich bitch."

"What?" Michael stepped back from the steaming water. "My turn to be lost. I missed something."

Time to bare his soul. "I was a poor kid and my mother, when she was younger, came from poverty.

My grandmother was widowed at the age of thirty and expected the kids to support her. My uncle did woodworking and odd jobs to bring in a little cash. My mother found rich boyfriends and eventually started escorting. Guys were a challenge. Find one, milk him for all the money she could, then get the hell out before someone got ideas. Then she met my dad. Why they fell in love is a mystery. I guess he was the one john she liked. Anyway, they had nothing in common and usually fought. Most nights, she threatened to leave. He is rumored to have had at least a dozen affairs. I came along shortly after they decided to get married. My mother liked to remind me I was the reason the love affair broke down."

Michael stirred the pasta into the water. "That's rough and nothing a kid should hear."

"Like your mother was better?"

"Never said she was." Michael half-smiled. "But now I understand you better. You're a product of your environment."

"I guess. If that explains me, then this will probably ruin me in your eyes." He bowed his head. *Christ. Why is being honest was so hard?* "My father's side of the family is rich. Like seventy years of old money rich. Dad spoiled Mom and, in turn, me. If I even considered doing something, I did it. Even if it wasn't legal, I tried it. I've got a record, had a drug and alcohol problem and partied my way through two colleges. I tried to kill myself twice." He hated admitting that part, but Michael needed to know who he was getting involved with so he could jump ship if that was what he wanted to do.

"Oh my God." Michael grasped Tristan's hand. "Tristan."

"I needed the experience. I thought the world revolved around me. I still think that to a degree. I have a penthouse in New York, a butler named Dennis and used to have a crazy social calendar. Writing started as therapy when I quit drinking and doing cocaine. But I replaced one addiction for another. Writing became my passion." He finally looked up at Michael. He had no idea how he would react.

"Wow." Michael stirred the pasta. "How'd you get published?"

"Really? That's what you want to know? Not why I wanted to screw up my life or that you want to ditch me because I've got a past? You're not afraid of me?" He had no idea what to think.

"We've all got things we've done that we look back and think…gee, that wasn't smart." Michael shrugged. "I had a one-night stand in college with a girl just to see if I could. I didn't think a woman would want me."

"Sly dog."

"The only reason she wanted me was to make her boyfriend jealous."

"That's harsh." Tristan relaxed. Things weren't going to fall apart like with other boyfriends. Michael wasn't turned off. He could do this. "Speaking of harsh, you asked how I got published. I had a friend help me, but that was only after I'd sent out forty-eight queries and was rejected forty-eight times."

"Really?"

"Have you read my books?" Tristan asked. "You're a librarian."

"That doesn't mean I've read everything that comes through the library. I'd never get anything done." Michael turned the heat down, then stood beside the stove. "But no, I haven't read you."

"You're not missing much. It's not great literature that will be recorded in the annals of time," Tristan said. "What I write are homey stories of real people. At least that's what I'm told. The closest I've ever come to real people was when I was here as a teenager."

"I see."

"I pushed a lot of those experiences down, but when I started writing, they came to the surface." Tristan left the counter and eased up beside Michael. "I tried writing under a pen name. Tate Pullman. He couldn't write, but, as Tate, I learned. I wrote practice novellas. I took the remarks from the rejections and internalized them, then set out to improve. I learned my craft by writing almost twenty-five currently unpublished works. I doubt they'll ever see the light of day and I'm fine with it."

"I never knew that." Michael returned his attention to the pasta. "You're more than you give yourself credit for."

He wound his arms around Michael and rested his chin on his shoulder.

"I love learning the stories of how authors create their works. It's fascinating. My creativity only goes so far and I respect anyone who is willing to put themselves out there in the form of a book, song or artwork. I can alphabetize a book shelf. That's about it." Michael laughed. "Sad, huh?"

"It's not sad. I bet you're the best librarian around. You're dedicated." He kissed Michael's bare shoulder. "Writing isn't easy and it's not for everyone, despite the prevailing notion it should be. It's hard and takes dedication. You have to have a thick skin."

"True."

"I'm not for everyone, either. I know that sounds blustery, but I'm not. Until I was twenty-eight, I thought the only way anyone would love me was if I threw my money around," Tristan said. "I didn't come out until I was done with college. Don't get me wrong. I explored more than I should've."

"I didn't." Michael turned the burner off. "Do you have a colander?"

"Yes." He'd just seen it. He let go of Michael long enough to retrieve the item, then leaned on the counter beside Michael. Talking to him was so easy. No judgment and they got along so well. He could confess everything to him. A thought occurred to him. Yes, this was happening at warp speed, but could Michael be the one? The possibility was there.

"I've got margarine in the bag. Open that container of milk." Michael drained the pasta. "Hand me the cheese when you're done. I premeasured everything but the milk."

"Smart." Yeah, he was falling for Michael. He didn't even care if Michael wasn't falling in return.

"Put the cheese and margarine in the pot. I'll dole out everything else," Michael said. He poured the pasta then milk into the saucepan.

"You're a taskmaster." He laughed. "It's a foreign concept for me, but I like it. It's exciting." Christ. He felt like a married old man. Where had Michael been all his life? If he'd known he could've had this kind of happiness with Michael, he would've skipped out of New York years ago and come back to Sullavan. The addictions of his past had nothing on writing and Michael.

"Almost done. Once you stir it all together and everything melts, we can eat." Michael nudged Tristan. "Keep the cheese moving."

Tristan did as told. Slowly, the mix came together. "Did Molly teach you how to make this?"

"She did. She said I needed to know how to cook something." Michael tossed the empty packets and carton into the plastic bag. "Have you heard from Jamie?"

"Lately? Yes." *Why lie?* "He stopped by with information about the community center. He seemed to think it would be best for the LGBT center. Why?"

"I passed him on the road." Michael shied away from Tristan. "He likes you. That's why he's going out of his way to help."

"He doesn't seem to like you." Tristan stopped Michael and turned off the burner. "Why?"

"Let's eat." Michael turned his back on Tristan. "Where are the plates?"

"In the cupboard," Tristan said. "Nice diversion, by the way, but it won't work. What is it about Jamie that makes you tense?"

"Nothing."

"Right." He ducked around Michael, forcing Michael to look at him. "I spilled my guts. Now it's your turn."

"There's nothing to tell. He hates me." Michael folded his arms. "Plain and simple."

"Why?" He refused to let Michael off the hook just yet.

"You really want to know?" Michael shook his head. Before Tristan could answer, Michael did. "I turned him down."

"Are you serious?" He hadn't meant to blurt that. "He's got an attitude because he was turned down?"

"Don't act shocked. It wasn't my brightest move, but I don't regret it." Michael tugged plates from the cupboard. "How much do you want?"

"I'll get it. Thanks." Tristan took the plates from Michael. "I'm shocked because he's pushy. Whether you're not smart for what you did is debatable. I think it was a good move. You're not a viable pair because he'd steamroll you. You deserve to be cherished and he seems like he just wants a score."

"He does." Michael balled his hands. "You like him. Don't you?"

"I'm attracted to him, but his attitude sucks. It drives me crazy." Tristan embraced Michael. "I like simple people and my drama in my books — not my life. I like you. You're too cute for words and have the sexiest dick."

Michael shook his head, but didn't say anything.

"What?"

"You'll get sick of me. You'll move on," Michael whispered.

"Don't be so sure." Now that he had Michael in his arms, he wasn't about to let go without a fight. Giving his heart away wasn't his style, but he'd practically offered it right up to Michael. Yeah, he'd found his soul mate. Now to convince Michael they belonged together for more than a few weeks.

Chapter Eleven

Michael tried tamping down his doubts. Tristan would be like Jamie and lose interest. He'd claim Michael was truly too boring. His boyfriends always got tired of his love of books and preference for staying in rather than clubbing. Tristan sounded like he'd turned over a new leaf, but come on. Tristan had flourished — according to him — in the trendy club scene. He'd want the party life back and to be the center of attention. Sure, Sullavan was a great escape, but it was a matter of time before he went full circle.

He sat beside Tristan on the couch and ate in silence. He couldn't wrap his mind around what Tristan had said. *Oh well.*

Tristan finished his mac and cheese first, then put his bowl on the table. "That was so good." He leaned over and kissed Michael on the cheek. "You should cook more often."

"Nah. All we'd eat would be pasta." He scraped the last few bits from his bowl.

"So we'd have to run a little more to exercise off the carbs...it's not an awful way to be together." He patted Michael's leg. "You're staying tonight, correct?"

"I am unless you tell me to beat it." He sounded confident, but damn, his hands were shaking.

"Perfect." Tristan stood. He stretched and rolled his shoulders. "Let me make a phone call and then we'll tackle the library."

"Sure." He almost asked who, but didn't. Whoever Tristan had to call was none of his business.

"Be right back." Tristan left the room and strode out to the front porch.

Michael didn't bother to listen in. Whatever Tristan had to say wasn't for him to know. He carried the empty bowls to the kitchen, then filled the sink with soapy water. He dunked the bowls into the suds. What else did he need to wash? The pans and utensils needed to be cleaned. He gathered up the items and put them into the water, too.

While he washed the bowls and pans, his thoughts turned to Tristan. As much as he wasn't sure about where things were going, he still couldn't believe his good fortune. Tristan was a catch—not for his social standing or financial status, but as a man. Tristan wasn't freaked out by Michael's connection with Al and seemed to like him. They weren't just sex partners, but friends too. He could see them starting the 'something epic' Tristan kept mentioning.

"Hey." Tristan strolled into the room. "You're cleaning."

"Of course. I made the mess. I'll take care of it." He laughed. "I take it you don't?"

"I usually have my butler, Dennis, follow behind cleaning up after me." Tristan shrugged. "It was part and parcel of my life."

"I know." He washed the second bowl and placed it in the rack, then turned his attention to the pan. "Everything okay?"

"Yeah. I needed to touch base with home, er, New York again." Tristan dried the bowls. "And I had to call my agent and publisher. They want my book, like, now and I have some done, but not enough. Then I had to check in with my butler. He's kind of my friend, but more like my keeper. It's strange, but it works for us."

Michael nodded. He'd never had a butler and had no idea how the butler and Tristan were so close, but whatever.

Tristan dried the pan. "You're quiet. What's up?"

"Nothing. I'm happy." Contented and soothed by washing the dishes. He liked the mundane aspects of life and being with someone.

"Yeah?"

"It's been a long time." Not only since he could say he was happy, but since he was able to admit it out loud.

"It's been too long and I'm going to do my best to make it up to you."

"Why? You didn't cause my issues." He shook his head. Sometimes Tristan made no sense.

"No, I didn't, but if I had come back to see my uncle, we might have met sooner and could be an old couple by now." He kissed Michael on the cheek. "I'd have been happier."

"I think this is when we were supposed to find each other." He pulled his soapy hands from the water and caressed Tristan's bare chest. "Any earlier and we wouldn't have been ready for each other or what we've got."

"Yeah?" He wrapped his arms around Michael. "Think so?"

"I do."

"I like the way you think, then."

He kissed Tristan. Being with Tristan emboldened him. If he didn't say what he wanted, he'd never get it. "I like the way you suck and you liked the way I did, too."

"Saucy. Am I bringing out your inner kinky side?"

"Yeah." He wasn't ashamed. For the first time in forever, he didn't care and embraced his needs. "Not kinky, but I'm comfortable enough to say what I want."

"I'm honored." Tristan licked the seam of Michael's mouth. "So, what do you want?" His eyes flashed.

"Sex."

Tristan threaded his fingers into Michael's belt loops and held him close. "I love the way you think." Tristan feasted on his mouth and, when he opened to him, he sucked on Michael's tongue.

The word 'love' had come up again, along with Tristan's dick. He ignored his concerns about romance and followed Tristan's lead.

Tristan tugged him to the library. "I had a feeling you'd want to be in here." He nodded to the box of condoms and bottle of lube on the writing desk. "I preplanned."

"You hoped." Michael snorted. "Right?"

"Yes." He pulled Michael into his arms again and kissed him. "I can't get enough of you." He peppered Michael's cheeks and chin with kisses, then nipped Michael's neck.

Michael groaned. Fire licked his body from within. He couldn't wait to get the rest of the way naked. He fumbled with Tristan's pants until the bothersome clothing slid down to his ankles.

"What are you doing to me?" Tristan's breath warmed Michael's neck. "Huh? Scrambling my brain."

"You like it." He withdrew his own cock and held it against Tristan's. Tristan raked his nails over Michael's shoulders. Power radiated through Michael. He met Tristan's gaze. He liked the passion he saw reflected in the blue depths.

Tristan ground his erection against Michael's and gritted his teeth. "Fuck me." He tipped his head back. "Love cock on cock."

The feeling of smooth skin on skin was pretty fucking hot to Michael, too. He stroked harder, mashing both dicks together. "Need some lube."

"Table." Tristan snagged the bottle. "Here. Fuck…"

Michael drenched both erections in lube. The slippery gel added a new dimension to the act of jerking him and Tristan off. Michael rocked faster, sliding the underside of his cock against Tristan's. Christ, doing this—being so bold with Tristan—blew his mind. Despite not being inside Tristan, he felt closer to him than ever. The bond was stronger.

Tristan placed his hand over Michael's. "Got me on the edge." He stroked in the same tempo as Michael. Another groan ripped from him.

"Yeah?" Good to know he wasn't the only one about to combust.

"Uh-huh." Tristan closed his eyes and rested his head on Michael's shoulder. A shiver wracked his body. He scraped his teeth on Michael's skin.

"What do you want?" Michael asked. He gave in to the desire in his veins. "My dick in your ass? Or my tongue on your hole? Bet you want me all over your cock."

"Fucking hell yes. All of it. Now." Tristan bit Michael. "Want you."

So, Tristan likes dirty talk? Nice. Michael kept stroking. His nerve endings were on fire. "Nah. You want to be on your knees and sucking me until I come. No, you want my dick buried in your ass. That's it. To be stretched and used."

"Jesus." Tristan tensed and pushed wildly into Michael's hand. "Let me come."

Michael squeezed his fingers around both dicks. He pressed his thumb on top of his erection. The change in pressure knocked him over the edge. He panted.

"Let me come." Tristan raked his nails over Michael's chest. "Fuck."

"Do it. I want your sticky cum on me. Mark me." *Brand me. I belong to you.* Michael couldn't ignore his feelings. He already believed what he knew in his heart—even if he couldn't say the words out loud.

Tristan growled. Cum shot up between him and Michael. Most of it landed on their hands. Michael met Tristan's heavy-lidded gaze. Seeing Tristan climax kick-started Michael's orgasm. He jerked forward and his seed stretched across Tristan's belly.

"God, that's hot." Tristan released his grasp on Michael's fingers. "Love." He dropped to his knees. "Let me." He licked the jizz from Michael's hand. "So good."

Michael leaned against the couch. Two orgasms in one night were just about his limit. *If this is going to be the norm with Tristan, then sign me up*. He ruffled his dry fingers through Tristan's hair.

Tristan rubbed his cheek against Michael's thigh. "Stay tonight."

"Already planned on it." If he wasn't careful, he'd fall asleep standing up.

Tristan cuddled against Michael's leg. "I've been looking for you all of my life." He kissed Michael's thigh. "Someone who likes my nervousness, my love of books and over-usage of the word love...who makes me laugh and is good in bed."

Michael petted Tristan's hair. "All you had to do was come home to Sullavan, I guess."

"Yeah." He gazed up at Michael. "I wanted to sort things tonight, but I'd rather tangle up with you on the couch a while."

"Let's do that." He helped Tristan to his feet, then stripped the rest of the way out of his clothes. He could have sex bent over the sofa later. There wasn't a rush. Once Tristan stretched out on the cushions, Michael joined him.

"Wait. I want to be on top." Tristan scooted out from under Michael, then rested on him. He snuggled against Michael's shoulder.

Michael caressed Tristan's arm. The moment was so quaint and perfect. The single lamp illuminating the room bathed the space in warm yellow light. Michael could get used to this — the couple-ness of the moment. He closed his eyes. Weariness overwhelmed him.

"Let me power-nap. Afterwards, we can have all the sex we want," Tristan murmured. He kissed Michael's pecs. "You're all mine."

Michael wanted to answer, but didn't. His? He should have been up in arms, but the moment of panic faded. Yeah, he was Tristan's. They were good together and the fear didn't have to be palpable. He had Tristan right now…and sex to come. Not a bad gig for a librarian who hadn't expected to fall for a writer. Not bad at all.

* * * *

Tristan rolled his shoulders and crinkled his nose. Sleeping on Michael wasn't the best for his back, but it was perfect for his soul. He liked being so close to his lover. To hear Michael's breathing and feel his soft skin. He splayed his hand on Michael's ribcage. The first fingers of sunlight stretched across the carpet. He could wake up like this every day and be happy. He noticed something blinking.

Fuck me. Tristan crawled off Michael and stood. He stretched, then rubbed his face. Why did the phone have to blink and dick with his perfect morning? He swiped his fingers across the screen. According to the icons, he had at least one email, a voicemail and a text. He tapped the email first. From his Aunt Salina…of course.

Don't forget the party is in two weeks. You haven't RSVPed. I expect you to be there. With your standing, you're important. Jean misses you.

No signature. No love. Just bluntness from his aunt. His cousin didn't care about him. *Good God.* He couldn't remember the last time he'd talked to Jean. Probably the last time he'd called her Babsy in her presence and she'd told him to fuck himself.

Tristan deleted the email. If he happened to be in New York around the time of the party, he might pop in, but then again, he might not.

He switched his attention to the texts. No subject. *What the hell?* He didn't open the messages, but rather only read the previews.

You're not writing.

Who was this person? The stalker?

Why aren't you writing?

He couldn't hide his irritation. The fan must've found his phone number. He archived the messages and debated his next move. Calling the cops would be smart, but what would he tell them? He'd been pestered? Bothered? They wouldn't investigate irritating emails and texts. They'd tell him, like they'd said in New York, to get a new phone number.

He shook his head and dialed the numbers to retrieve the voicemail. He knew the number. Dennis.

"Hi, Tristan," Dennis said in the message. "I'm passing along information. I doubt you'll care, but your aunt can't say I didn't try. Number one, your cousin's engagement party is in two weeks and you should let them know if you're attending. Number two, your agent called the apartment. The outline is good and she'd like you to move forward. I'm not sure if she contacted you, but now you know. Number three, Cody stopped by. He claims he's moving in. I prevented him from doing so. Might I suggest you come home so you can sort out your affairs? Your vacation to deal with your uncle's things should be about over. Your friends think you've abandoned them. I hope you're getting everything accomplished and life can get back to normal soon."

Tristan stared at the phone. The message was the most Dennis had ever said. He sighed. Cody could look elsewhere for a free place to crash. Unless something drastic happened, he had little intention of attending the engagement party. Auntie Salina and Babsy weren't going to con a fancy gift out of him. The rest of the family would surely shower them with presents.

He erased the voicemail. He had to focus on his current situation. The agent wanted him to keep going with his manuscript. Good. He and Michael could create a schedule. He'd work and write while Michael was at the library. Afterwards, they'd fuck until they dropped. If he had a more constant situation, he'd have the book done in no time. Then he'd focus on advancing the relationship with Michael.

"Hey." Michael sat up. His hair stood on end and red infused his cheeks. He blinked. "I fell asleep."

"We both did." He abandoned his phone. "Good food and orgasms tend to make one tired."

"Yeah. I guess so." Michael's dick stood tall. He chuckled. "I've got a boner."

"That tends to happen." He wanted to wrap his lips around that cock and suck him until Michael cried out his name. "Why's a boner funny?"

"I haven't woken up this way since the last time we slept together." Michael stretched. "I was beginning to think my dick didn't work."

This time, Tristan chuckled. "Then I showed up and overused it." He strode over to the back of the couch and waggled his ass. "Speaking of using...I've got a place you can stick that morning wood."

"You do?" Michael left the sofa and picked up the lube and a condom as he rounded the piece of furniture. He tore open the foil wrapper, then sheathed himself in the rubber.

The condom snapped and Tristan groaned. He grabbed the back of the couch and widened his stance. "Yes. Do it. I want you in me." His balls ached. He mashed his cock into the back of the sofa and flexed his asshole. He tensed when he heard the snick of the lube cap. The chill on his ass and down over his hole soothed him.

Michael dug his fingers into Tristan's hip. "Ready?" The blunt head of his dick rubbed against Tristan's asshole.

"Never more ready." He backed up, trying to impale himself on Michael's erection. Tristan bowed his head and gripped the couch. Being together seemed destined and he didn't want the pairing to end.

"You are. Breathe for me." Michael breached the tight ring of muscle and pushed into Tristan.

He exhaled. The pain and stretching excited him. He laughed, to hide his momentary discomfort. How could he breathe or relax with a hot guy behind him? Easy. He couldn't.

Michael gripped Tristan's hips tight. Tristan didn't mind. He liked how Michael seemed to blossom when given the chance to take control. Michael came alive and excelled.

Tristan moaned. He wanted a partner — an equal. He wanted Michael for more than a few weekends or a couple of months. He clunked into Michael. "Please? Come. I need to..." His voice broke. "Uh..." He couldn't think or speak. Michael consumed him in every sexy, fantastic way.

"Yes." Michael kissed Tristan's shoulder. His warm breath and wet mouth excited Tristan. "Do it."

Tristan braced himself on his left hand and used his right to stroke his dick. He pulled and tugged, getting close to orgasm. He wouldn't last long.

"Fuck," Michael said. His thrusts turned feral and rough. "Tristan."

Tristan met each push until he and Michael were in perfect rhythm. The sound of skin on skin echoed in the air. Perspiration tingled on Tristan's upper lip and a droplet slid down into the corner of his mouth. The salt exploded on his tongue. He writhed. Christ, he swore he felt Michael in his soul.

"Shit." Between the pressure from the back of the couch on his cock, his hand on himself and Michael in his ass, Tristan's resistance shattered. Cum shot down the back of the sofa.

"Fuck me." Michael rammed hard into him. His dick throbbed and he added a few more thrusts before he stilled. He wrapped both arms around Tristan, holding him close. "You scrambled my brain."

"Mine too." Tristan collapsed on the couch and laughed. They'd made a mess. Somehow, he didn't care. He wanted memories made in each room of the house. He twisted enough to look at Michael. "I'll never get enough."

"I doubt I will, either." Michael laughed with him, then kissed Tristan's neck. "We're so sloppy. I'll help you clean it up."

"After we shower." He clasped Michael's hand. "I don't want this to end."

"Me either." Michael pulled out of Tristan and ditched the condom. He swatted Tristan's ass. "We'd better get going, though, or you'll have a stain."

Tristan shrugged. He managed to stand and wandered upstairs to the bathroom. He turned on the water and nudged Michael into the shower first. Instead of pushing his way forward and taking charge, Tristan lingered in the back of the stall and watched Michael. The man didn't understand just how sexy he was, or how pretty. All sinewy muscle and taut pale skin, Michael could've been a model. He had a boy-next-door look that would have everyone drooling to be with him.

"Are you going to stand there or what?" Michael blushed from his hairline to his chest. "What?"

"I'm watching you." Tristan took the soapy washcloth from Michael. "You're captivating."

Michael didn't say anything. His blush deepened.

Tristan kissed Michael under the hot spray, then resumed cleaning himself off. He and Michael reminded him of an old married couple. Comfortable with each other, but still learning.

"What are you going to do today?" Michael stepped out of the shower. "Writing? Sorting?"

Tristan rinsed, then turned the water off and opened the curtain. "I thought I'd deal with the clothes in my uncle's closet and dresser first, then figure out what to do with what I don't want." He dried off. "Got any ideas where I can donate used clothes?"

"There's a second-hand store in town and the consignment one. You'd be better off going to the second-hand one because I don't see you wanting to price a bunch of clothes." Michael shrugged. "My stomach rumbled while we were in the shower, which reminded me...we should eat, too."

"We don't have anything else food-wise." Tristan wrapped the thick bath towel around his hips. "We should run to the store."

"Could order in." Michael dried himself. His hair stood on end again. "The diner delivers. Or I can run into town."

"Need a break from me already?" Tristan dropped his towel, then snagged Michael in his arms.

"No." Michael frowned. "I thought it might be faster since I know my way around town."

"I'd rather order in. Then we can get stuff done and spend time together." Tristan tweaked Michael's nipple. "Or have sex on the couch again…"

Michael shrugged. "Okay by me on all accounts. I've got the menus on my phone. Let me get it." He stepped into his boxer briefs, then strode past Tristan.

He grasped Michael's hand, stopping him. "If you weren't so irresistible, I'd be able to let you go."

"You just like sex." Michael's eyes sparkled.

"With you."

"Horny toad."

"Duh," Tristan said. "But you made me this way." He kissed Michael, then let him go.

Michael glanced back at him and laughed, then left the room.

Tristan shook his head. Michael was such a good distraction. So sexy and handsome. But he needed to get some writing done. He turned his phone over and the screen lit up with an incoming call. Jamie. He tapped the connect button. "Hello? Jamie."

"Hey, you. What's your Sunday look like?" Jamie asked.

"I'm writing." Not a total lie. He'd be writing eventually.

"Oh. Want company?"

"I already have it. Michael's here." He didn't want to be on the phone with Jamie. Yes, the man was his lawyer, but he still grated on Tristan's nerves.

"Oh. When is he leaving?"

"I don't know." The more Jamie spoke, the more he irritated Tristan.

"How are you writing if he's there?" Jamie asked.

"Because I'm on a break."

"Ah. Well, I need to see you."

"Why?" He hoped Michael wasn't on his way back upstairs yet. He didn't want Michael to think he'd replaced him or was in the process of doing so. He'd seen the fragility in Michael's eyes and remembered what his uncle had written about Michael. No wonder the man was wounded and didn't trust. Sure, Michael had a few issues, but so what? Who didn't have a few quirks? Besides, Tristan still liked him. Still wanted him.

"I need to see you about the foundation," Jamie said.

"The shelter situation, right. You looked into the community center?"

"I did."

"And?" Tristan massaged his temples. "What did you find out?" Did he sound as irked as he was? He hoped so.

"It'll be tight, but with your writing income and your notoriety, we should be fine. I've talked to the corporation who owns the building and they'd like to work with you—as long as you're willing to work with them. We should be great."

We? He suppressed a groan. "How about you see what can be done with the hundred grand first? Yes? I'd rather work with guaranteed money, not projected.

I can't be sure the next book will hit." And he wasn't ready to dip into his trust fund cash. Actually, he would for the shelter, but he didn't want Jamie to know that yet.

"Uh-huh."

He tipped his head. *Is that footsteps? Fuck it.* "I have to go."

"To see Michael?"

"Yeah." He disconnected the call and tossed the phone onto the dresser. He wasn't in the mood to argue with Jamie or defend his blossoming relationship with Michael.

Michael strode into the room and stopped. "We can get— What's wrong?"

"Nothing. I had to deal with a telemarketer." He shouldn't lie, but he didn't want to worry Michael. The poor guy was already touchy about Jamie. Knowing they were talking on the phone would cause problems he didn't want to deal with.

"Oh, okay." Michael shrugged. "Want farmhouse, pasta or Chinese?"

All three options sounded good. "Farmhouse." He'd have to run more to work off the calories, but it'd be worth it if he could be with Michael. Besides, he could use the running time to work through his story.

Michael offered up his phone. "Here's the menu for the diner. They do a special farmhouse feature on Sundays. Let me know what you want and I'll put in the order."

He perused the listing and stole glances at Michael. He'd lost his mind, but he wanted this moment and more like them to continue. "Move in with me." His comment was bold and off-the-cuff, but felt right.

Michael froze. "What?"

"Move in here with me."

"Tristan." Michael tugged his shorts on. "You've only been in Sullavan for a little while and what you and I are doing is new. You're jumping the gun."

"No." Michael didn't understand. Tristan had moved too fast, but he went with his gut feeling and being together felt right. How could Michael not see that? He needed Michael there.

"I have my doubts. Not about us, but about living together already. I'm not moving in." Michael folded his arms. "Here's my suggestion. You spend the time I'm at work writing. When I'm done, I'll come over. If you're not writing, we'll hang out. If you're busy, then fine. I can't go so fast. We need to see where this goes at a slower pace."

Tristan groaned. He hated not getting his way.

Michael splayed his hand on Tristan's chest. "If I move in with you, it'll prove to me that this is just a whim for you. I don't want to be someone to occupy your time."

"You're not." Michael wounded him. Occupy his time? How didn't Michael see this was fated? Tristan groaned. "I don't say what I don't mean."

"But I'm not ready."

Tristan sighed. Michael had a point—quite a few, if he had to be honest. His idea was too quick and moving in wouldn't work—not yet. Part of him wanted Michael there for the stability he craved, but another part didn't want to be lonely. He wanted to force the relationship, but that wasn't healthy.

"What do you want?" Michael asked.

"You." At least he was being honest.

"Besides me." Michael tweaked Tristan's nipple.

"There's plenty of nutritional value in you," Tristan said. "And emotional value."

Michael chuckled. "What did you want to eat for lunch?"

"Oh." He met Michael's grin with one of his own. "Wedge salad, ham steak and potatoes. But you're going with me to run off the calories."

"I can work with both and will do." Michael dialed the phone and wriggled his eyebrows. "You can eat me later." He left the room again.

Tristan pinched the bridge of his nose. His impulsiveness would be the death of him and drive Michael away. He could rein it in. If chilling out meant proving to Michael they could work, then he'd do it. He didn't have roots in Sullavan, but wanted to put them down with Michael. He needed stability and love—with Michael. Damn it, he deserved both and he'd get them. He wasn't about to quit on what his heart desired.

Chapter Twelve

Tristan rolled his shoulders. He glanced over at Michael and grinned. Having Michael at the house for the last week, leaning on him and just being together had done wonders — not only for sorting through the contents of the house, but also for his writing. He spent most mornings writing while Michael worked. Once Michael came over, they sorted through items for two hours, then existed together for the remainder of the night.

"Have you heard anything about the house?" Michael fiddled with his glasses and rubbed the bridge of his nose. "Did Rose get back to you?"

Tristan paused. *Shit.* He should know who Rose was… "Um…"

"Did you call her?" Michael abandoned his laptop and crossed the living room. "The real estate agent?" He settled on Tristan's lap. "The person who will help us get the house so you can start the foundation?"

Now he remembered. *Duh.* "I did call her. She told me how much the Gladden estate was and what the asking price was for the house on Second Street. The Second Street building will be more in the price range. We're supposed to go through both on Sunday. As for the former community center, there's no way. I can't swing the rent for it for a week just to use it…let alone taking over the building."

Michael rubbed his crotch on Tristan's and draped his arms around Tristan's shoulders. "Who said we needed the community center? Start small and build it up. Get the thing solid, then worry about adding on."

"Jamie." As soon as he said the name, he wished he'd kept his mouth shut. "Sorry."

Michael froze. He sagged on Tristan's lap. "I see."

"Don't get upset about him. He suggested it when we read through the will. He had a lot of ideas and I wrote them down. I liked yours better and agree with you." He palmed Michael's ass. "Hey. I didn't ask Jamie to move in with me. I asked you because I like *you*. I want you here. Not him."

"I know."

"I don't think you do." He slid his hands into Michael's back pockets. "You've got it in your head I'm going to dump you. I'm going to decide I don't want to be here and I'll pull up roots to go back to New York. I've thought about it, but I can't see being there when you're not. I want to be where you are." He pulled Michael forward, forcing Michael to look him in the eye. "I get it. You've been shafted in the past and you're worried. I would be if I were you. Hell, I am and I'm not you. I have a reputation for screwing people over, but when I look in your eyes I want to be better than that."

"I know," Michael murmured.

"I need you to trust me." He cupped Michael's jaw. "It's hard and scary. You have no reason to believe I'm a man of my word."

"But you are?"

"I am."

Michael closed his eyes. "I don't trust. It's hard."

Tristan nodded. "I know, baby. I wouldn't trust me, either."

"You don't understand. After your uncle, I tried to date again. Some of the guys were okay. A few were horrible for me. Then I met Ian. I thought he was the one. I loved him. We were together for six years. For me, that was an eternity. I settled into a good life with him." Michael pulled away from Tristan. "Then things changed."

"What?" He led Michael to the sofa. "Sit with me."

Michael collapsed on the couch. "Christ, I hate angst, but that's all I seem to be lately." He sighed. "Ian walked out. One day he was there and the next he was gone. I didn't understand why. I called him, went to his work…nothing. Then he showed up at the library. He hadn't wanted our life together. He wanted to be with someone else. He'd been doing that guy during the last year of our relationship, but he couldn't tell me because he wanted to be sure the thing with his new love was good before he moved out."

Michael's words were jumbled together, but Tristan caught everything. "He used you for a place to stay."

"Yeah." Michael scrubbed both hands over his face. "I don't trust myself to find the right guy. I know how I feel about you, but I'm worried I'll ignore my gut and stay where I'm not wanted."

"I want you."

"I'm not sure you won't change your mind," Michael said.

"I want you, though." He wasn't sure what to say to fix this. "I'm following my heart and using my head. It's usually one or the other. I've never felt so comfortable with my decision, either. I'm writing more. We've got the house fifty percent in order and we're looking good to finish the rest of it in the next week."

Michael disengaged from him. "But you've forgotten the center."

"No. I'd like a base camp here at the house and for it to be set up before I work on the center."

Michael bowed his head. "I'm not sure."

"I know. I wouldn't trust me if I were you, but I'm begging. I love you." He'd taken a huge step and prided himself on being honest. His stomach hadn't lurched when he'd said the words and he wasn't instantly regretting it.

"Right. You're saying love like you love blow jobs or peanut butter. It's not special."

"You're wounding me, but you might be right – kind of. This instance is different." He wasn't getting through to Michael. Why not? Sweet and pouting had always worked for him before.

"Let's keep riding the wave. I'll help you with the center, but then we reassess." Michael left the couch. "I should go."

"You have no faith in me." Tristan wanted to chase Michael, but his legs refused to cooperate.

"I'm being cautious."

He wished Michael wasn't playing it so safe. He wished Michael would open up and let him in. But he couldn't force Michael. Not now or ever. "Okay."

"Okay?"

Michael shrugged. "Yeah, okay."

Maybe he had made an inroad… "Babe?"

"We'll figure something out," Michael said.

"Together."

Michael nodded.

Tristan left the couch and breathed a sigh of relief. He could keep the relationship working. He'd get the story done, the house in order and the foundation for the center created. Once he had all that in the works or finished, he'd work on Michael. He had a positive feeling about him and Michael and refused to let that goodness go to waste.

* * * *

The next afternoon, Michael stood behind the desk at the library. He'd shelved everything that had been turned in and sent the inter-library loans out. For the first time that day, the library was quiet.

The bell over the door dinged and a man strolled into the building. He smiled at Michael.

"May I help you?" Michael folded his hands. "Welcome. I hope you're having a good day. It's sunny out, isn't it?" He'd cocked up his delivery, but oh well. The last time a hot man had come into the library, Michael had ended up in bed with him.

The man nodded. "It's quite nice out, thank you. I do need some help. Where are your Tristan Paulson books?"

"Are you a fan or a first-time reader?" He wasn't sure why he'd asked that since he had no idea what order the books went in. He hadn't read any of Tristan's work.

"I'm a fan. I'm new to Sullavan and wanted to curl up with something familiar. My stuff hasn't arrived yet, but I have." He gave Michael a sly smile. "Tristan and I are tight."

"Oh." He wasn't sure what that meant—they were tight? "The books are right over here." He directed the man over to the shelf featuring Tristan's work. "Are you looking for a specific title?"

The guy grinned and nodded to the corner. "There is a specific title. It's called *Keep Your Hands the Hell off My Boyfriend*. Heard of it?"

Michael almost blurted that the title wasn't one of Tristan's books, but kept his thoughts to himself. "I see."

"I hope you do." He glared at Michael. "I've been patient while he goofed off here in Sullavan. I have no desire to move here. It's a dump, but he's here, so I am. Now stay the fuck away from him. I've given him space, but I didn't know he'd hooked up with you. So much for trust."

Michael stood his ground, but said nothing. He didn't understand what was happening, although he wasn't surprised. He knew Tristan had other lovers and guessed there were a few broken hearts left in his wake, but did Tristan have a guy in New York? Still?

"Are we clear?" the man snarled.

"We are."

"Good." He soft-punched Michael in the arm. "I trust he won't see you again."

"Right."

The man winked and brushed past Michael. Within minutes, he'd left the library.

Michael stayed in the midst of the books and waited for the door to shut before he peeked around the corner.

He patted his pocket, then retrieved his phone. Maybe he wasn't supposed to interact with Tristan, but a text wouldn't hurt.

Got a visitor @the lib. Someone you know

He got an instant reply. *Oh? Who?*

Didn't say, but claimed to be your BF from NY

Truth be told, he hadn't asked the man's name.

The next reply popped right up. *Don't have one.*

Michael gritted his teeth. If Tristan was playing coy, it wasn't helping. *Well, he was here*

U sure?

Positive. Tall, blond, handsome. Could be a celebrity.

Doesn't sound familiar, Tristan wrote back.

Think it could be the stalker? He said you were tight. Michael held his breath. Talking about the fan was playing with fire.

That guy never showed up before in person. Let me do some checking.

Michael pinched the bridge of his nose. Something about the new guy didn't feel right. *Fuck it.* He'd wear his big boy britches and talk to Tristan in person. He needed to know the score. He typed one more text.

Okay. Guess it was a misunderstanding.

He tucked the phone into his pocket. He was an adult and had to act like one. He'd worry about Tristan later. The guy could be a sham or could be the real thing. Who knew? Right now, he didn't know which way was up.

"Are you okay?" Dicey wrapped her arm around Michael. "I saw the new man."

"I'm fine."

"Don't lie." She rubbed his back. "What happened?"

"Honestly, I'm not sure. Could be something. Could be nothing." He shrugged. "Could be…anything."

"With Tristan?" she asked.

"I don't know." He seemed to be saying that too often.

"I hope not. I had my misgivings about him, but you've been the happiest I've ever seen in the last two weeks. The smile is back and genuine. The spring is in your step. I haven't worried about you." Dicey walked him over to the counter. "That's big for me."

"I know and I appreciate the concern, but I'll be okay." He hugged her. "Things will work out." Once he spoke to Tristan, he'd be happier, but he understood part of what was going on. He'd jumped into a relationship with Tristan too fast. He'd gone against his better judgment and followed his heart. Big mistake. He didn't have the looks or swagger to compete with the new guy.

At ten minutes to eight, his phone buzzed. He'd almost forgotten he'd left the device in his back pocket. Michael checked the text from Tristan.

Meet me at the old Victorian on 3rd Street. Got the realtor there for a tour.

He debated ignoring the text, but gave in. *Will do.*

Another text popped up — also from Tristan. *Love you.*

He paused. Did Tristan love him? He tucked the phone away. Giving in to his feelings right now wouldn't do him any good. Besides, if he didn't answer that text, he couldn't get into trouble later.

He clicked the lock on the main library door, then went through the closing-down-time checklist. All doors locked, computers off, lights off…patrons out. *Good.* He met Dicey at the main entry. "Ready?"

"Let's go." She strolled out in front of him and waited for him to set the alarm then lock up. "Nice night."

"It is." He breathed in the chilly air. "See you tomorrow?"

"No." She clasped his forearm. "It's your required weekend off. I'll see you on Monday. Don't come in unless there's an emergency and even then, we can handle it. You need a break."

He'd forgotten about the forced vacation days. He'd worked too many regular shifts in a row… *Drat.* Well, he'd have a long weekend doing his own thing alone. No way Tristan would want to be with him after the new guy made a move.

Dicey waved, then drove off.

Michael unlocked his bike. He put his helmet on and switched on the headlight. The little safety features didn't make him feel all that secure, but whatever. He pedaled over to the specified house. Three cars waited in the driveway and Rose, the realtor, stood on the porch.

"Hello, Michael." She waved to him. "I'm glad you're here. Maybe you can talk sense into these two."

He doubted it. If Jamie was one of the men there, then he'd have little say. He steeled himself and parked the bike. "I'll do my best." He strolled into the house. The rich wood and old paint smell wrapped around him. He'd always wanted a home like this, but the place hadn't been in his price range. When he stepped into the parlor, the guy from the library stood with Tristan. Michael should've guessed…

"Oh, hey." The guy nudged Tristan, who had his back to Michael. "Why'd you call him over?"

Tristan stared at the guy for a moment, then turned. His face lit up, then dimmed. "Michael." His eyes widened. "I forgot you were coming over. That my boyfriend was coming over."

"What do you think of the house?" Michael asked. He forced himself to stay focused. "There are plenty of bedrooms and lots of space for common areas. It's in your budget — for you and the boyfriend."

"Right. Wait — no." Tristan held hands with the guy — or rather the guy held onto Tristan. "Shit."

"But that's just my take." Michael shied away from the pair. He'd had enough.

"Have you met Cody?" Tristan let go of Cody. "He decided to visit me." He hurried over to Michael. "This looks bad. Just…trust me. I can explain." The pleading in his voice resonated in Michael's brain.

"I met your *friend*." Cody? Of course, the handsome man would have a trendy name. Michael wasn't sure what to think — be mad? Uh, yeah, he was pissed. Tristan was holding on to someone else. Be jealous? A little. Cody was better-looking than he'd be on his best day.

"Oh, honey, we didn't meet. You've got me confused with someone else. I've got that kind of face," Cody said. "I'd remember a sweet thing like you." He winked. "But it's a pleasure to meet you now. Michael, is it? Hon, you're wearing a bike helmet."

"Right." He'd forgotten all about his helmet. *Fuck.* Every cell in his body screamed to have Tristan explain himself, but Michael kept quiet. He'd ignore the Cody in the room. "Did Jamie come by?"

"No." Tristan snapped to attention. "He had other business."

"You probably should get his opinion." Michael sighed. He'd had enough. "Well, I'm heading out. I still have to bike home and it's getting dark."

Tristan fidgeted in Cody's grasp.

"It was good to meet you," Cody said. "When Tristan and I decide on the house, we'll have you over for the shower. We'll need lots of stuff to fill this huge place."

Michael's mind swam. Fill the place? They were a couple and he'd been a fool. He turned on his heel and left without looking back. *Just pedal home.* He rode until his legs ached and his chest damn near exploded. Tristan owed him an explanation, but not right now. He wasn't in the mood for more drama.

* * * *

"What the hell?" Tristan swatted Cody's had away. "What was that about?"

Cody shrugged. "He's not needed."

"*He* is my *boyfriend*." Anger welled within Tristan. How had he managed to stay quiet when Cody practically shoved Michael out of the door and why hadn't he chased after Michael?

"*Was.*"

"Jesus. Yeah. It's probably past tense now." He glared at Cody. "What'd you say to him?"

"Me? I just met him a moment ago." Cody held up both hands. "You heard everything. I don't see the big deal."

"You're lying," Tristan snarled, angry at Cody, but also at himself. "I know you. There's always an angle. You saw him. I know. He texted, so either you tell me the truth now, or I do something I'll regret."

"Oh Christ, you drama king. You're with me." Cody shook his head. "You never want to admit the obvious."

"I'm not with you." His throat hurt from growling and arguing. He held on to his composure, but not by much. Rose had to think he'd lost his damn mind. He narrowed his eyes. "Cody, you were at the library. What did you do?"

"I don't even know where it is."

Rose ventured into the house. "Gentlemen, I'd like to lock up."

"Wait." Tristan needed a moment. "Are we zoned for a non-profit in this area?"

"As long as the center stays non-profit, yes." Rose nodded. "You turn it into a for-profit and you'll have problems."

"What's the asking price?" Tristan massaged his temples. "What…eighty thou?"

"Yes, but they'll come down. There's work needed on the back porch and general upkeep that hasn't been done. We can get them down to sixty, I think." She fiddled with her cell phone. "I can ask."

"Fine." Tristan nodded. "Put in an offer for sixty-one and see what they say."

"Our dream home," Cody shouted. He clapped his hands. "I'm so excited."

He ignored Cody. "I'll sign whatever. I want this moving forward."

"I'll make the calls." Rose pointed to the front porch. "But why don't we lock up and you can sleep on it. I'm sure they will."

"Sure." Tristan turned to Cody. "I'm not buying this house as a place for us. Why? There is no us. Why else? Because the money isn't for me or my needs. It's from my uncle and it's earmarked for a shelter for the LGBT youth of Sullavan."

"He's dead and this doesn't look like a Mecca for LGBT youth." Cody rolled his eyes. "Whatever. You always want to be the savior."

"Someone has to be." He hated Cody. How in the world had he ever carried on a relationship with such a narcissistic asshole?

"You sound like Dennis," Cody snapped. "Is the book done?"

Where did that question come from? "Not yet, but I'm close."

"He'll be happy then."

Tristan left the house and stood by his car. The moonlight stretched across the lawn and illuminated the vehicles. "What are you talking about? You switched on a dime again. Who is going to be happy?"

"Dennis." Cody toyed with his keys. "Don't you know?"

"Obviously I don't." Tristan leaned against the fender. "Is this so I'll come back to New York? Fake interest or something?"

"Uh, yeah." Cody laughed without humor. "You don't know, do you?"

"Know what?" Now he was confused. "Make sense please?"

"Dennis hasn't told you?"

"What?" One more question and he'd lose his temper.

"You'll have to ask him, then. Holy shit." Cody threaded his fingers together on top of his head. "Wow."

"What? Say it before I blow my cork and I'm really close." He balled his hands. "Cody."

"He's in love with you. You're supposed to go back to New York so he can tell you how he feels," Cody said. "How did you miss that?"

"He's my butler." *He's in love with me? How?*

"Right. Because no one ever does the help. Really? You're not this naïve." Cody shook his head.

"He's like a father to me." And not at all on his dating radar. He wasn't even in the ballpark for possible hook-ups.

"Well, he wants to be your daddy in other ways. I don't know how you couldn't tell. He's stuck around a lot longer than you deserve and put up with a lot of shit from you." Cody sagged against his car. "I'm shocked."

"Cody." He wasn't sure what else to say. He glanced over at Rose, who paced the length of the porch and remained on the phone.

"Okay. Let me spell it out," Cody said. "Why do you think he told you I was moving in? So you'd come home. Why'd he leave you a long-ass voicemail? So you'd come home. You don't belong here. You and he had a great thing in New York."

"Cody." He sounded like a broken record.

"I got rid of your boyfriend because Dennis asked me to. Pissed me off, too. I've been Dennis' freaking piece of ass for the last two years." Cody's voice cracked. "Does he love me? No. Why? Because he loves your goddamn ass. I love Dennis, but he doesn't love me." Tears streamed down Cody's face. "Now you know."

"I'm sorry." He hadn't suspected Cody and Dennis of anything, but he could see them together. Hell, they made sense together. Dennis was soft-spoken but firm, and Cody liked someone who could take control.

"Yeah, don't be sorry. If you don't love him, then you don't." Cody wiped his face and shrugged. "I brought this on myself. I knew how he was. It's been you for a long time, but I thought I could change his mind."

"I had no idea." Maybe he'd seen them as a twosome at the apartment. There were the odd conversations at night. The creaking in Dennis' bedroom and hours where Dennis wasn't available, but he'd chalked it all up to Dennis wanting alone time.

"You're prettier than me."

"Cody." There was the petulance he knew so well. "Who cares who looks better?" Besides, he'd always thought Cody was the better-looking one. Cody wore his clothes effortlessly and grabbed attention at whatever club they attended.

"You're stronger. You work out and run. I just diet. It sucks." Cody stuck out his bottom lip. "I can't compete."

"You're very handsome." He shouldn't have to compete with Cody. They deserved to be taken on their own merit. Cody was smart and savvy with money. Tristan didn't know how to balance a checkbook.

Cody sobered and hooked his fingers in his belt loops. "Look, you need to get your shit in order."

"I know." He had to figure out how to get things with Michael back on track, if only so they could be friends. He wanted to stay lovers, but that was asking a lot.

Cody tipped his head to the side and stared at Tristan. "Where are you happy? Really, truly happy?"

"Here." Tristan stuffed his hands into his pockets. "I'm centered." He hadn't thought about where he belonged, but the moment he said the word, he knew. When he drove into Sullavan, he remembered all the good times and the slower pace. He had the chance to do what he wanted with his life and make good on his promises to his uncle. He'd been able to turn his life around. He hadn't touched booze or pills since he'd arrived. Hadn't thought about either addiction. Was he cured? Not by a long shot, but he had new fixations to divert his attention and he liked the reinvented Tristan.

"Because it's new?" Cody asked.

He had to be honest and spill his guts. The words tumbled out fast, but they were the ones in his heart. "Because it feels like home. For the first time in my life, I feel like I belong. I never fit in at the house. Certainly not at the apartment. Mother wanted a token gay child, but I write, not act or whatever, so she doesn't care. My aunt only wants me around so I can be the token gay person at her parties. She doesn't even like me. I'm too sarcastic and mean. Yeah, maybe I am sarcastic and mean, but I've had to be in order to survive. Here, I don't have to do those things. I can be me. I can write and breathe and exist. I want to be here. I want to keep what I started going. I want Michael." He hadn't realized he'd held all of that in, but letting go freed him. Things weren't perfect, but he'd been real with someone — mostly with himself.

"He is cute."

"He's fantastic." A smile curled on his lips as he thought about Michael. Michael's scent, the softness of his skin, the way his eyes widened when they made love...how Michael listened to him when he complained, but didn't let him wallow in self-pity. Michael was special.

"I hated splitting you up." Cody kicked at a rock on the driveway. "Like, really hated it."

"Well, since he's seen us together...I'm guessing his trust in me is shot. It should be. I told him I wouldn't fuck him over, but with your help, I did." He'd promised his love was true and his heart belonged to Michael. The charade with Cody had been just that, a sham, but the damage was done. Only a miracle would get him and Michael back together.

"It can be fixed."

"No." He knew better. Besides, Cody sounded like a greeting card.

"You're giving up? Like that?" Cody frowned. "I know you. When you really want something, you don't quit and you *really* want Michael."

"No. He's got trust issues and I played into it. I screwed up." There weren't enough sorries to make up for what he'd done and been caught in the middle of. There'd never be enough.

"If you really like each other, then you'll find a way."

Again with the greeting card lines... "Since when did you get so philosophical and wise? Have you swallowed the encouragement cards from the store? Or is this another act?" He hated to doubt Cody, but he knew the man's act. He'd been the butt of Cody's jokes and worse. "Huh?"

"I've always been this way, but, like you, I've had to hide my true self. If I keep up the dick persona, no one can hurt me. I hurt them first, but the real Cody suffers." Cody sighed. "I'm fucked up."

So many more things made sense. He'd seen flashes of the real Cody plenty of times. When Cody worked at the animal shelter, when he'd donated time to the food pantry and helped with the soup kitchen. But then the asshole side of him came to the surface. Cody could rip into people without a second glance. He'd work a crowd at the clubs and get men to buy him just about everything. Still, Tristan liked the toned-down side of Cody. "No, you're not fucked up. I like the real you."

"You *like* Michael."

"Correct, but I also like you. The real Cody is better than the fake one."

Cody wriggled his eyebrows. "We wouldn't have a chance at a second go-round, would we?"

And the dick side had come back. Tristan groaned. "No, but we can be friends."

"Okay. I can handle friends." Cody laughed. "Friends is good."

"What about Dennis?"

"That's your problem to work out. He quit on me. I can't go back." Cody bowed his head. "Speaking of going back, when you see Michael again—and you will—tell him I'm sorry. I would do it myself, but I think he'd deck me."

"He might." And he might take a swing at Tristan, too. "I'll see what I can make happen, but I still think you should say the words in person."

"You work it out with him and I will." Cody offered his hand. "Friends?"

"Yeah, friends." He shook hands with Cody, then hugged him. "As for New York, I should go back. I owe my aunt a visit and my cousin has a party, like, tomorrow. I want things settled and I want my life back in my control. Where are you staying tonight?"

"The B&B. I saw it was highly rated and I wanted a place to go if things went to hell. I'm glad they did." Cody waved. "I'll see you."

"Yeah. See you." Tristan unlocked his car, then glanced over at Rose. "Everything okay?"

She nodded and strode over to him. "We'll see what they say in the morning, but I did get the offer in. We won't fill any paperwork out until Monday because their realtor is out of town until then, but they sounded receptive, so keep positive thoughts." She waved the sheath of papers at his car. "You're leaving? You've got me parked in."

"I am. Thank you. I'll look forward to your call." He winked at her, then climbed behind the wheel of his car. Cody drove off first, then Tristan backed down the drive. He had too many thoughts in his head. The house, the argument, Cody...Michael.

His brain ached as he motored down the street. How had he missed the signs from Dennis? The man was his butler, his friend and nearly old enough to be his father. Sure, he liked Dennis and trusted him more than almost everyone, but he wasn't in love with him.

Tristan gripped the steering wheel. The more he thought about Dennis, the more he realized he hadn't missed anything—he'd chosen to ignore. He'd brushed off the shoulder massages as butler stuff. When Dennis shooed away Tristan's former lovers, Tristan had considered it the act of helping a friend. The special dinners, offers to go along to signings and family events... Dennis wanted to be involved and more.

Tristan pulled the car into one of the parking spots lining the main thoroughfare through town and stopped the vehicle. He had to deal with the fires in New York. Cody was right — *damn him.* Tristan needed grounding, but he also needed to sort out his life. He'd walked away from a lot. Did he want to stay away from the action and glamor of New York? Could he handle being with one person in the middle of Ohio and without the noise? What about being noble and running the shelter? His uncle had expected a lot out of him. He wasn't sure he could shoulder the pressure.

Then there was the stalker.

He didn't know what to do. For all his bombast about being done with New York, he missed it. The lights, the food, the friends, the anonymity...

He stared at the blinking light over the intersection. The choice wasn't clear. Stay or go? Follow through or hide? *Fucking hell...* He raked his fingers through his hair. One thing was certain — he needed to see Michael. If nothing else, Michael deserved an explanation and an apology.

Chapter Thirteen

Michael closed the garage door and flicked on the additional security lights. His head swam. He'd been a fool to get involved with Tristan. All the warning bells had gone off in his head. Tristan still had someone in New York. Someone who wasn't him.

He wandered through the house and stopped in the living room. He tossed his bag onto the sofa. His legs ached from the ride and his sinuses were raw from the night air. He collapsed on the couch and sighed.

Self-loathing took over. He should've fought more for Tristan. At the very least, he should've stood up for himself. No, he'd been weak and left. He'd kept his thoughts to himself. *Get away before shit happens.* Now, he was neck-deep in shit. Retreating hadn't helped. He felt worse...like a piece of him was missing. It sucked. He liked Tristan—maybe even loved him. How was that possible? The one guy he'd fallen for, the one he could see a future with, had played him.

Of course.

He massaged his forehead and clunked his knuckles on his bike helmet. *Jesus. I still have the thing on?* His hair was probably glued to his head. Oh well. He wasn't out to impress anyone tonight. He removed the helmet and kicked off his shoes. When he wriggled his toes, the bones creaked. He sighed again. At thirty-five, he was falling apart.

He closed his eyes. Life was strange. One minute he'd planned his life around dinners by himself and working until he forgot his loneliness. Then next, Tristan had swooped in and gotten him thinking about being part of a twosome. Then reality had ripped everything to shreds, leaving him to pick up the pieces. Not that he had much choice—he had to move on with his life.

He opened his eyes and unbuttoned the collar of his shirt. The desire to leave the sofa crossed his mind, but he didn't move. Why bother? Moping seemed like such a better alternative.

White light flooded the living room, then disappeared. Michael sat up. He hadn't ordered pizza or takeout. Knowing his luck, a hot delivery guy had the wrong address. He rifled his fingers through his hair and stood. A shadow moved across the picture window. Instead of giving the wayward delivery man a chance to speak, Michael intercepted him from behind the door.

"You want the next house. Two-thirteen. This is two-eighteen," Michael called. "Two doors down and across the street."

"Michael."

He froze. *Tristan?* What? He had to be cool in case his mind was playing tricks on him. "I didn't order anything." The voice sure sounded like Tristan, but he didn't trust himself. Besides, Tristan was with Cody.

"I know. I want to talk to you," Tristan said. "Please?"

No denying that was Tristan. He grasped the door handle, but didn't open up. "Why? You said enough at the house." Come to think of it, Tristan's body language had been all wrong, but it was too late to take the statement back. Tristan hadn't said much and had seemed confused back at the Victorian. Still, he hadn't argued when Cody had said they were together.

"Please?"

Michael opened the door, but stared at Tristan through the mesh of the screen door. "We can talk, but no sex." He twisted the lock on the storm door. "I'm not in the mood." Wrong again. He'd spread out for Tristan. He craved the man's body and soul, but neither was up for grabs.

Tristan didn't smile or push his way in. His shoulders slumped and his hair was a mess. The circles under his eyes were deeper.

Michael stepped out of the way as Tristan inched into the house. "I just left you at the Victorian. I'm the one who should be winded. Have you been drinking?" He offered his arm. "Come on. I'll make coffee and sober you up." He'd inferred a lot from Tristan by just being at his home. There wasn't an invitation for sex and Tristan hadn't said a word about drinking.

"Michael." Tristan touched Michael's forearm. "I'm not drunk. I haven't had a drink in days. As for sex, I'd love to be with you, but I can't."

"Because you're with Cody." He closed the door. "I understand."

Tristan shook his head. "Because it wouldn't be fair to you."

"I don't understand, but then a lot of what's happened in the last couple hours makes no sense." He gestured to the sofa. "How about we sit and chat?"

"Your hair is standing on end." Tristan brushed his fingers across Michael's cheek. "It's cute."

"Yours isn't much better." He sat opposite Tristan. "Want coffee or some water?"

"I'm fine." Tristan scrubbed both hands over his face. "When I left New York, I'd effectively run away from my problems. I had a kind-of boyfriend who wanted fame, but not really me. Then there's my aunt, the social climber. She wants more of everything and will stop at nothing to get it. Add in my lack of writing, my desire to drink too much and my tendency to pop pills to function… I used the uppers to get through the day and downers to sleep. It's only by sheer willpower and a doctor's help that I got off them before I came here." He sighed. "I kicked some of my addictions, but I ran away from the rest of my problems. I didn't force myself to write or do anything. I just got the hell out of Dodge."

"Sounds like." Michael wasn't sure what else to say. His heart broke for Tristan, but then again, he was a little envious and disgusted, too. How could someone with so much going for them not realize what they had? Or better yet, how could Tristan want to throw it all away?

"I got a new start when I came to Sullavan. My mother seemed to know when I was a kid that my being here was a sort of reset button. Maybe my uncle knew that, too. I haven't taken any pills, drunk except the beer I had with you and I'm writing. The story is nearly done. I'll have the first draft to my publisher this weekend."

"Good job." Michael clapped Tristan's knee. "Proud of you." He met Tristan's gaze and eased his hand away. "But?"

"I'm scared," Tristan said. His voice cracked. "Part of me wonders if this trip to Sullavan wasn't what it seems. You know, like I'm only seeing the bright side so I can hide from the negatives back home."

"Could be." He'd done his fair share of hiding at the library to avoid his issues. "They won't go away, though."

"I know." Tristan leaned back on the sofa. "The bigger part of me thinks I needed the change. All I've ever known was the dysfunction of my family. If you can't fix it, you either toss it or buy a new one. Still won't work? Sweep the problem under the rug. Still not enough? Ignore it and shove more money at it. Want something? Use the family name and cash to get it. That's a crazy life." He stood, then paced the length of the living room. "I don't know."

Michael picked at the band of his watch. He didn't have a grand answer. Hell, his life was its own ball of crazy. But he had to help Tristan. "I've always been told to follow my heart. Good or bad. My heart is my compass. It's steered me in odd directions, but none I've regretted." He looked up at Tristan. "What does your heart say? Look deep and think about it."

"Michael." Tristan's shoulders slumped again.

He stared at the man he'd fallen for. He'd kept so many things bottled up and needed a release. "My heart wants you. I've got a good chance at being dicked over again, but I'm not shying away. I'm happiest with you. I don't want you to go. If I could, I'd tether you to me." He paused to consider what he'd said. Shit. "Okay, that's extreme, but I like the way you make me feel. I like your overuse of the word love and your tendency to leave stuff everywhere. Your smile disarms me and so does your laugh. I want you to stay here, but I can't force you."

Tristan sank onto the overstuffed chair. "Do you love me?"

Yes. "I'm... I don't know." Why was he holding that last part back? Fear?

"You don't."

"Tristan." He knew, but terror swept over him. What if Tristan didn't love him, too, despite his declarations? What if every time he'd said love, he didn't mean it?

"Come to New York with me." Tristan hopped over to the sofa and grabbed Michael's hand.

"Now?"

"Yes." Tristan's eyes shimmered.

"No." He couldn't just drive off to another state. Not right now.

"Why?"

"How? It's a long-ass drive." Besides, he didn't want to be cooped up in his car for that long.

"We'll fly. I called my friend Reg. He's sending his jet to the county airport. It'll be here in an hour." Tristan squeezed Michael's fingers. "Please? I can't do this alone."

"We have an airport in this county?" Michael blurted. He pieced through what Tristan had said. "What can't you do alone?"

Tristan scooted to the edge of the cushion. "Come to my world. I need you with me."

"To do what?" He shook his head. "I don't understand. This is irrational. All of a sudden you want to go to New York. *We* aren't even a *we*. Besides, you're not answering my questions."

"I'm horrible at relationships. Until you, I imploded every one of them. I couldn't handle the stress. Here, in Sullavan, I'm myself. I'm not stressed. I'm level and doing things. But I have a life in New York. Just come with me and help me prove to myself that I don't need whatever it is I can't shake in New York."

"Tristan." He knew damn well what Tristan couldn't shake. "You've got Cody."

"Hon, I don't have him. He's the one who I thought was using me to climb the social ladder. Turns out, he had eyes for someone else." Tristan shrugged. "The man Cody wants doesn't want him. We're just friends, but I'd love to get him paired up. The one I want to be with is you."

"What?" He had to think this one through. So Tristan had been with Cody, but Cody wanted another guy who wasn't interested? *Jesus.* He had a soap opera going on in his life and he was only a bystander.

"You'll get to ride in a jet. Where else are you going to get to do that?" Tristan grinned. "It'll be fun."

"You're spoiled." Half of Michael wanted to give in, but the rest still wasn't convinced.

"You think I'm bad now, you should've met me two years ago. This is nothing." He tugged Michael in close. "I need this. I need you. No one grounds me like you."

"And Cody isn't in the picture?" He wanted to be sure.

"He's not. The whole reason he came here was to split us up. Just…" Tristan shook his head. "It's complicated and part of the reason I'm begging you to come to New York."

"But…"

"The only person I want is you."

"I heard him say you were going to live in that house together."

"Yeah, he did so you wouldn't trust me. Him coming here was all part of a plan to get us split up, but it wasn't for his gain." Tristan cupped Michael's jaw. "I can see the question in your eyes. You want to know who would do that? Long story short...my butler."

"Tristan." His butler? Now Michael had heard everything.

"Grab your stuff and I'll explain along the way." Tristan tugged Michael to his feet. "Before you ask, I'm sure." He waggled his eyebrows, then kissed Michael. "I'm also scared. I'm worried you'll see New York and realize you can do better than me. Or maybe you'll meet my family and refuse to see me because of them. Or what if we decide we aren't a twosome? I'm petrified, but I'm willing to put everything out there for love."

"Right, because a trip always helps." Michael allowed Tristan to pull him forward into his arms. Going to another state wouldn't bring them closer together. Hell, it might tear the relationship apart.

"It can't hurt."

"Tristan." Every cell in his being screamed to stay home. A change of scenery wasn't going to fix anything. But he wanted to be with Tristan. His heart yearned for Tristan. Christ.

"If you say my name one more time, I'm going to climb on you. You're wicked sexy in that bike helmet."

Michael paused. Then tucked his hands into Tristan's back pockets. "Will there be privacy on this plane? At least enough to...I don't know...allow you to climb on me?"

"You want to join the mile-high club?" Tristan laughed and held Michael closer. "Would you believe I've never joined?" He nodded. "Yeah, I think we should stamp our memberships together."

"Then I'll go."

"So we can have sex?"

His resistance melted. Tristan had won him over and there wasn't any turning back. "So we can figure out whatever we've got going on here and maybe move forward."

"I won't let you down."

Michael hoped not. His heart was in Tristan's hands.

* * * *

Four hours later, Michael sat in the back of the limousine and stared at the lights ringing the ceiling. He still hadn't wrapped his head around what he'd done. Against his better judgment, he'd gone with Tristan to the jet, flown to New York City and was now riding across town — one he didn't know — to Tristan's penthouse. He snorted. Tristan hadn't been kidding about the jet or the luxury. There were leather and wooden details everywhere in both vehicles. Every bell and whistle was included. He'd never seen anything so over-the-top. He hadn't expected the limo at the small airstrip or for Tristan to be so at ease in this lifestyle. Christ, there was so much he knew but didn't know about Tristan.

Tristan patted Michael's thigh. "I'll make the mile-high club up to you." He handed Michael a little bottle of water. "Reg said he'd sent the jet, but I didn't realize he'd upgraded to the open floorplan one. The only privacy was in the bathroom. Yeah, I've done sex in the teeny bathroom. Not again."

Michael wasn't sure if he should be reassured or mildly horrified. He tried to laugh, but the sound wasn't right.

Tristan bowed his head. "Sorry. I forget how overwhelming this can be. I'm used to it." He met Michael's gaze. "You've flown before, right?"

"I have." He nodded. "But I'm more used to cracked upholstery and long car trips. The only time I got on a plane was to visit Florida when I was twenty." He wished he was in the quiet and safety of his library. At least there he knew what would happen. Being with Tristan had become an adventure he wasn't sure he wanted to take.

"I understand." Tristan draped his arm around Michael's shoulders. "With any luck, I'll have ninety percent of this straightened out and we can go back to our lives in Sullavan. Have you ever thought about cats? Dogs?"

"I like both, but I'm lost. What are you talking about?" Why does he keep changing subjects?

"How about we adopt two of each—two cats and two dogs. They'll have the run of the farmhouse." Tristan sighed. "Our own little oasis. You, me, the critters and peace. Yeah?"

Oh boy. "Don't you think you're biting off an awful lot?" *Like, way too much?* Yeah, he'd admitted he wanted Tristan, but whatever the craziness was in New York, would they be able to withstand it and come out stronger on the other side?

"Nah. I know what I want." Tristan kissed Michael's temple. "You." He sat up straight and clapped his hands. "Here we are. My other...the other place I sleep." He grabbed Michael's wrist.

Michael fumbled with the bottle of water. He hadn't even opened it. He shook his head. Things had moved too fast. "What about this? I can't stuff it in my bag for later because I didn't bring a bag."

"Stuff it in your pocket, for Christ's sake." Tristan shrugged, then left the vehicle. When Michael climbed out of the back seat, Tristan stopped him beside the car. "Sorry. I've shifted into asshole mode."

Michael gripped the plastic. He wasn't fond of wasting and sure wasn't thrilled about Tristan's change in attitude. He shook hands with the driver. "Thank you for the ride. This was my first time in a limo. It was fun." He sounded like an awkward kid. *Damn it.* "Thank you."

"You're welcome," the driver said. He smiled and stood beside the car.

Michael rushed up to Tristan. "What'd I say?" he murmured. "Did I just insult him?"

"No, but you stunned him. My family never thanks him—which is sad. We should." Tristan hurried into the building, then the open elevator car. "I forgot how many manners I don't have."

"If I said something wrong, then tell me." Manners or not, he didn't want to embarrass anyone. "I'm not good in these situations."

"Better than me." Tristan pinned Michael between his body and the wall of the car. "I should learn a few things from you." He brushed his nose along Michael's. "Now for the hard part. Just...don't run away."

"Oh?" His heart sank and his stomach soured. "Why would I run away?"

"Well...convincing my butler I'm not in love with him won't be easy and, if there's more to the story like I think, it'll get complicated fast." Tristan let go of Michael. The bell *dinged* and the doors opened. He marched into the penthouse.

Michael wasn't sure what he'd expected from Tristan's New York home, but the high-end items weren't a shock. Maybe it was the sparseness of the space or the lack of character. No framed photos or trinkets from vacations. Nothing was out of place. Just cold, boring functionality in the form of futuristic furnishings.

"You don't like it." Tristan grinned. "Back when the stuff was delivered, I liked it, but I've come to realize I'm more of a country chic kind of guy than I thought." He tossed his keys onto the plastic table. "Dennis?"

"Tristan." A man with at least fifteen years on Tristan breezed into the room. He didn't wear a suit or even a dress shirt, just a polo shirt and jeans. The look certainly didn't scream butler to Michael. More like father-figure or friend.

Michael lingered back a few paces to stay out of the way.

Tristan embraced Dennis. "It's good to see you, old man."

"I'm thrilled you're here. Shall we get down to business?" Dennis clapped his hands. "Is this my replacement? He's a bit young and too pretty. We should look elsewhere."

Tristan met Michael's gaze, then scrubbed the back of his neck with his palm. "Dennis, I'm not replacing you."

Good for him, Michael thought. Tristan had backbone, but sometimes refused to use it. Besides, something about Dennis annoyed Michael, but he couldn't figure out what.

"You don't honestly think I'm going to be the bottom? I've cleaned up after you for long enough. It's someone else's turn." Dennis folded his arms. "Correct?"

"You're right," Tristan said. "I agree."

"But not him," Dennis said, clipping his words.

"I'm too pretty." Michael hadn't planned on saying those words, but they slipped out before he could take them back. "Story of my life." Not really. Hearing himself described as pretty was laughable. Passable maybe, but not handsome.

Dennis faced Michael. "Then what *are* you doing here?"

Michael held out his hand to Tristan. "I'll allow Tristan to explain." After his last outburst, it was best if he let Tristan handle the situation. "Tristan?"

Tristan sat on the arm of the couch. The slender strip of wood bit into his backside. Why in the hell had he purchased such ugly furniture? Because he'd had his aunt telling him it was the best. He'd guess she got a cut from whoever sold it, or at least a discount on her own stuff.

"What's going on?" Dennis met Tristan's gaze. "What's he talking about?"

"I should ask you that." Tristan folded his arms and glanced back at Michael for a moment before focusing on Dennis. "I'm here. The book will be submitted for first edits next week and I'm still not done going through my uncle's house. I have commitments in Sullavan."

"But you belong here. Hire someone to deal with the house," Dennis said. "I need you."

"Why? I'll get you another job with someone else. I'll bet my aunt can use you." He'd be better off there anyway. Tristan didn't want a butler in Sullavan. He wanted time with Michael and a new, quiet life.

"Your aunt isn't you." Dennis reached for Tristan, then recoiled. "Come on."

"I'm glad I'm not her." He shuddered. His aunt drove him crazy.

"We're supposed to be in this together." Dennis grabbed Tristan's hand. "You and me."

"Why?" He pulled away from Dennis. "You're expecting more from me than I can give."

"You don't understand. I love you," Dennis said. "Have since I hired on."

Tristan crooked his eyebrows. *Shit.* He'd seen this coming, but hearing the words out loud still rocked him and not in a good way. "Denny, you don't love me. Cody loves you. Why not stick with him?"

"Cody?" Dennis snarled. "He's a child."

"He's a year older than me." Tristan left his spot on the couch and stood between Dennis and Michael. "He's in love with you."

"You're mature." Dennis' voice cracked. "You need me. He doesn't."

"I'm not all that mature." Tristan hadn't been when he'd still lived in New York. But leaving and resetting his brain had helped him to gain insight. He did better in the slower pace.

"We've got a good thing." Dennis blushed. "I can't imagine life without you. You write and I'll hold you up."

"I've got Michael for that." Tristan stood firm. "I need to get out. I'm in a box here. I'm trapped. My creativity went to shit. When I changed venues, it came back."

"No." Dennis grabbed Tristan's shoulders. "You owe me this."

"Owe you?" *What the hell?* Tristan splayed his hands on Dennis' chest. The rush wasn't there—not like with Michael. The desire and need...he felt nothing. Michael was the one he wanted and he owed Dennis nothing.

"Yes. I've been here. I've put up with your shit. I've watched you be a self-indulged asshole. I've cleaned up your messes and pushed you to write." Dennis shoved Tristan. "Yeah, I fucking pushed you."

"You encouraged me, sure." He didn't understand.

"No, you fucknut. *I'm* the one who sent all those messages. The emails. Don't you get it? I told you not to go to the police because I'm the one who sent them. The fear made you great," Dennis said. The veins in his forehead stuck out. He gritted his teeth. "Understand?"

"Dennis?" He froze. Everything made sense and scared him to his core. The man he'd trusted with his banking, his career, his life...wanted to help, but in return for something. "What are you thinking?"

"I've seen what you've got. I know you. That tidy trust fund money would be great. Share it with me and I'm gone." Dennis grabbed Tristan's shirt. "A quarter million should do it. I'll keep my mouth shut and you'll never have to worry about me again."

"Dennis." *Shit, shit, shit.* He'd thought Dennis was the one person who wouldn't fuck him over. He'd been wrong.

Michael eased between Tristan and Dennis. "Slow down." He shoved his phone into Tristan's hand. "If you truly love this man, then you don't want to extort him. Come on."

"You don't understand. I've spent years cleaning up after him." Dennis lunged at Michael, but somehow

Michael kept them both upright. "He owes me. He's got the money. His family is filthy rich. They can afford this."

"That happens." Michael nudged Dennis away from Tristan.

"I want my due," Dennis screamed.

Tristan didn't know what to do. He'd had Dennis or various other wait staff cleaning up after him all his life. *What the hell?* He glanced down at the phone. Michael had left the notation function open.

I texted the police and your chauffeur. Someone should be up in a moment. If the police call, ANSWER IT.

He glanced up at Michael. *Holy shit.* He nodded when Michael looked at him. Tristan sent another text from Michael's phone, but this time to the building security.

"What's it going to be?" Dennis asked. "Money or we're together?" He notched his chin in the air. "Or do I kill him? He's the one in the way." He pulled a small revolver from behind his back. "I'll do it, then blame you."

Tristan typed out a text for Michael.

Need help in penthouse 2. Being held at gunpoint. Help.

He hit send, then met Dennis' gaze. Tristan turned on the camera function and aimed it at Dennis. "Don't hurt Michael. You're mad at me. Not him." He put the phone on the table, then inched over to Dennis. He needed to buy more time for the police and security to arrive. "Just stop. Kill me. Hurt me, but not him." He put his hands up. "Please?"

"Stay with me. This ends if you stay." Dennis threw his arms around Tristan and pointed the gun at Tristan's head. "You're really doing it?"

The blunt barrel of the revolver pushed into Tristan's scalp, reminding him the danger wasn't over. He fought to stay calm. "Yeah. I'm staying." He rested his hands on Dennis' hips. "Let him go."

"Whatever." Dennis moved the gun and waved it. "Go."

Tristan noticed Michael out of the corner of his eye. Michael shook his head. "Put the gun down. You don't want to do this. You don't want to hurt Tristan...not if you love him. If you truly care about him, you wouldn't extort him. You'd show him how you feel and bring him closer."

"What are you? A therapist?" Dennis waved the gun again. "Shut up."

"Am I wrong?" Michael asked.

Michael might not have been wrong, but Tristan wished he'd stop talking. He wasn't buying time, but rather pissing Dennis off.

"No." Dennis aimed at Tristan. "But I'm not losing you."

"I'm not going anywhere." Tristan opened his arms and enfolded Dennis in his embrace. "I'm here. Michael, go."

Dennis wrapped himself around Tristan. He held the gun, but wasn't aiming at Tristan. "You ignored me and my messages."

"I was writing." Tristan bit back bile. *God damn it.* He worked the gun free from Dennis' grip and put the firearm on the floor. He kicked it out of the way. "We don't need that gun. I'm not going anywhere."

Tears stained Dennis' face and his cheeks reddened. "I've wanted to call you mine for so long."

"We're good." He nudged the gun once more, pushing it farther away from Dennis. "Yeah." He angled Dennis with his back to Michael. He wasn't sure what to do, but he didn't want Dennis getting an eyeful of the cops until the last minute. Besides, where in the hell were the police?

Michael scooted the revolver the rest of the way from Dennis, but before he could do anything else, the door to the penthouse flew open. Building security and police strode into the living room.

"What the hell?" Dennis squeezed Tristan hard. "What did you do?"

One of the officers rushed across the room to Michael. Another intercepted Dennis. Tristan collided with the sofa, but managed to stay on his feet. "I'm sorry, Dennis," Tristan said. "I can't be with someone who'd kill me or take my money." He picked up Michael's phone and handed it to the closest officer. "We've got the whole thing on video."

"Tristan. No." Dennis struggled against the policeman's grasp. "I wouldn't. It was the other guy. He did it. I wouldn't hurt my Tristan."

"Take him downstairs." The officer led Dennis through the room. "We'll need statements."

Tristan wobbled against the couch. He saw the investigators in his home and photographing everything, but he barely paid attention. His life had been in the balance. His butler, one of the few people he'd trusted, had fucked him over. He scrubbed both hands over his face. When the police officer approached him, he answered every question, but his thoughts continued to race. He willed his stomach to settle and rubbed his clammy hands on his pant legs. When he'd decided to come home, he hadn't planned on being held at gunpoint by his butler or bringing Michael into such a disaster. He'd begged Michael to come along, but then everything had blown up. He couldn't shake the feeling of disgust. He stole a glance at Michael. Would he and Michael be able to continue their relationship after this or would the danger be the last straw for him?

"My heart belongs to you, Michael," Tristan murmured. "Please let yours still want me, too."

Chapter Fourteen

Michael stood on the balcony and stared out at the New York skyline. The lights twinkled and the breeze wrapped around him. He noticed the roar of planes overhead and the hum of traffic below. He wondered how many people were in the surrounding buildings. Probably hundreds or thousands. More than he could count.

Could he live amid such commotion? He'd meet a lot of people if he nabbed a job at one of the branch libraries. But could he live here? His chest constricted and he couldn't breathe. He clenched his hands and fear overwhelmed him. The thought of so many people and so much action sent panic to his core. He panted, trying to catch his breath. If he and Tristan were going to make a go of their relationship, he'd have to compromise on a few things. But living arrangements? He wasn't so sure. New York from the vantage of Tristan's penthouse was too much for him.

The door creaked behind him. He didn't bother to look back. The only people left in the penthouse were him and Tristan.

Tristan stopped beside him at the railing. He crinkled his nose. "Would you believe I rarely came out here? I never saw the point. I hate heights and the smell of exhaust churns my stomach."

"Really?" Michael blurted. "The view is phenomenal. I bet the sunrises and sunsets are beautiful." He gripped the railing, then blew out a ragged breath. He needed to move away from the edge. "I'm not wild about heights, either."

Tristan said nothing. The breeze caught his hair, moving some of the strands off his face. He rested his elbows on the concrete wall.

Michael inched backwards to the doors and willed himself to calm down. The danger was gone. No one would rush in and threaten them. Besides, he had to say something. "Are they all gone?"

"Yeah." Tristan didn't move.

"Cool." Michael flattened himself against the inner wall of the balcony. "I was told I'd get my phone back tomorrow. Good thing we didn't take any nude selfies." But bad if the library had to contact him. *Fuck.* If anyone from Sullavan wanted him, he was unreachable. He'd better have Tristan contact Dicey at least so someone knew he was still alive.

"Probably just as well we didn't make any sex tapes, either." Tristan's half-hearted chuckle faded. He stared at Michael for a long moment. "I'm sorry."

"For what?" Michael shrugged to hide his residual fear. "Life didn't end. I got to ride on a plane and see your place." He'd left out the scarier parts, but oh the fuck well.

"I'm sorry for everything. I thought I'd talk to him and get this settled...not what happened." Tristan left his post at the balcony wall and crossed over to Michael. "I wanted to show you my life here and treat you to something special. We're supposed to go to my cousin's engagement party tomorrow. I thought maybe you'd wear something from my closet and we'd be handsome bastards together. I'd blow my auntie's mind and convince her to leave me alone. Then this happened."

"Hey." He stuffed his fingers into Tristan's front pockets. He tugged his lover close. "First, you couldn't know your butler was writing those stalker notes." He nodded. "Yeah, I heard his confession and put the pieces together."

"Faster than I did." Tristan blushed. "Yet another thing I'm sorry for."

"Don't be. Your heart was in the right place. I've never been to a penthouse before or on a jet." He brushed his nose along Tristan's. He wasn't sure what to say, but he had to reassure Tristan. "I don't want your money or your status. I like you."

"You do?" Tristan's voice cracked. "Michael?"

"Yeah, I do. It's more like love." He laughed and the sound vibrated in his throat. "Jesus. I never thought I'd say that ever again, but it's true and what scared me the most was the possibility I'd lose you before I could tell you the truth." He'd have stepped in front of the bullet in order to save Tristan. He loved Tristan too much to let him go.

"I love you so much," Tristan said. "That's not me being flip. It's the God's honest truth. I can't see my life without you."

Michael sighed. He'd longed to hear those words from Tristan. "Then we'll figure this out and do the long-distance thing for a while."

"Long distance?" Tristan laughed this time and threw his arms around Michael. "I'm nowhere near done going through my uncle's house and the shelter isn't even started. I have so much left to do in Sullavan. I'm not leaving. My time in the Big Apple is done, yeah, but not with you."

"Tristan." He had no other words. Excitement and desire wound through him. He wanted to show his lover just how much he cared.

"The police released the penthouse, so we can stay here tonight. We'll order takeout tomorrow and be lazy until the party. Yes?" Tristan cupped Michael's jaw in both hands.

"I can't think of anywhere else I'd rather be." Michael kissed Tristan. His life had gone from boring to colorful to dangerous, then had settled down. He'd probably never be bored with Tristan, but that was fine. He loved the writer and every plot twist Tristan could toss at him.

Tristan kissed Michael, then wound his arms around him. He tucked his hands into Michael's back pockets. "I wanted to show you New York and a piece of my world."

"I'm seeing all I want." He returned the kiss. Heat shimmered in his veins. He feathered his mouth over Tristan's. "I'm not sure I'm cut out for the city or this world. It's too...much." He paused. His big admission could push Tristan away.

"I'm not sure I blame you." He withdrew from Michael, then tugged him into the penthouse. "This place isn't my preference anymore. I like the view and

I love everything being within walking distance, but you're not. I want to be where you are. To be where I feel free and with you." He walked backward through the living room to the hallway, then the bedroom. He held onto Michael. "But that doesn't mean I won't let you fuck me senseless right here."

"Oh?" Blood rushed below Michael's belt as Tristan nudged him onto the bed. "So you'd stay...even if I go?"

"Nope. I'm following you." Tristan straddled Michael's thighs. He removed his shirt. His hair stood on end and the shadows deepened around his eyes. Still, he grinned. He slid his hands over Michael's chest and the move sent shivers down Michael's spine.

"Tristan." He loved the delicious pressure on his dick. He memorized the taste of Tristan's kiss.

"Uh-huh?" Tristan feasted on Michael's neck and nibbled his way down to his collarbone. He pinched Michael's nipple.

"You're making me crazy." Making it hard to think, but easy to lose himself in Tristan's arms. All he wanted to do was feel.

"Good." Tristan ground on Michael's lap. "I want to be irresistible."

"You are." He grabbed Michael's ass. "I'm not done with you. Up. I want to be inside you."

"Even better." Tristan scrambled off Michael's thighs long enough to shuck his pants and boxers. He stood nude before Michael. "I've never told anyone I belong to them. You're different." He tugged Michael's shirt up over his head, then knelt and worked on opening Michael's jeans. "I want to belong to you."

Michael propped himself up on his elbows. His cock stood tall. He'd never been so turned on. He shimmied out of his jeans and briefs, then reached for Tristan. "Come here."

"Not yet." Tristan retrieved a bottle of lube and dribbled the clear fluid over Michael's cock. Fires lit in Tristan's eyes as he massaged Michael's dick. "I want this in me."

Michael grunted. He pushed into Tristan's fingers. "You're dangerous."

"I'm trying to show my man I love him." Tristan whimpered. His touch seared Michael to the core. When he crawled onto Michael's legs, he leaned forward and kissed him. "I want you more than my next breath."

Michael swatted Tristan's ass. "Then I want you on all fours so I can make us one." He raked his nails down Tristan's hip. "Do you want me balls deep in you?"

"Fuck yes." Tristan shivered as he climbed off Michael. He perched on his hands and knees. When he looked back at Michael, he waggled his ass. "Take me."

"You bet I will." He dribbled lube over Tristan's ass and slid his middle finger into him. Forget finesse. Raw need took over. He groaned as Tristan clamped down tight around him.

Tristan tensed. "God, yes." He rocked onto Michael's finger. "This won't take long."

"I know." He wished it would, but the desire to be one with Tristan was too much. Tristan had him on a hair-trigger.

"Please?" Tristan backed into Michael. "Need you."

"Yeah." Michael withdrew his finger, then added more lube. He lined his dick up with Tristan's hole. One push would do the trick. Just one and he'd find completion. Inch by inch, he slid into Tristan. *Holy fuck.* Joining Tristan was like coming home. Freeing, yet so tight. He filled Tristan to the hilt and paused. "Is this what you wanted? Me right here?"

"Yes," Tristan said, drawing the words out. He shuddered. "Need you."

Michael grasped Tristan's hips. Power and desire rushed through him. He wanted Tristan more than anything. He moved in time with Tristan—when he pulled out, Tristan backed into him. When he pushed to the hilt, Tristan writhed on his dick. Michael swore he saw stars. He didn't think. Instead, he just moved. He lost himself in the rhythm of being with Tristan. Skin on skin and soul to soul. His balls ached and his cock throbbed. He tensed. *Holy shit.* "Tristan."

"Do it," Tristan bit out.

So calm. Michael could barely think straight and Tristan sounded so...normal.

Another shudder wracked Tristan. "Please?"

He tried to answer, but his words disappeared. He slammed into Tristan and dug his nails into Tristan's hips. His control snapped and he squeezed his eyes shut. He filled Tristan's ass. From head to toe, he sighed. He added a couple more thrusts, then slumped over Tristan and opened his eyes. He panted.

"Christ. That felt good, but I need to come." Tristan flexed his asshole. "Please?"

"Yeah." He eased out of Tristan and plopped onto the bed. He stretched out to enjoy the view. "I want to watch."

"Oh?" Tristan stood tall and his eyebrows rose. He palmed his dick with one hand and caressed his balls with the other. He stroked himself. His nipples were hard and sweat slicked his pecs. He blushed from hairline to chest. He clenched his teeth and his strokes increased.

Michael had never seen anything so pretty. "Come. Fall apart."

Tristan inched toward the bed and his pace quickened. He met Michael's gaze. "Can't hold back." He settled between Michael's open thighs.

"So don't." Michael sat up and added his hands to Tristan's. He watched Tristan. "Now."

Tristan curled forward. Cum shot across Michael's chest in a hot mess. Michael tipped his head back and basked in the warmth.

Tristan collapsed onto Michael's thighs. He draped his arms around Michael's neck. "I loved that." He curled into Michael. "So much."

"Me too." Michael cradled Tristan against his body. "I loved it a lot." He meant every word.

Tristan didn't say anything for a long moment. Michael swore he could hear Tristan's heartbeat. He held his lover and petted his hair. No more kidding himself or trying to deny the truth. He loved Tristan down to his soul.

"You said the word love," Tristan murmured. "About me."

"I did." He kissed the top of Tristan's head. "You're pretty special." He'd started to offer his heart. Time to finish the job. "When I saw the gun pointed at you...my stomach ached and my heart dropped. I got so scared I'd lose you."

"I'm here."

"I don't know if I can live here in New York, but I know I want to be wherever you are. I love you, Tristan. I don't care about the fame or your family's money. I only want you." He brushed his cheek over Tristan's hair. "I never thought I'd say that again. Not to anyone." He chuckled. "I'm in love with you."

Tristan sat up. His cum smeared between them and shimmered on his chest. He curled his fingers under Michael's chin. "I love you, too."

Michael smiled. For the first time since he'd met Tristan, he didn't doubt the truth in his words.

"I'm serious about what I said. The lease here runs out in a couple of months and I never liked it here all that much. I'm betting my cousin and her soon-to-be-husband would like this place better." Tristan nodded. "I'm guessing my aunt would love it, too, because they'd be closer."

"Okay." His heart raced. He had a good idea what Tristan was about to say, but he wanted to hear the words to be sure. "And that means?"

"I'm moving to Sullavan for good. I want you to live with me at the farmhouse. We'll get the shelter going and be better than we ever thought. Promise me you want to," Tristan said.

"I do." No hesitation. No thought. He believed in his gut and his heart.

"Michael?" Tristan's eyes widened. "You're sure?"

"I agree with all of it." He hadn't expected his life would come full circle this way, but he wouldn't change much of it. Tristan was the future he'd never believed possible.

"I bet Reg would bring my shit home if I asked." Tristan threw his arms around Michael's shoulders. "We should shower and sleep. We've got a party tonight and cops who want to talk to us again."

Michael sighed. *So much for forgetting our troubles.* "What party?" He didn't have to ask about the police.

"My cousin's engagement party. I wasn't going to attend, but that was the other reason I dragged you here to New York. I want everyone to meet my boyfriend." Tristan beamed. "I've never brought anyone home before. My aunt will lose her shit, but I don't care. I want to be comfortable in my own skin and you make me feel that way."

"I'm honored." And petrified. He hadn't planned on a party. "But what am I supposed to wear? All I brought was a T-shirt and jeans."

"I know. It was rather spur of the moment." Tristan sagged on Michael's lap. "I've got stuff here you can borrow. You're a tad thinner than me, but I've got the feeling you'll look better in my clothes than I do."

"I doubt that, but I'm doubly honored." Michael palmed Tristan's sticky chest. "We'll make a date of it and have the time of our lives."

"See if you feel that way after you've met my aunt. If she thinks you're not cultured or wealthy enough, she'll turn her nose up at you," Tristan said. "Sad, but that's the truth for her. For me, you're perfect."

"It'll work out. Promise."

"I've got you. Everything's already worked out."

Michael held Tristan and laughed. One minute he was lonely and looking for love at the library, then the next a sexy writer walked into his life. Would he have changed any of it? Probably the being held at gunpoint part, but that instant had proven to him just how much he loved Tristan.

"Shower with me. I promise we'll get clean and crash." Tristan left Michael's lap. "Once we've had a power-nap...then all bets are off."

"I'm counting on that." He followed Tristan to the shower. He'd never get enough of the view of Tristan's ass as he walked. Someone must've shown Tristan favor to have a butt like that, but then they must've liked Michael, too, if they'd ensured he and Tristan would meet. He'd won the guy lottery.

* * * *

Tristan strode up the front steps of the art gallery and his heart lodged in his throat. Coming to the party wasn't such a big deal, but introducing Michael was and he worried what his aunt would say. He squeezed Michael's fingers. "You look fantastic."

"Your clothes are too big," Michael muttered. "I'm afraid the belt won't hold and my pants will fall down. I've never worn a tuxedo in my life."

"You're fine." He stopped just before the main doors and tugged Michael aside. "Plus, it'll make it easier to take them off when we get back in the limo."

"True." Michael grinned.

Tristan palmed Michael's ass and nudged him into the gallery. He'd forgotten just how opulent the place was and how much money had been spent to rent the space. Marble floors, rich wood around each painting and along the staircase and everyone in evening gowns and tuxedoes...plus a string quartet... Good heavens, his aunt must've spent the family riches just to throw the party.

Before Tristan could warn Michael about his family, his aunt strode over to them. Salina waved. "Shit," Tristan groaned. "Wait for it."

"Tristan Milo...what a surprise." Salina threw her arms around Tristan. "Let me get a look at you." She swept her gaze over him. "You need to eat more. Too thin and people will talk."

"Thanks." He should've known her compliment would be backhanded. "It's been tough since Uncle Al passed."

"Oh, I'm sorry. I didn't know he was sick." Her smile returned. "You're here now with your family. We'll take care of you."

"Well, it's funny you say that. I've been doing a good job of caring for myself." He draped his arm around Michael's waist. "And speaking of family, I've got mine right here. I want you to meet my partner, Michael."

"Him?" Salina's eyes widened. "Are you…?"

"Yes, this is Michael Kane—like the actor, but not. He's my partner and we're very happy together." Telling anyone who would listen that he and Michael were a couple never ceased to please him.

"Hello, ma'am." Michael extended his hand, but Salina didn't move. "Okay. It's a pleasure to meet you."

She glared at Michael. The lines deepened around her eyes and her makeup crinkled.

"Salina," Tristan growled. "Remember you're in public."

Her glare increased. "Are you kidding?" She yanked Tristan away from Michael and out of earshot. "What are you doing?"

He frowned. He'd expected her to be resistant, but not this mean. He hadn't done anything wrong by introducing Michael. "I'm sorry?"

"You should be. This isn't your party. You're taking the spotlight from your cousin," Salina snapped.

"We walked in, said hi to you and were on our way to speak to Jean. No one else approached us." Tristan balled his hand to hide his anger. "What's wrong with Michael?" He wanted the real reason for her negativity.

Her mouth opened but no sound came out.

"Salina." He refused to back down. "What's the deal?"

"Don't refer to me by my name." She stared at him. "I'm Mrs. Delaney."

He rolled his eyes. "Answer me. What's wrong with Michael?"

She smoothed her skirt and shifted her gaze around the room. "Where did you meet him?"

"Sullavan."

"Is that a club?"

"It's where my uncle lived. Michael's a librarian." He gritted his teeth. She had to be making this deliberately difficult. "He's an intelligent and mannered guy."

"Are you kidding?" she asked a second time. Her jaw slackened and her brows crinkled. "He's not even from a good family."

"How do you know?" Why would she think he'd pull her leg?

"First, his haircut is horrible. Second, he's wearing a tuxedo off the rack and it fits horribly," she said, clicking her tongue. "He's classless."

"That's my other tuxedo and it's worth more than some cars." He folded his arms. "Just stop. You want to hate him. You do. Fine. Don't take it out on him just because you're being snooty."

"He couldn't afford a proper tuxedo. That's awful." Salina notched her chin in the air. "Just go."

"You want me to leave without saying hello to Babsy?" He tamped down his anger. He should've expected this level of displeasure from his aunt. "That would be terrible." He left Salina where she stood and returned to Michael. "Sorry. She wanted to read me my rights." He held Michael's hand. "Let's visit my cousin." He navigated his way through the crowd.

"What happened?" Michael asked. "What'd I do?"

"Nothing. It's my aunt. I told you she'd find fault with you." He stopped in the middle of the throng of people. "You didn't measure up and she wanted to make a scene. I didn't take the bait and neither should you."

"She's that petty?"

"Oh yeah." He started away, but Michael stopped Tristan.

"Tristan." He held on to Tristan's lapels. "I'm sorry. Next time I'll buy a tux that fits."

"No." He cupped Michael's jaw in both hands. "This is one of the reasons I'm ready to leave New York. I can't do the fakeness. I can't allow someone I love to be treated like shit because he's not from the right family. That's crap."

"I knew I shouldn't have worn your tux." Michael chuckled. "Oh well. Next time I'll show up naked."

"Yes." Tristan nodded and laughed until his ribs hurt. "But only if the party is a party of two." Christ, he loved Michael. He'd wanted a man who knew how to break the tension and buoy him while being his equal. Michael fit the bill. "Let's visit with my cousin a moment, then we can go. I have the feeling my aunt would like us out of here as soon as possible."

"I say we stick around a little longer and annoy her." Michael half-shrugged. "I enjoy irritating her."

"You're so bad." He kissed Michael hard. "But I'd rather go home so we can do naughty things to each other."

"Oh?" Michael's eyes flashed.

In the middle of so many people, with the noise and music playing, Michael managed to make it seem like he and Tristan were the only ones in the room. Tristan shifted his hips to hide his burgeoning erection. When could they leave? Now?

"Where is this cousin and her beau?" Michael asked. "Since you're offering up your penthouse, the least you can do is let her know in person." He tucked in close to Tristan. "Then we can go home for lots of sex."

He shivered and desire hit hard. "Yes."

"Then let's go." Michael kissed Tristan. "Now."

"Uh-huh." He needed a second for his brain to defog. He wandered with Michael through the crowd until he spotted his cousin.

Jean and her fiancé, Antonin, stood beside a swan ice carving. A fountain with pink water flowed behind them. Tristan strode up to her. "Jean," he said. "Antonin. So good to see you. Congratulations. When is the happy event going to be?"

Jean blushed. "Uh...how'd you know?"

Antonin kissed her knuckles. "He meant the wedding, but you might as well tell him the rest...he's family."

Her blush deepened. "Uh...who is this?"

Tristan tipped his head. What was she hiding? He flattened his hand on the small of Michael's back. "This is my partner, Michael. Michael, this is Jean and Antonin."

"It's a pleasure to meet you." Michael shook hands with Antonin and kissed Jean on the cheek. "Congratulations. Your secret is safe with us."

Antonin laughed. "I knew I liked this guy for a reason. Thank you."

Jean clasped Antonin's wrist with both hands and nodded to Tristan. She glanced around before speaking. "The baby will arrive in April so we're getting married next month. I don't want the situation to be so obvious. My mother will die. As soon as she finds out, she'll try to take control."

"It's a small beachside gathering, but I want you both to be there," Antonin said.

"We won't say a word." Tristan kissed her temple. "But speaking of secrets, I've got one for you. Since Michael and I are permanent, I don't need my penthouse here in town. If you'd like to take it over, then the place is yours."

Antonin's eyes lit up. "Are you kidding? We'll get out of her house. Yeah, we'll take it. Thank you."

"Jean?" He leveled his gaze at his cousin. "What do you think?"

She hugged Tristan, then Michael, before settling against Antonin. "That's the best gift we could receive. I'm tired of living under my mother's thumb."

"I'll bet." Tristan nodded. If his aunt could be hellish to him, he couldn't imagine what she'd be like to her daughter on a daily basis.

"She's pushy, mean and hates anyone who can't help her advance." Jean blew out a ragged breath. "Wow. I've held that in for too long."

Tristan clapped his hands. "If you feel better, then that's what matters." His pride in his cousin swelled. She deserved the best. "I worked out the lease situation with the building supervisor. Since it's technically my penthouse and I bought it, all we have to do is transfer it to your names. I just rent the mailbox or something like that." He shrugged, then handed her an envelope. "I put the information in the card plus a little something to help out." He draped his arm around Michael. "Count us in for the wedding."

"Both of you." Jean beamed. "Thank you."

Tristan glanced over his shoulder, then groaned. "Your mother is incoming and she's not fond of Michael, so we'll go. Enjoy the evening."

Antonin shook hands with Michael, then Tristan. "Thank you and I'm sorry, Michael. At least you're not marrying into that side of the family."

Jean blushed again. "She's a handful."

"True." Michael waggled his head and started away.

Tristan winked, then followed Michael through the crowd. He waited until he and Michael were in the limo before he spoke. "You survived." He massaged Michael's thigh. "I apologize for my aunt. My father would've laughed at her and my mother would've encouraged her behavior."

"Is that a good thing? Me not meeting her approval?" Michael rubbed his forehead. "She seemed a little more than annoyed."

"She, like my mother, had her moments, but neither is bad." He settled in his seat and tucked Michael to his side. "Jean has become more of her own person, which is good."

"Yeah," Michael murmured.

"Are you okay? Is the collar too tight?" He faced Michael. "Hey."

"Marriage," Michael said.

"Okay...what about it?" He wasn't following.

"Did you catch what Antonin said? Marrying into that side of the family?" The creases at the corners of Michael's eyes deepened. "If I'm not good enough..."

Tristan laughed, cutting Michael off. "Don't let Auntie Salina rattle you, but it's just as well she's not going to be your mother-in-law."

Michael's eyes widened. "Are we even in a position to look that far ahead? Are we thinking of marriage? You kept calling me your partner, but are you sure?"

So that was what had Michael freaked out... "Eventually I'd like to get married. When I take that step, you're the one I want to marry. No questions or having to think about it. Why? Don't you want me that way?"

Michael shifted in his seat and faced Tristan. "I *do* want to marry you and it scares me. I've never been this far in over my head. I thought I loved one other guy and he decided to leave. I'm worried. I trust you, but I know me. I'm worried you'll realize I'm not enough."

"No." He kissed Michael and palmed the back of Michael's neck. "Things happen for a reason and we came together when we were supposed to. I've never felt this much for anyone outside of my family and I've never craved anyone the way I do you. We'll be ready and we'll figure it out together. I'm not going anywhere."

Michael rested his head on Tristan's shoulder and his hand on his thigh. "One of these days my self-esteem won't reside in the basement. I just needed the reassurance."

"I'll give it whenever you want." He kissed the top of Michael's head. "Although running off and making you an honest man does sound like fun."

"It does," Michael said. "But we've done so many things at breakneck speed. We need to live with what we've done and make sure before we jump into something so permanent."

"You might be right, but I like our pace."

"I do, too."

"Do you love me?" Tristan asked. He didn't doubt Michael's affection for him, but hearing the words pleased him.

"Yes."

"I love you, too." He tipped Michael's chin and met his gaze. "I'm not changing my mind. You're the one for me — whether we're living together in the farmhouse or married and locked in...I'm happy because I'm with you."

The corner of Michael's mouth kinked.

"I know you believe me. You wouldn't have flown off to New York if you hadn't." He kissed Michael. "I love my librarian. The best part of Sullavan is in my arms."

"I love you, too." Michael brushed his nose along Tristan's. "But being an honest man does sound good."

"Yeah."

Michael laughed. "An author and a librarian meet in the center of town... Sounds like the start of a bad joke."

"Or our forever story. I've got an idea for the ending. How's this? They lived happy ever after in the farmhouse, having sex each night and most days while spending time with their animals and books. Good?" Tristan asked.

"Sounds perfect."

Tristan nodded. Sullavan was supposed to be a side trip, not forever, but he couldn't think of anywhere else he belonged. Michael was the one man he could live without, but didn't want to. He'd found his missing piece in Michael. Thank God Al had had a plan when Tristan hadn't a clue.

Epilogue

Michael toyed with the picture frame and sighed. The last six months of his life had consisted of working at the library, more sex than he'd thought imaginable with Tristan and too many hours refurbishing the Victorian house. The shelter Al had imagined was about to open and already had three guests.

Tristan eased up to Michael. "The sign is ready out front. What're you waiting for in here?"

Michael leaned into Tristan's chest. "I never thought this day would come."

"Opening the shelter? Or finally seeing all of my uncle's wishes come to fruition?" Tristan laughed and embraced Michael from behind. He rested his chin on Michael's shoulder. "I'm thrilled John was able to bring his expertise to the shelter. He's a dynamic counselor. Between him and Dicey, I have the feeling anyone who sets foot in the shelter will be well cared for."

"I'm sure." Michael hooked the photo on the nail, then admired his work. "Your uncle would be thrilled."

"He'd be happier knowing I helped finance the rest of the project." Tristan kissed Michael's neck. "I kept holding on to the trust fund cash. I didn't know why, other than I wasn't going to use it. Now I'm glad I waited."

"Me too." Michael admired the photo of his one-time lover. He wouldn't change his past because it made him more appreciative of his future, but still. If he'd met Tristan a little sooner and could have had this level of happiness, he would've done anything to have him.

"When do we find out if the board approved of my donation to the library?" Tristan asked. "We have to move some of those books out of the house. I need room for more."

"They accepted it. The letter came through the mail at the library yesterday, but I've been neck-deep in painting so I didn't get a chance to bring it home." Michael turned in Tristan's arms. "They loved your idea to create an annex for the special volumes out of the original schoolhouse and a brand-new library for everything else."

"I do have strokes of genius from time to time." Tristan grinned. "Like not giving up when I saw the farmhouse."

"Well, the idea to use the old community center was just as smart." Michael cuddled against his partner. "You're going to be broke, though." Tristan had spent so much money to bring the shelter into being and for the library. The farmhouse was paid for and they had a tidy sum from the sale of Michael's house, but adopting the twin black Labrador retrievers and four cats… He wondered how they'd be able to afford everything.

"Call it investing in my town." Tristan shrugged. "It's only money." He placed his finger over Michael's mouth. "I'm happy and writing. As long as we're doing what we love with each other, we'll be fine."

Michael nodded. He loved Tristan's positive outlook. The man could put a happy spin on anything. One thing bothered him. "What about Jamie? He's been pretty heavily invested from the start. He'll want his name on this shelter and the library project."

"I don't think he'll be a problem. He's shifted his attention to other places. Cody's been hanging around Sullavan more than I thought," Tristan said. "He doesn't bother me, so I don't care."

"Ah." Cody and Jamie would be a good pairing—if they'd get past their egos and give each other a chance. Michael kind of liked the idea of Cody and Jamie being a couple.

"I'd rather Cody find someone decent, especially after the...incident." Tristan pulled away from Michael.

Since the night of the encounter with Dennis, Tristan refused to refer to it as anything but 'the incident'. Michael didn't blame him. He'd been traumatized, too.

"If Cody and Jamie hook up, then cool. Cody just wants someone who doesn't see him as a male model or stepping stone," Tristan said. "But I'm not interested in Jamie. I believe I asked *you* to marry me, not him."

Michael's cheeks burned. He hadn't forgotten Tristan's proposal. He'd waited until everyone left the night before and dropped to one knee on the back porch of the shelter house. He'd accepted Tristan's ring and knew Tristan loved him. Maybe one day his damn low self-esteem would go away for good.

"I've got you, a library full of books, my writing mojo, the dogs, the cats and a purpose. I'm better than great." Tristan held out his hands. "Didn't I say we'd be epic?"

"I never should've doubted you." Michael grasped Tristan's fingers. "Should we go outside and cut the ribbon to make the shelter official?"

Tristan nodded once. "Of course. Then we'll go home and celebrate. The last one naked has to fuck the other." His eyes flashed and he let go of Michael. "See you outside. Better hide the boner."

Michael glanced down at the front of his pants. *Well, fuck.* The erection was plenty visible. He shook his head. Life with Tristan would be an adventure and he embraced everything Tristan had to offer. Tristan held his heart and soul in his hands. For a guy Michael had tried to avoid, Tristan had been irresistible and just who he needed.

Want to see more from this author?
Here's a taster for you to enjoy!

Cedarwood Pride:
Home to Cedarwood
Megan Slayer

Excerpt

"Hello. Welcome to our single fathers' group. My name is Colin Baker. I own the Books, Comics, Vintage and Memorabilia Bookstore on Main Street. I'm thirty years old, gay and I have a son. I've been single for the last year, and I'm not sure I'm ready to start dating, but I'm positive I'm tired of being alone." Colin rubbed his hands together and stood behind the podium. He hated being the center of attention. Being terminally shy, he preferred to play the role of the wallflower. Then he and his partner had adopted their son. Everything had changed when they'd welcomed Gage into their lives. He gripped the top of the podium.

"I'm glad you're all here." Colin folded his hands to hide the shaking. "I created this group for the single gay parents in the Cedarwood area—especially the guys. As you know, Cedarwood isn't exactly welcoming to the LGBT community. There aren't many of us, but I figured we all need a support system. Feel free to add your name to the outreach list and invite anyone you think might like to attend. In this group, we share our stories and support one another. Now I'll open the floor."

He stepped away from the mic and made his way down the steps of the stage. Meeting in the basement of the former Reserved Church of the Open-Minded worked better than he'd expected. People knew the building, but no one seemed to care if anyone gathered there—unless the people were gay. The church for anyone who wanted to worship had only lasted long enough for a sign to be erected. Bad for the church members but good for Colin and his people, who now numbered only five. He grabbed one of the chairs and listened to the others share their stories.

He'd been asked once if the group was intended to hook up the single fathers. Colin had smiled at the time, but inwardly seethed. *God.* Yes, they were single, but not everyone wanted to hook up. Okay, that wasn't true. He wasn't interested in a hookup. After Nicolas, he dreaded jumping back into the dating pool. But the loneliness wouldn't go away.

Two and a half hours later, the meeting broke up. He helped put the chairs away, turn off lights and locked the building. The guys in the group were a good bunch. Everyone seemed interested in the problems of the others. Some of the men were making headway in their love lives. Others weren't. Some were happy to be in Colin's not-yet-ready-for-dating camp.

Despite the town's location outside Cleveland, the population numbered only around six thousand. Most people worked in the bigger city and spent their weekends in Cedarwood. People moved to Cedarwood for the schools and the safe small-town feel. The children tended to live idyllic lives. The kids belonging to gay parents were the subject of bullying more than most of the other children. He knew because he'd heard stories from his son.

Colin drove home to the duplex he shared with his brother, Farin. The light shone in the living room of his half of the building. Farin must've brought Gage home for the night. Colin checked his watch. Nine p.m. *Shit.* He'd stayed out fifteen minutes past his son's bedtime. He preferred to be home before Gage went to sleep to kiss him good night. He strode into the house and dropped his coat and keys on the chair by the door.

"Heya." Farin stood. He rolled his shoulders and groaned. "I've been on that couch for the better part of forty-five minutes. Gage and I read every book he's got on every superhero known to mankind."

"He likes his superheroes." Colin rubbed his temples. "Police too. I don't know why. I tried to get him interested in baseball, but that hasn't worked."

"It's a phase. Remember how I used to get silly over fire trucks?" Farin patted his brother's shoulder. "I was five, but I loved those trucks. But we were talking about Gage. He hit the hay ten minutes ago. He didn't want to go to bed. When I asked him why, he said there's a kid at school giving him hell. He didn't say hell, but you get the idea."

Colin pointed to the chair. "Sit. He hasn't said a word of this to me. What's going on?"

"Okay." Farin perched on the edge of the armchair. "Some kid in his class—he wouldn't say who—has been talking crap to him. Saying his dad is gay, so he must be gay. Kids are rough at that age."

"He's seven." A dull ache grew behind his eyes. The next thing he knew, the kid would be teasing Gage because he was adopted, too. His younger brother had definitely inherited the listening gene. Where Colin moved first and thought second, Farin knew how to get people to talk. Apparently, he'd worked his magic on Gage.

Farin rested his elbows on his knees. "Don't let it bother you. Kids say stupid shit all the time. I talked to Gage, but he wanted me to keep quiet. He just wants to know that Dad has his back, but he's scared to talk to you because he's worried you'll get upset. Let him know you'll go in and talk to the principal, too, if that's what needs to be done."

"You bet your ass I'll talk to the principal." Colin bit back his anger. He hated the way the residents of Cedarwood refused to accept the differences in society. *So some people are gay. Who cares?*

"Calm down before you do or you'll blow a gasket and get yourself into trouble." Farin left the chair and headed to the front door. "Give Gage a kiss, tell him it's cool and you and Uncle Farin love him. If you need help, I'm right over there." He saluted Colin, then headed out of the door.

Colin jumped up from his seat and ascended the stairs two at a time. When he reached Gage's bedroom, his son was already asleep. The kid did have a talent for crashing once his head hit the pillow. He kissed Gage on the forehead and whispered, "Love you, big boy."

Colin crept out of the room and left the door open a bit. He went back downstairs long enough to lock up and turn off the lights. He paused at the picture window. The lights of Cedarwood twinkled against the dark sky. In the silence of the night, the small town was almost pretty. He should've been happy to live in the community. The schools were all located in one central campus and the sports programs were highly ranked. The graduating classes featured only around a hundred and twenty-five kids each. A person could still shop in town and get everything needed in one trip down the main drag. The cost of living wasn't horrible, either. But the cost of living in Cedarwood as a gay man rose by the minute. He managed to fuck himself over doubly by co-owning the lone bookstore in town. The people wanted the books, comics and collectibles he sold, but that didn't stop them from making derogatory comments.

He raked his fingers through his hair. He wasn't part of the star baseball team and he wasn't the naive kid from high school anymore. He had a kid, a business and a life. He'd worry about Gage's problems at school in the morning. Maybe by then he'd have a fresh perspective or better advice to give his son. Maybe.

* * * *

The next morning, Colin stood at the island in the middle of the kitchen and drummed his fingers on the faux marble surface. Two months into school and his kid was late…again.

"Come on, Gage. You're late." He glanced up the back set of stairs one more time. The light glowed on the wall from the second-story bathroom. "What are you doing up there?"

Gage rounded the corner and bounded down the stairs. "Sorry, Dad." He kept his head down. "My belly hurts."

"Really?" Colin stopped Gage on the steps. "I heard about the kid at school. Besides, you're only a week away from the Halloween parties. You love those parties."

"Harvest parties. We can't have Halloween ones. It's against the law."

"It's not against the law." Probably against something else, but Colin didn't want to discuss that with Gage. "So, talk. What's with the kid at school?"

"Uncle Farin blabbed." Gage ducked under Colin's arm. "He wasn't supposed to talk to you. He promised."

"You do realize your uncle and I talk about everything?" Colin followed his son into the kitchen. "So, spill your guts, kid."

Gage stared at Colin. He might have been adopted, but from the way the kid glowered at him, he could've sworn Gage shared the same gene pool. With the same blond hair, blue eyes and thick lashes, Gage reminded Colin of a mini-version of himself.

Colin squatted in front of his son to put them at eye level. "What did the kid say?"

"That my dad is a fag." Gage stuck out his bottom lip. "Why would he do that? You're a dad."

Colin sighed. "Okay." He needed to explain the situation for Gage to understand. "Some people say mean things. No matter how hard you try to get away from them, they'll always be there." God, did he know that lesson well. He'd tried to shake the memories of the guy from high school who'd insisted on making his life hell.

"What do I do?" Gage rested his hands on his hips. "Uncle Farin said to ignore him."

"That's a good idea. Don't let him know you're upset. It's hard because you're going to be mad, but once he realizes you're not going to react, the kid should stop," Colin said. *Unless you have a secret crush on the guy being the dick.* He shook his head. He wasn't about to tell his son that little tidbit of information.

"Fine." Gage picked up his tennis shoes. "But I'm already late. Why don't you just let me skip today?" He grinned and batted his lashes. "A mental health day, like you say you want to have?"

Kids were such sponges. He'd have to remember to think before he spoke in the future. "No mental health days. Grab your book bag. You have art today, don't you? You love art."

Gage yanked his bag from the hook. "I do." He hurried past Colin and headed out to the garage.

Colin picked up his tablet, wallet and keys. He'd get Gage to school late, but at least he'd conned the kid into going. He locked the back door, then climbed into the car beside his son.

Once the garage door opened, he backed out of the garage and closed the door. Colin eased the rest of the way down the driveway, then turned onto the street. He glanced at his son's reflection in the rearview mirror.

"I'm going to take you in to school and write the excuse then, okay?" Colin asked. He barreled down the back road to the school complex. The speed limit sign read twenty-five. He snorted. Did anyone actually drive that slow anymore? He checked his speed. Thirty-nine. *Fuck*. He tapped the brake. He needed to get his head in the game and pay attention. The speed limit was there for a reason, not a suggestion. *God*. He was a dad and getting his kid to school safely should've been utmost in his mind.

Colin let off the gas and continued down the road, but something in the mirror caught his attention. Red and blue lights. What the hell? Realization washed over him as he recognized the reason for the lights. *A cop. Fucking balls.* He'd been caught speeding. He pulled over to the side of the road and parked.

"What's wrong, Dad?" Gage asked from the backseat.

"Daddy went too fast on this road and the cop is calling me out. I was wrong. I was speeding." He sighed and leaned back in his seat. *Shit.* Of all the times to screw up, he had to do it in front of his kid.

"Sorry, Dad." Gage curled up in his booster seat.

"Me too, kid. Now you're super late." Colin pressed the button to roll down the window, then reached across the dash to the glove box and retrieved his registration.

"Excuse me, sir." A shadow darkened the window. "License and registration, please?"

Colin slid the card from his wallet. "Here you go." He refrained from looking at the cop. Not because he disliked cops, but because the shame of his actions washed over him in epic proportions. He'd been speeding, in a school zone more than likely and with his kid in the car.

"Do you know how fast you were going, sir?" the officer asked.

"Probably twenty miles over the limit." He closed his eyes and rubbed his forehead.

"Thirty-nine in a twenty. This is a marked school zone. The lights were flashing."

"I'm sorry, Officer." Colin opened his eyes. The stress was no excuse to be a jerk. "I was trying to get my son to school and wasn't paying attention. I accept responsibility for my actions." *And I've learned my lesson.*

"I see." The cop paused. "Colin Baker? I knew a guy named Colin Baker when I was in school. We played ball together. Huh. Well, I'm going to give you a ticket. Give me a moment."

Colin slid his gaze to the officer as the man retreated to the cruiser behind Colin's car. He didn't need to read the man's badge to know his name. He'd recognize that body anywhere — Jordan Hargrove. Why in the name of God did the guy who'd featured prominently in all Colin's high-school fantasies have to be the guy who was currently writing him up for breaking the speed limit?

The dull ache from the night before developed behind Colin's eyes. So much for being a good role model for his son. Horrible fucking luck.

PUBLISHING

Sign up for our newsletter and find out about all our romance book releases, eBook sales and promotions, sneak peeks and FREE romance books!

About the Author

Megan Slayer, aka Wendi Zwaduk, is a multi-published, award-winning author of more than one-hundred short stories and novels. She's been writing since 2008 and published since 2009. Her stories range from the contemporary and paranormal to LGBTQ and BDSM themes. No matter what the length, her works are always hot, but with a lot of heart. She enjoys giving her characters a second chance at love, no matter what the form. She's been the runner up in the Kink Category at Love Romances Café as well as nominated at the LRC for best author, best contemporary, best ménage and best anthology. Her books have made it to the bestseller lists on Amazon.com.

When she's not writing, Megan spends time with her husband and son as well as three dogs and three cats. She enjoys art, music and racing, but football is her sport of choice.

Megan loves to hear from readers. You can find her contact information, website details and author profile page at https://www.pride-publishing.com